THE GLASS OCEAN

THE GLASS OCEAN

Lori Baker

THE PENGUIN PRESS
New York
2013

THE PENGUIN PRESS
Published by the Penguin Group
Penguin Group (USA) Inc., 375 Hudson Street,
New York, New York 10014, USA

USA · Canada · UK · Ireland · Australia
New Zealand · India · South Africa · China

Penguin Books Ltd, Registered Offices: 80 Strand, London WC2R 0RL, England
For more information about the Penguin Group visit penguin.com

Portions of Part One first appeared, in different form, in *Common Knowledge*,
Volume 16, Issue 1, Winter 2010 (Duke University Press).

LIBRARY OF CONGRESS CATALOGING IN PUBLICATION DATA
Baker, Lori, date.
The glass ocean / Lori Baker.
pages cm
ISBN 978-1-59420-536-1
1. Man-woman relationships—Fiction. 2. Domestic fiction. I. Title.
PS3552.A43148G53 2013
813'.54—dc23   2013007696

Printed in the United States of America
1   3   5   7   9   10   8   6   4   2

Book design by Meighan Cavanaugh

This is a work of fiction. Names, characters, places, and incidents either are the product
of the author's imagination or are used fictitiously, and any resemblance to actual persons,
living or dead, businesses, companies, events, or locales is entirely coincidental.

For Peter

Contents

I.

VOYAGE OF THE *NARCISSUS*   *1*

II.

THE BIRDCAGE   *97*

III.

THE GLASS OCEAN   *223*

IV.

ON A WINTER NIGHT A TRAVELER   *327*

THE GLASS OCEAN

I.

VOYAGE OF THE *NARCISSUS*

I write in retrospect, from the vantage of a distant shore.

Carlotta Dell'oro is my name; I am eighteen years old; mother I have none; father either. My hair is long, red, bright as a flame; I stand six foot two in my stocking feet; or would, except I am very seldom in my stocking feet, having planted my boot firmly on the backside of the new world—up to the hilt in it, in its mud and its muck and its offal—a commitment of a sort; my hair, like a flame, has lit the new and savage shores, the hills, the craggy, wooded paths of this new world, coming now, briefly, to rest, in this bright, hard, hot, blue place. Here I rest; here I write.

Outside, beyond the screen, is a jeweled line where sea meets sky; a single tree trunk, bowed, elliptical, smooth as a rib, its shaggy top pendant with the brown, rough-skinned nuts of this land; there is a rustle of anoles; high-pitched alarm of cicadas winding up, then down, then away, into deceiving silence. Before me, on the table, are spread my father's things, what was left of him, his diaries, his drawings, his letters. Of my mother I have nothing—just his drawings of her (many of these), a single roguish photograph, and memories—poor uncertain objects, from which to try to reconstruct a world.

Spiders stir in the high, bright corners above me as I write, knitting their webs; the fan ticks rhythmically, *tock-tock-tock-tock*; it does not stir the air; this is a hot place; innocent, relentless in its innocence; without shadows; remorseless in its brightness; begging to be filled in. From the other room, the room where I am not, comes the sharp, sudden creaking and croaking of springs, a screen door snapping, sharply, open and shut.

Carlotta? It's time to go. Carlotta.

Her step is soft, compared to mine; her hair still dark, supple, repelling reflection, like a raven's wing. She has packed our bags, bought our tickets.

Carlotta.

We are about to step off the edge of the earth together, she and I. It takes great faith, to do a thing like that, with anybody. Let alone with an orphan like me.

First steps are hardest. When we step outside, onto wooden sidewalks that loft us up, in our long skirts, an inch or two above the muck of the new world, the men will call out to me: *Hey, Red! Walk my way!*

Ginger hair being no impediment here, in the new world. In this savage place.

Wait—I'm not ready.

Then hurry up, she says, *hurry up*, she's impatient, with her little valise buckled up tight, lengthwise, crosswise, she's ready to go; while I'm the picture of laxity, everything loose, scattered, unpacked, unorganized, unready; falling apart, oh, all falling apart, from the hairpins on down, with the past spread out before me on this desk, the future a willful flinging into the abyss. There is such complexity in this thing, of orphaning, and being orphaned; of leaving, and being left behind.

I am one, you see, who has slipped through; fallen down, unnoticed, through a gap in the fabric of things; settled softly, in a quiet, nearly forgotten place.

Hurry up, Carlotta. Or we'll miss the boat.

Well. This is true.

It's not that I'm angry. They couldn't help themselves, my parents; nor could anyone else have helped them—they were, like all of us, each in our own way, doomed right from the start, just by being who they were: she, with her vague blue eyes, her pink, sulky pout, her distractedness—that peculiar air she always had, of being somewhere other than where she really was, or of wanting to be, until at last she was nowhere at all; he, with his pale white stalk of a neck, his nervous stutter, his pad and pencils, his ill-fitting suit, hunching over his lamp; hardly more than children themselves, when I came into the world; and unmoored, the both of them, terribly unmoored; all at sea; and so it was inevitable; and where blame cannot be placed, nor can anger be. They did not belong together, it is true, though he would chase her to the ends of the earth, and has done, and is doing—or so I believe—

Carlotta, it's time—

No blame to be placed for their serial disappearances, first she, then he; she, as I am about to be, off over the edge of the earth; he—willfully—off over the edge of a boat into the cold—the slithering—the grey blue—the unblinking—the sea—

Don't dwell on it, don't dwell, that's what they say. But I dwell nonetheless, casting my shadow onto this new and bright, un-sullied and heretofore shadowless world.

Scraping of bootheel. Slamming of door. She's given up on me for now. Out of patience. Crossing my line of vision, out there beneath the palms. Calmly regarding the horizon, that sharp, seamless glitter of blue. Balancing, for a moment, from my per-spective, the sea on her back; then stooping to touch—to touch— I don't know what. A coconut. A cockleshell. The sand.

. . .

Let her go. It will pass, this feeling, as of sinking into cold black and wet, the bubbles rising swiftly around me, silver and white, and the buzzing—

There. All right again now. It's only for a moment that I'll be alone.

That's how it was when he went, into the cold North Sea. A sea far darker, and colder, than the one outside this window.

Tell Clotilde, he said.

Unwitting last words. Or not? She'd been gone a long time already, when he finally went, too.

It's hard to know what he meant by it. This is ambiguous.

Down then. Into the murky unknown.

We were in the smallboat together, he and I, and Harry Owen; just before dawn we'd sought our purchase on that slithering sea, with the cliffs still shadowed in the distance—Black Cap, Mad Molly, Devil's Brow, their faces indistinct—Whitby itself somnolent, the whitewashed houses with their red-tiled roofs clinging like barnacles to their cranny in the cliff, limpets in the crevasse, holding tightly, tightly, such memories. Shadows aplenty there, in the old world. And all asleep among them. Outside the protective embrace of the breakwater, which in all weathers flashed its lights, one red, one green, our smallboat bucked and turned on the waves, while, from the harbor, fishing boats essayed, with their accompanying chorus of gulls, all in ignorance of us, our business none of theirs on that playfully cavorting sea: sea like a cat, batting us languidly with a tireless, disinterested paw. My father had the diving suit on, the entire ridiculous getup, the lead-soled shoes, the horizontal steel tank mounted on his back. Going down he was, to gather specimens for his glass ocean. These to be sketched, remade in glass.

It was Harry Owen's job, up top in the boat, to work the pump. He it was who would play out the length of hose, press the air down beneath; an esoteric job for an esoteric man. My job was simpler: I helped my father adjust the helmet.

Tell Clotilde, he said, before taking the mouthpiece between his teeth. Then I battened the seals, and he sank, with a last, businesslike nod, into the wine-dark sea.

What was I to tell her? How was I to tell her? He didn't say, I didn't ask.

No matter. No matter. My mind was elsewhere mostly. I inherited that from her.

I may have been irritated with him, just for a moment.

Then he was over the side. I saw the silver crown of the helmet descend into the greeny-black void. All gone then. Not even a ripple remained to mark the place. The ocean unzipped and swallowed him up. The air hose played out vertically. Stopped. Harry Owen said, *He's struck bottom.* The hose played out some more. Harry Owen said, *He's walking.*

How deep? said I. But Harry didn't answer. He was too busy tending to the pump. As was only right. Suck and hiss of air, mischievous *lip-lop* of waves, cat's paw softly batting. And then the sun rose, sparking light in the black bituminous shale of the cliffs, awakening from their nests the fulmars and kittiwakes, which began to wheel with haunting cries above us.

Harry Owen said, *He's off the tether.*

This in itself was not alarming. The tank on my father's back allowed for that, for several precious minutes at least.

Ten minutes passed. Fifteen. Twenty-five.

Seven minutes the apparatus allowed. But by no means twenty-five.

There was a silence then, but for the playfulness of the cat, batting at the gunwales.

Harry Owen said, *He's gone.*

What else could he say? Reluctantly, we hoisted in the tether.

Harry slowly rowed back, while I remained holding tight to aft, staring out to sea. There was no splash or scar to mark the place where I became an orphan. No matter how I looked I could not find it; nor would I ever, in the days to come.

The days to come.

Ironical positioning, that.

For it seemed to me then that there were no days to come. Seconds, minutes, hours; passing time, keeping it, counting it; what were these to me? I was done with all that. Time was stopped, and I with it. Though I was aware, in my dim way, of tumult around me, of running feet, of voices raised, and banners, too,

upon stern, upright masts; of shrill police constables and of fishermen who set out upon the water to troll for the body of my
father who, it was presumed, had slipped his tether, gotten lost
down there in the dark, and drowned.

The diving suit weighed more than he did. Much was made
of that, after the fact.

His body, though, was never found. Of course it wasn't. He
was too subtle for that, far too subtle, he was a subtle man, a
tactful man, oh father mine. And gone.

Suddenly there's a scratching at my window screen. Look—it's
she, outside. She's holding something up, something she found
out there beneath that stark, polished rib of palm, something
she wants me to see. Two halves of something, bone white, brilliant, unmatching. Disarticulate. Occluded by glare.

She doesn't want me to tell it, that's the problem.

Too late. Too late. I am launched now, in one sense, at least.

———◦◦◦———

I'D LIKE TO BE ABLE TO SAY: THEY MET AT SEA. THERE
is a gracefulness in that, an ease of telling. An economy. They
met at sea, they were at sea, they parted by sea, exeunt. But no.
It was never that simple. The problem is they should not have

met at all, at sea or anywhere else, neither on the street nor in a room, in a field, on a beach, he and she, Leo and Clotilde, two opposing elements that should have repelled, resisted; that did repel, resist, for a time; that still resist me, at any rate. The two of them, unmeant; of emphatically disparate stuff. Until brought together. A collision, I the result. And then once again: the molecules fly apart, will not hold.

She was a beauty then, though. That's what Harry Owen said of her. *She was irresistible, your mother. Irresistible. Who knows what fantasies took root and blossomed in that charming little Eden, the pale and tender hollow of your mother's heat-bared shoulder.* That's what he said. He rhapsodized all right.

From which it may be seen that he was a little bit in love with her, too. As were they all.

But I'm getting ahead of myself now. Best reserve her entrance for later. She deserves a good one; such drama.

My father, of course, is a wholly different matter. Unprepossessing. I imagine him as he was then, a young man, very young—young as I am now—a little older, perhaps—eighteen, nineteen; dressed very properly in a dark suit, yellow waistcoat with small silver buttons, white shirt with a stiffly starched collar. These clothes are of fine quality, evidently expensive, purchased on the eve of his long journey from the north; but he is uncomfortable in them; unaccustomed; see how he pulls at the collar, fiddles with the cuffs, nervously pulling, nervously fiddling, with his pale, small, delicate hands. Small. Yes. He is a small man, my father. Neat and small. A pale man, dark haired, with bright, dark eyes the most expressive feature in a face otherwise unrevealing. Fiddling with his cuffs and collar in a hot, dark room. Pressed close, he is.

I can easily imagine it, the closeness. And the smell: very sour. For it is a very hot day, the hottest of that very hot summer of 1841. Outside the small, dark room wherein my father is contained (wherein I have contained him), close pressed, in his very proper suit, the roads are a steaming clamor of dust and dung, the garbage tips expelling everywhere across the city their noxious gases, cinders carrying thick and hot on a dry, southwest wind. He's lucky to be indoors actually, on a day like this. Despite the fug.

It is arbitrary of me, perhaps. I could have chosen differently. But I've decided that this unpleasant day is the day on which I will begin. On which they will. He and she. In late August. All the parks burned brown, the leaves on the trees like galvanized metal, uncompromising sky the color of steel. Water in the Long Pond stippled. Crackling. Conducive to chemical reaction.

My father is in Bury Place. I have contained him upstairs, in the peculiar pink-and-blue confection of a building, so unexpected among all the red brick and whitewash of Bloomsbury, where are located my grandfather's lodgings.

Is this precise enough?

No. I can be more specific yet. The pink building is at the corner of Bury Place and Great Russell Street, just around the corner from Montagu House. On the street level there is a shop, very dark, that bears the placard: A. PETROOK, ANTIQUITIES; COINS; CARPETS; OLD COINS; PAPER MONEY BOUGHT AND SOLD. Small, intriguing objects are contained within this shop, displayed in its windows. A head of Isis, for example. Another of Aphrodite. Greek vases and other odds and ends of pottery. An iron Celtic figure of a horse and rider. A red terra-cotta hand and arm, very roughly made, probably broken off an early Roman figurine. Something Mayan.

Arthur Petrook is there as well, at the back, one among his objects, like them rough, with an unfinished quality, as if poorly cast, by old-fashioned methods. A short man, squat, dark, balding, foreign looking (not unlike my father in this), apparently untouched by the heat (in this very unlike my father indeed), surrounded by old, piled newspapers, dusty bound squares of carpet, a jumble of packing crates and boxes from which straw stuffing protrudes. He sits at—or rather, it seems, crouches over—a desk, though, of course, this isn't true, he doesn't crouch, not really, more it's that he's leaning over something, leaning avidly over an object that lies before him, on the desk. It's a page from what must be (have been) a very old book, lettered in Latin, brilliantly colored in the margins in gold and crimson and deep blue, borders illuminated with strange, deformed figures, some human, some not, cavorting, coupling, consuming themselves and each other and the text in an infinite, uncheering roundelay that, from the look of it, Arthur Petrook finds infinitely cheering.

There are only two ways he could have obtained a single plate from a manuscript this old. He cut it out of the book himself, I bet. No stranger Arthur Petrook to this and other profitable mutilations.

How can I say such things? What do I know about it? It's not like he's got the knife in his hand right now.

It's something else, that sharp glint, something else altogether.

Anyway, that's no business of mine. Look away, look away.

And find, in the corner, behind a narrow door surrounded by stacks of crates, the stairway leading up to my grandfather's lodgings.

Like the shop itself, this stairway, dim and airless, is choked with objects—papers, books, boxes, terra-cotta heads, grimy textiles—that almost completely occlude the passage up. It is very like a burrow, dug with tooth and claw by some eager, gnawing mammal. At the top is a landing piled with carpet samples, and a door with a card upon it that reads: PROF. F. GIRARD. Behind the door: a dim, low-ceilinged room, antechamber to the warren, carpets rolled and leaning against the wall, large packing crates, some with the lids pried off, from which protrude rocks and bones partially wrapped in old newspapers. In one corner hangs the skeleton, strung together with wires, of some kind of ape, orang-utan, perhaps, how should I know, this is not my area of specialty; in another corner, a stuffed vulture, the feathers grown patchy with mange—El Galliñazo this is, wattled, beloved companion of my mother's childhood. The collection continues into the adjoining corridor; here are shelves crowded with seashells and birds' eggs and butterflies of great beauty, side by side with glass jars containing dark things pickled in brine, all kinds of things: fish, insects, tree tumors, parasitical worms; here again a box in which somebody has mounted, perfectly, an exquisite set of colorful dried beetles with enormous mandibles, like something from a dream; there, anemones and hydras in fluid, indifferently prepared, poorly preserved, hardly worth keeping, but kept nonetheless. Stinking, in the heat.

My grandmother, Marie-Louise Girard, has already left my grandfather by now. By '41 she's returned to her father's house in Paris. Very soon she will remarry. This, perhaps, explains the state of my grandfather's lodgings. Or does the state of his lodgings explain her departure? And anyway, the house doesn't belong to my grandfather; it belongs to the one downstairs, him with the cutting eye and edge, Petrook. My grandfather is a kind of employee, a procurer, who, by supplying Petrook with antiquities and curiosities from foreign lands, obtains a favorable deal on the rent.

I imagine the two of them, Petrook and my grandfather, as two vultures sitting side by side on a single branch, each guarding his pile of decaying treasure, pecking and squabbling, biting and squawking, eating, shitting, shedding, scratching, as vultures will do.

Really, though, it's more complicated than that. The households Girard and Petrook are intimately entwined in a cheerless roundelay all their own, one that will prove unfortunate for my grandfather (and my mother) in the long run.

Little wonder my grandmother left this place. Who could blame her?

To think I've put my father in here.

It's all right. I'll let him out soon. And anyway, he feels at home. He's in the study, safe and warm. Like part of the collection.

It's hard to see him really, it's so dark, the room so crowded, with books (both on shelves and in stacks, rising up like stalagmites from the floor and from the surfaces, nearly submerged, of a drowning desk and a few weary armchairs, paddling for their lives among the debris), as well as with rolled-up carpets smelling of incense and cloves, with grimacing carved stone heads of Central American origin, and with the ubiquitous specimens, swimming in their bottles of murk.

Not one to be deterred, my father is poking among these objects, ferreting, sorting, examining things in the very dim light provided by the room's single window, narrow, dirty, and distant.

Bit of a collector himself, my da. Crumpling something soft into his pocket, left pocket, something that doesn't belong to him. I can't quite see what it is. But the sly, shamefaced expression, that I can see. Even in this lousy light.

He starts then, gives a sudden, sharp little quiver, surreptitious creature that he is, all alert, scenting the air, listening, ears and whiskers turning like pinwheels because he's heard, from somewhere within the softly swaddled chambers of the burrow, a reedy distant susurrus that might or might not have been a *Hallo—*

Yes. There it is again. *Hallo* from the next room, rattle of hand on doorknob, minor rupture followed by inward collapse, a geometry of light and dust containing a figure, unfamiliar. Round glint of glasses, sharp spade of beard, tweedy sleeve, inserted. And a voice. *Hallo! Is somebody there?*

This will be Harry Owen. He's been waiting, too, in another part of the burrow. Drawn by my father's scrabbling. Something else alive in here! It's not just me! Or so it seems.

My father comes toward him eagerly, emerges from the

shadows, hastily checking his pockets, gasping slightly, as if rising in a very great hurry from a very great depth.

Yes, yes, it's me, he says, *I'm here. Leo Dell'oro—ship's artist.*

Harry Owen is startled by this. It shows. Slight retraction of the beard. We aren't on a ship, we're in a burrow. But being impeccable in manners, introduces himself nonetheless.

Yes, says my father. *I've heard all about you.* And unhelpfully adds, *Felix Girard is out. Would you like to see my pictures?*

Oh my dear my father I miss him so. Such a child, scampering off into the warren in search of a sketch pad with which to impress the tweedy stranger. Where has he gone? I don't know; I can't see that part of my grandfather's kingdom. And anyway, he's back now, already, panting, sketch pad in paw. The stranger, encompassing this, draws book and boy both out into the passage, where the light, such as it is (an aqueous matter no matter where, in this house), is somewhat better for looking.

The sketch pad is a ragged, well-thumbed thing, thickened by interpolation into it of other matter—pages torn out of books and periodicals, letters heavily annotated in the margins, daguerreotypes, restaurant menus, old postcards, tickets, pieces of carpet, a swatch of wallpaper—no wonder my father feels at home in Felix Girard's house, and will soon possess an impulse to make the collecting a family matter. Nasty, unhygienic stuff. But in among it—the drawings. These are very good, precociously good. Pencil sketches mainly, flora and fauna, North Yorkshire coast, moors. And bones. These are his drawings of the Whitby ichthyosaur, which was excised from the cliff called Black Cap by my grandfather, Felix Girard, several years ago.

The ichthyosaur was and is my grandfather's most famous

find, crowning achievement of his career as a bone monger, the career for which he left his other, previous, more respectable career, that of surgeon, in Paris, at l'Hôtel-Dieu.

Charnel house on the Seine. All those infected linens hanging out on metal clotheslines on terraces above the river. Bloated monster, breathing sickness on the city of light.

He had to leave it. *So much death*, that's what he said. *Ah, the stink, Marie!* Without irony. And so my grandmother left him.

I can't blame her. There's an issue here of contracts, as well as of expectations.

So this is how my father met my grandfather: by sketching his ichthyosaur. The drawings, amazingly exact and to scale, accompanied Felix Girard's paper on the find, and were published, along with it, in the *Proceedings* of that year. My father was very young then, just a boy. That is why, now, the drawings look familiar to Harry Owen, a man of science himself. He saw them in the *Proceedings*. But he doesn't remember that he did.

My father received no credit for this work, nor any money either.

Nor did the cliff Black Cap receive any money, though it very conveniently collapsed, exposing the ichthyosaur to my grandfather's opportunity-seeking eye.

Which just goes to show that success really does consist, first and foremost, in being there.

Why, says Harry Owen, evidently surprised, *these are very good! You have an amazing quality of—of—tact—with your living creatures especially—they really look alive—*

This is excruciating to my father, this praise. He never could accept a compliment. He blushes painfully, begins rubbing his left wrist rapidly against the heel of his right hand, cannot look Harry Owen in the eye. Unbearable, unbearable. Now he has to run off—run off!—with his sketch pad, back into the warren, and disappear. Gone to ground. Leaving Harry Owen alone.

Or not exactly alone.

Many eyes, in that place.

I don't know where my father's gone. Some parts of the burrow lie too deep even for me to excavate. Nor do I desire to dig there. I'll remain with Harry Owen instead.

Here he is, left alone in the hallway with my grandfather's jars of pickled fish and a number of those grinning Mayan heads Felix Girard trades to Petrook in lieu of rent. Clearly, he's as taken aback by my father's abrupt departure as he was by his unexpected appearance. At a loss, he stands in his tweeds (it isn't just my father: they all wear too many clothes in this August heat, sweat trickling down behind the very proper collar and cuffs, soaking the starched shirtfront beneath the tightly buttoned waistcoat, dampening the worsted trousers, pooling around the garters at the stocking tops, such a way to live, so very, for lack of a better word, Victorian); he flashes his spectacles this way and that, intelligently pointing his spade of a beard, patting down his smooth, fine hairs, looking around, looking around, looking around at all the *stuffed, pickled, and preserved*. Then, finally and suddenly giving up on my father (now classified: *Homo enigmaticus*, form *juvenilis*), retreating back into the study, removing a stack of books from one of those poor groaning easy chairs, sitting down, and lighting a cigar.

I can see the red spark of cigar ash wavering in there, in the semidark.

It is very rude of my grandfather, is it not, to leave his guests sitting around like this?

Poor Harry Owen, sitting around in the semidark with his cigar in that oppressive room. I can see now that he's noticed the smell, the sour-sweet smell of death, not quite disguised by the pungency of the cigar. He's running his finger around inside his collar, shifting uncomfortably on his hams. There's a large, poorly stuffed, mottle-coated, buck-toothed South American rodent on the low table by his elbow, this for company, such lousy conversation. *Mrs. S—, is that you?* No. No. Though it looks quite like her, it flirts less well. All communication is by other means, other channels. Harry Owen sniffing slightly, there, in the dark.

. . .

Honestly, I don't know why he waits. He lacks my father's aptitude for snooping, he's far too proper, this is all just tedium to him. And he doesn't even know my grandfather. When the summons came to him at the house on Half Moon Street, he hesitated, even, over whether he ought to come. Debated, pro and contra.

My grandfather has something of a reputation, hardly any of it good. Though his books are quite good. *Felix Girard's Ghosts of Bain Dzak* in particular. That's the one about Mongolia. I like it very well, myself. But Harry Owen hasn't read it, not yet.

It must have been very dull, that summer of 1841, to keep Harry Owen waiting in that study.

And my father, where has he gone? Honestly, I don't know. He's still there somewhere, in Felix Girard's lodgings. I can hear him, the soft little rustlings. Keeping himself busy among the collection. If only Harry Owen had that knack.

But he lacks it, and having waited half an hour, is just pulling himself together to leave—first shifting in the hams, a tensing of the knees—when, with great tumult, my grandfather, Felix Girard, arrives.

There's always tumult when Felix Girard arrives. He's a large man, coarse and broad, with a fierce feral thicket of red whiskers interspersed with sparse tendrils of grey; often he's loud, sometimes drunk, usually dirty, and peculiarly dressed— bombachas, bolas, a moleskin coat, all stuff he's picked up in his travels, affectations in anybody else but in my grandfather unself-conscious, worn to suit the weather; no moleskin today, because of the heat probably, but still remarkable enough, in his unraveling yellowed shirtsleeves, all unbuttoned and awry, and exuding an unmistakable sweaty musk.

There are two people with him. One is a man, wiry, thin lipped, upright, with steel-grey hair and a cool, severe, unblinking predator's eye   this is Hugh Blackstone, captain of a small ship for hire, *Narcissus,* at anchor in the Thames. The other is a young woman, pale as a flame is pale, white gloved, elegantly muslined, with a cunning, sharp-toed boot and a pert yellow flounce. Seeing Harry Owen sitting there in the murk with his rodent companion, she immediately lets forth three melodious trills of laughter, crying, *Oh, Papa, it's a new specimen! Did you stuff it yourself? Oh, no, of course not—that's Johnny Twomey's rotten handiwork—I'd recognize it anyplace!*—pointing at the pendulous ash clinging to the tip of Owen's cigar—*You can tell by that funny little fringe left hanging loose there!*

Laughter then, among the three. Even Hugh Blackstone's stony visage contorts in that muscular rictus meant, by him, to signify a smile.

Hilarious, isn't she, my mother?

And irresistible as well, for not a moment after she's insulted him she's offering Harry Owen her hand, saying, with a charming absence of guile, *You must excuse me, Dr. Owen. I'm afraid my*

father's new assistant, Johnny Twomey, isn't working out very well,
and I can't seem to stop myself making jokes at his expense! Please
forgive my very poor manners. I am Clotilde Girard.

Then she touches his hand, just barely; or rather, she does
not quite touch it, creating, instead, by her motion, a small,
warm current of air, suggestive of a touch, at the same time
looking steadily into Harry Owen's eyes with her own, those
distinctive eyes, pale grey-blue, like a sea held close beneath
cloud, as if to say, *There, this is just between us!*

Oh, she's expert, my mother; expert at making it all disappear. Harry Owen will forgive her anything in that moment,
and he does, taking her hand, squeezing it, pleased to meet
her, my dear, despite her quick, small, triumphant smile; or
maybe he doesn't see that, so speedily is it replaced by another of such sincere friendliness and cordiality as to belie the
first.

Dr. Owen, I am so glad you have come.

She leans very close when she says it, her breath warm on his
cheek, her skin with its sweet, soft scent—she's fresh pastry, my
mother, warm croissants, meringues, Bath buns with orange
icing.

She's irresistible all right, delectable, oh mother mine. What
chance will poor Leo have, scrabbling creature that he is, with
all his antennas twirling, confronted with such as she?

None. None whatever.

It attracts sometimes, that which ought repel.

. . .

Awright now, Tildy, leave Dr. Owen alone. Don't let her tease you, doctor. She gets the best of us all with that stuff. Tildy, you go out for our supper. I gave you the list, remember?

Yes, Papa.

And make sure the bread's fresh this time—none o' that moldy stuff.

Naturally, Papa.

And keep away from the cat's-meat man today, eh, Tildy darling?

He winks, my grandfather, the bear, and presses a coin into her small, gloved hand.

Oh, Papa! says she, with a blush. *Now it is you who are teasing!*

Ah, Tildy! cries Felix Girard, gripping her arm, holding it tight in a sudden, fond, yet melancholy rapture, *what won't you do, my dear, to add another penny to your pretty little bank, toward that pretty little hat you are wanting? You see, your Papa knows you truly, my dear, no matter what these gentlemen might think! Only the best for our guests this time, petite!*

Yes, Papa.

Now off with you.

Yes, Papa.

And obediently she hurries away, the flounce of her skirt sliding demurely down the stairwell behind her, like the lowered tail of an exotic bird.

She is a naughty girl, but good, says Felix Girard, gazing affectionately after. *Where does she get it from, gentlemen? From her*

mother, of course! Don't they all, eh? You have already met Dell'oro?
Gone back down his rabbit hole, has he? We shall ferret him out quick
enough. Dell'oro! Show yourself! Now then, gentlemen, this way. We
will talk.

He leads them then down the hallway, past all those mute
reproachful gazes, into the room he calls his workroom.

I like this best of all the rooms in my grandfather's lair.

Here a dim and sultry daylight filters down through three
stingy windows set high up in the wall; some enterprising person has propped these open, just barely, with broken shards of
renegade terra-cotta—casualties, no doubt, and rejects, from
Petrook's shop—so that the sashes rest heavily upon the cracked
foreheads of the gods. Slack, battered window shades hang
limply up there, stirring, with an eerie, papyrus rustle, in the
infrequent and unrelieving hot zephyrs of air. Just beneath—
arranged along the wall, for maximal light, I suppose, in this
vague and dusty place—stand Felix Girard's worktables, with
his many incomplete projects spread out upon them: the rusty,
red skull of some small reptile, who knows which, its teeth bared
in a perpetual impolite snarl, vertebrae laid out beneath, like
broken links in a lady's necklace; a bowl of water in which
brightly colored snails are crawling; nearby, empty shells,
recently denuded of their occupants and stuffed with white,
antiseptic tufts of cotton wool; beetles and butterflies and drag-
onflies, recently treated with prussic acid, pinned in their setting

boxes, the sparkling wings fastened down with little cardboard braces; and plants as well, nothing escapes him, laid out flat to dry on sheets of coarse brown paper. In a long, low cage on the floor, pea doves bow and coo; in another, jewel-bright lizards cling to the mesh, lazily expanding and deflating their red and yellow throats, like gentlemen about to utter unwise remarks of which they have suddenly thought better. Orchids growing on clumps of wood hang from pegs in the walls, some displaying dreamlike, colorful blossoms, others the roots alone, tangled and knotted, with spidery, delicate filaments reaching out for props to cling to, finding only each other or themselves, intertwining to form weird webs, miniature dangling forests. Lines have been strung from the walls and run in various directions just above the guests' heads; from these hang innumerable cones of paper, bobbing gently, with an aura of muted festivity, like small, enigmatic Japanese lanterns. Inside are the skins of birds, hung up to dry, safe beyond the reach of pests. A pronounced and disturbing buzzing, like the buzzing of bees, fills this peculiar, junglelike space; these are my grandfather's hummingbirds, battering themselves cheerfully against the window shades, hovering in the high, hot corners of the room. Felix Girard has placed a cup of sugar water on the edge of the table for them; every now and then, one darts down, drinks, sits for a moment on the edge of the cup before once again taking flight, with a flash, ruby red, emerald green.

Get out! Hey! Get out of there, you, Johnny Twomey! We gentlemen must talk in private, eh? Gather your bits and get out. Where? How should I know where? All of London is at your disposal! But see you are back before seven if you want your pay! cries Girard; there is a sudden, frantic stirring at the far table, and a small man, about fifty years old, dressed in a smeared smock and apron, pushes past, softly muttering—whether apologies or imprecations, I don't know; nor does anybody else; so let it go, let it go. It is my grandfather's ill-fated assistant, Johnny Twomey, who will be fired for incompetence before the end of the month. On the table he has vacated lie a dozen dead birds he was in the process of skinning, along with the tools of his grisly trade: scissors, knives, nippers, needles and thread, cotton wool, a jar of arsenical soap—and several more of those paper cones, idly awaiting their occupants.

He is bad, very bad, says Felix Girard, carefully picking up, and then lovingly rubbing, between his thick forefinger and thumb, a delicate skin with feathers of deep cobalt blue, which he then turns, exposing a large bald patch, like a scorched tract in a forest, which Twomey has left on one side. *Careless. It is ruined! I have hired him as a favor to my friend Petrook, but . . .* he shrugs mournfully . . . *What more can I do? He ruins too much. Some can learn, some cannot, is it not so, Dr. Owen?*

Harry Owen in his tweeds gapes slightly, hung now on my grandfather's hook. *Some persons have more potential than others . . .*

Ah! You are an idealist at heart, I see, doctor! You would like to say to me that poor learning is often the fruit of poor teaching, and that the pupil's failure is the teacher's fault, but you fear to offend! Anyone can learn, eh? It is a good thing, this idealism, it does you credit. But I, well—

He sighs, shrugs. Great eloquence of shoulders.

I am an idealist no longer.

Then pushing aside the table's contents, he plunges beneath

it, broad back exposed, like an island, like the hump of a seal, and emerges with a large book bound in black leather, which he spread-eagles on the tabletop, contemplates, with eyes moist, red rimmed, while fingering the blazing thicket of his beard.

Yes. This is the one.

Looking up sharply.

Where is Dell'oro? Is he still not here? Leopoldo Dell'oro! Come out, shrinking violet, come out! It is time, and past time, to show yourself!

Honestly I expect no result from this. My father has interred himself in some secret space, he is lost, I can hear him rummaging, rummaging; no one will extract him; but my grandfather knows him better than I, for here he is; he has emerged; evidently he was nearby all the time; sheepishly now he insinuates himself into the room, still overdressed, hot, disheveled, sleepy. Tugging still at cuffs and collar. Nervous twitching.

Very well. Now we shall begin.

They gather around the table where lies my grandfather's map book, opened to the sapphire Gulf of Mexico and Caribbean Sea, there where the Greater and Lesser Antilles, the Leeward Islands, and the Windward Islands sweep, like the snap of a serpent's tail, from the southernmost tip of Florida to the north coast of Venezuela.

Gentlemen, my grandfather says, *she is here.*

Gently he lays his great thumb on the green protruding bulb of the Yucatan.

Let me explain. As reported by my colleague Lord Willoughby in the Proceedings *of 1840, which I for you now quote, "The fossil remains of an ancient cetacean, measuring thirty feet long, were found here imbedded in a sheltered plateau approximately three miles inland from Punta Yalkubul; but could not be excavated due to difficulties of approach and terrain and resistance from the native peoples." There, gentlemen, she lies; and so she shall continue, unless we go, and dig her out.*

Beatific smile then, rapture of the beard, so incongruous, he radiating joy, drooling with it practically, this big, rough man, my grandfather.

I propose we shall go in October. Harry Ellis of Montagu House has agreed to fund us. Hugh, what do you say?

Blackstone narrows his expressionless yellow eyes, cocks his head, says, *It could be done.*

From Hugh Blackstone, it is an endorsement. And you, Dr. Owen?

Some dithering now. *Willoughby's reports are still unconfirmed . . .*

So you do not believe our colleague Lord Willoughby? His word is not enough for you?

Wicked provocative gleam of eye from Girard, the angelical banished, now the devil behind the beard.

It could prove unfortunate to undertake such a venture without proper confirmation and corroboration.

Laughter at this from Girard, Blackstone meanwhile following, with his cool glance, a hummingbird's trajectory along the perimeter of the wall; brilliant green, bumping and bobbing beneath the moldings. As for my father, Leo Dell'oro, he glances anxiously from one party to the next, antennas twirling; rubs, quickly, one wrist against the heel of the opposite hand. Rub himself raw he would; and did, when I was a child.

But that's not yet. Not yet. I don't exist as yet, not even as a gleam in my father's eye. Maybe I'm the intimation of a gleam.

Dr. Owen, says Felix Girard, stifling his laughter, *you are the soul of caution! It is you who will save us all from our doom. If Harry Ellis, and the museum, trust Lord Willoughby's report, what more is there to think about? If they will pay, what else is it to us?*

It should matter very much to us.

Ah.

Disappointment now, a frown among the russet fronds. Yet warmly he grasps Harry Owen's elbow. *Promise me at least to think about it, Dr. Owen. I would like to have you with us. It will be a very great thing for us, and a very good thing, I think, for you, too, if you would come. But now I think I hear my Tildy in the salon. We will talk more later.*

He takes Hugh Blackstone by the arm then, and together they depart the room, whispering of the necessary preparations, while my father and Harry Owen linger behind.

He touches my father's arm.

Have you decided to go, then?

Oh, yes. My father is quick about this, has no doubts, smiles his gentle smile. *Yes, of course I shall go.*

Where does it come from, this unexpected certainty?

Harry Owen releases him then, but my father remains behind among the orchids, which seem to float, like hallucinations, in this very hot room. Feverflowers: my grandfather's pets. Gently he caresses the ice-green blossom, *Angraecum funale*—the corded ghost. It is smooth, soft, cool, lightly furred. Whose cheek is this I touch? Then a sudden stirring, a sibilant, soft rustle; Clotilde is in the doorway. Her skin is pale and cool as ivory; so pale, so cool; like one of Petrook's sculptured goddesses.

This though is an illusion.

She laughs. Flesh and blood.

Papa says to tell you dinner is served, she says, and half lowers herself in a hideously ironic curtsey. Then she runs away, like a child, boots clattering noisily upon the floor. Leaving him gawping.

Delectable. Delectable. Oh mother mine.

They will speak no more this night about the journey that is to come (for it will come, despite certain reluctances, it approaches them already, slipping quickly toward them across the waves). Instead, in a hot, dark, dining room, as the dead look on, they raise and lower their spoons and listen as my grandfather speaks of journeys past. He is eloquent, and he has been everywhere:

Bain Dzak, Cyprus, the Canary Islands, the Basque regions of Spain, Argentina, Baalbeck . . . he speaks of these with affectionate nostalgia, as another might speak of long-missing friends. Yet what a dismal company they make! My mother is not there; the procuress only, she does not eat the meal; or eats it elsewhere; somewhere; in another room; somewhere else, in the warren. So it is the four men. My father, gazing at the tablecloth, starting slightly each time anybody speaks to him—Hugh Blackstone, eating little, saying less, regarding them all with his cynical yellow eyes—Harry Owen, wrapped up in his tweed, growing appalled as his glance explores the collector's cases, finding here, stretched out in supplication, the black leathery hands of a gorilla or a chimpanzee, so like ours, yet so unlike; there, the famished, begging grins of cayman, alligator, crocodile.

What can it mean, this collecting of my grandfather's, all of it, any of it? These creatures in their sullen, half-rotted profusion represent not the multiplication of knowledge but instead its opposite—the impossibility of knowing anything at all. Many things, dead; corpses, carapaces, shells; collected, catalogued, cut open once, then cut again—flayed—essence gone, destroyed in the cutting, if it ever was there at all.

They are no different, these four. Grist for the mill. As they know. Anxiously sipping their soup through clenched teeth.

And him, too, the servant with the Asiatic features who stealthily slips in, lights the lights, departs again. Him especially.
    Objects in the collection of.

Lacking only the ether, the scissors, the arsenical soap, and
the pin.

There is one thing living, though. It is the sound of my mother's
voice. A trill of laughter, musical, soft, is coming from somewhere in that place, from some unseen room or unknown corridor (filled, no doubt, with other carcasses, other carpets, other
artifacts). My mother, alivest thing in that cabinet of mummies,
living and dead, is laughing.
    Leo hears her. His eyes are round, startled, his spoon sus-
pended in dense midair. What's that look on his face? It's not
surprise; it's something else. Something like surprise. Apprehension, that's what it is. Apprehension, bordering on fear.

He knows already, of course. He already feels the trouble she
will be. It's there, in her voice, for he who has ears to hear it.
Attraction and repulsion. He wants to run away, but he can't.
It's too late already.

What can Harry Owen think, glancing up from his soup, seeing the fear on my father's face? And then, too, seeing the

cayman grinning at him from behind my father's shoulder. Grinning confidentially, with something like a wink.

He hears her, too, of course, this Harry Owen. My father isn't the only one with ears.

Dash! cries Felix Girard. *Open another bottle of '28!*

Alcohol does help sometimes, it's true.

They are waiting for her to appear again, Harry Owen and my father both. If the truth be told.

But she's hidden herself. She, the desired one. She's plaiting her long golden hair, tucking herself into bed with lizards and vultures looking on, so that in the end, when my father and Harry Owen can bear to wait no longer, it's the bell suspended above Petrook's shop door that bids them a cheerful good night, not she. Despite their hopes. The man himself is still sitting there, hunched like a spider over his desk, with a sallow cup of tea at his elbow, tepid, grassy liquid gleaming dully in the well of the saucer; when he sees them he pauses in his work for a moment, glances up with those dark, feral eyes, then quickly away. Not much of a leave-taking this. They two will part disappointed on the pavement, Leo Dell'oro, Harry Owen, two friends well met, one turning left, one right, into that stinking garbage tip of a city. The night air heavy, hot, black; thick with cinders. A red glow on the horizon, sulfurous stench. Analogy to hell artlessly implied. Thick guttural vibration, this is the life of the city, its arteries pumping, darkly, warmly, all the engines turning over, then turning again. The vital essence sparked. It is a place on the verge of the future. Upstairs, oblivious to all, my grandfather and his friend Hugh Blackstone will go on, and on, the exotic servant opening another bottle, then another. Behind that lighted window. There are so many lighted windows in this city, curtains drawn, a scrim descending, shutting out, shutting in; and so much is going on behind them, who knows what. Vertiginous thought. Best look away. These two are done anyway, for now.

Such an awkward parting. *Perhaps I shall see you again. Perhaps.* One toward Mayfair, the other, God knows.

Of course they will sail, in the end. Despite all doubts. They haven't any choice, not really.

My father has decided already, on the strength of a certain blue glance. This is foreordained. The other will dither for a while, finally read *Felix Girard's Ghosts of Bain Dzak,* find it brilliant, say he is sailing on the strength of it, when really prompted by boredom. Ambition. Rebellion. Because his father prefers him to pursue the clove trade, while he prefers not. Hence: dislike of hearth and home. Restlessness. Dissatisfaction. And something else he cannot name. Will not.

Such is *her* influence.

Like a planet, she draws her acolytes.

Not that she does it on purpose. Misunderstandings that

might arise are never her fault. She's innocence in a tower, guarded by dragons, plaiting her golden hair.

———⇒•⇐———

OF COURSE SHE, TOO, WILL SAIL. THIS IS HER DESIRE. Regardless who may disapprove: and many shall. But she's willful, my mother, and fiercely attached to her father, the bear.

Papa will stay with Clotilde always. Papa will never go away again!

She is a child, sitting on his lap, poring with him through books containing exotic colored plates of faraway places. He has just completed his own book, *Felix Girard's Ghosts of Bain Dzak*, after years holed up in the attic in his father-in-law's house with his fossils spread out around him on two long, scar-topped, spindle-legged tables. All day and all night he spent there, in those two cramped, inconvenient rooms, writing; my mother as a baby crawled among his loose and discarded papers on the floor, as a tot leaned on his shoulder while he wrote, contaminated his inkwell with spiderwebs, whirled like a dervish through all his accumulated research until she finally collapsed, exhausted from her games; then he read aloud to her from his work. She was too young to understand much, but what of it? It is the voice that matters, and all these years later she still recalls the sound of it, her father's voice, intoning: *In the distant steppe, the camels stride* . . . Wherever she was, curled up at his feet on the floor, or against the wall among the piles of discarded papers, dropping into sleep with his words in her ears, the simple line, *In the distant steppe, the camels stride* . . . , like an invocation, heavy with the fragrance of the unknown. *In the distant steppe* . . . *the camels.* My mother is in her father's arms. She is asleep, and sleeping, dreams of the things he has seen, of which he has written and then read aloud to her, of the bazaars of Khuree, of swift, small horses and of courageous horsemen whose boots curl up at the toes, of fantastical sandstone buttes weirdly shaped by fierce desert winds, of the skeletons of dragons he has carved single-handedly out of the stone; dreams, until it seems as if she has seen these things herself, has been there with him, with her father, the bear.

But then it all is over, the book is finished, the manuscript wrapped up in plain paper, and mailed to London. He begins to think, once again, of travel.

Papa will not go away. Papa will stay with his Clotilde always. One babyish hand on his cheek, the other buried in the luxuriant ginger beard. *Papa will never go away again.* Attempting to extract, in the unguarded moment, a promise she can use against him later. *You know I'd like that, Tildy. Better than anything else in the world. To be always and ever with my Tildy!* And reaching into one of his pockets, he pulls out a sweet he's hidden there especially for her.

. . .

But never does he promise. Felix Girard will not make a promise to Clotilde unless he intends to keep it.

And he does travel: bravely, selfishly, mercilessly, relentlessly—once he has finished his book, he travels. First, briefly, to Spain; then southward, staying longer, down into the Canary Islands, and on to Morocco. Then another trip, to Greece, is extended into Malta, and then on to Tunisia. In between, the stops home, to Paris, and more gifts. An egg from which she is allowed to raise a wild dove that perches on the curtain rods and shits on Madame Girard's curtains before escaping out the open window. Then a pair of spice finches in a gilt cage—she'll spend hours watching these, with their brilliant red beaks, pert black eyes, brown-speckled breasts. Their movements are like clockwork, their songs like high notes plucked upon taut wires. She feeds them bits of apple and orange, trains them to perch on the heel of her hand, to let her spread out, with her small fingers, their small fragile wings. She is enamored; but in a few weeks the spice finches are forgotten, and Felix Girard is leaving once again. He is departing for Sfax; his cases are packed, they are in the entry hall. *Papa does not love me! If he loved me he would take me with him to Sfax—*

Ah, Tildy! Sfax is no place for a little girl. It's a hot, rough, nasty place. They eat goats' eyes for dinner in Sfax. Would you like to eat goats' eyes, Tildy? Of course not. Nor anybody else's eyes neither.

You shall come with me when you are older, to someplace better than Sfax.

But he does not tell her when, or where; my mother is not fooled, she grabs hold of his beard, pulls fiercely, all the while screaming, *Papa does not love his Clotilde! He does not love her at all!*

My grandmother, Marie-Louise Girard, has her own ways of coping with this. She floats off, with a resigned air, among the bright blooms in her father's conservatory. This is the world she came from, the world she will return to. There, surrounded by the yellow and white winter orchids, with a watering can in her hand, she hums quietly to herself, *Mmmm. . . .*

She has surrendered my mother to Felix Girard long since. Clotilde's first word, pronounced a month after her father returned from Mongolia, was *Up*, by which she meant to say that she refused to lie for one minute longer in her bassinette. Her second word, after Marie-Louise picked her up out of the bassinette, petted her back, and pressed her affectionately to her breast, was *Papa!*

Marie-Louise can say only one thing about this daughter who runs wild, ripping all the curling papers out of her hair, crawling in the mud beneath the shrubbery looking for worms, who spends all her time in the garden playing "camels and tigers" with the Mongolian servant, Dash—carried round and round, dizzyingly, on those exotic brown shoulders:

Qu'est-ce qu'un sauvage!

What else can she say? It's true: my mother is a savage. And she is lost to Marie-Louise: sometimes it is impossible to get back that which has been taken. It recedes, is ever out of reach, a blossom on a branch that bends infinitely away, a bird retreating to a higher and higher perch; pursue it too sharply, and it will fly.

But Clotilde has her wish now. At last she will travel with her Papa.

———⟫◦⟪———

THEY MET AT SEA, THEY WERE AT SEA, THEY PARTED by sea. Launched now, on a roundelay all their own.

———⟫◦⟪———

THIS, THOUGH, IS SEPARATE FROM THE LAUNCHING OF the *Narcissus*. Weeks yet before that will sail. Not until autumn. Cold winds will blow. For now: there she lies, at anchor on the Thames. A small, seaworthy vessel, restless perhaps, listing slightly at the bows. Preparations come first. Where or what she has been before, unknown; nor does it matter. Felix Girard will fit her to his own specifications, using Harry Ellis's money. She will be stripped down, recaulked, refitted. Two scientific laboratories and a naturalist's workroom are installed on board. It will all be there all right, everything they need—the benches and stools, the nets, specimen jars, calipers, scalpels, hammers, brushes, vials, tweezers, magnifying glasses, microscopes, beakers of formaldehyde, jars of ether—the entire clanking, juddering, swaying machinery of science, all this is provided at the museum's expense, and an accountant, too, pale-mustached MacDowell, with his *Ah yes, just so, just so, indeed*, the lone and constant companion of their departure—see him noting it all in his book of accounts, a book as thick with papers and as carefully kept as the devil's own? *Ah yes, just so*. The museum is concerned for its property: concerned, but not interested. MacDowell's shrug will be sufficient to see them off; then they'll know themselves truly disowned.

The *Narcissus* is growing heavy in the oily, black water. Her belly is full of ballast: not just the weight of science but also of potatoes, salt beef, biscuits, bread and onions, cabbages and beans, pickles, tobacco, bolts of cloth, soap, bottles of bitter and of claret, barrels of water, all that's needed to keep body and soul together at sea. There is a floating farm as well, squealing piglets, chickens, a goat, these are the ill-fortuned charges of the cook. I think it will not go well with them, but we'll see, we'll see, it's a capricious thing, that wheel.

Just before sunrise on a cold October morning the tugs will take her off: the *Narcissus* sliding out low and gravid from between the tarry hulls of her neighbors, sleek wayfarers lately returned or shortly bound for Singapore, Ceylon, Bombay, black bellies looming threateningly close, then sliding back into a silent oblivion of fog. The Owen family's latest fortune in cloves no doubt lies somewhere among them, somewhere close, unseen. And yet.

No room, now, for second thoughts.

The sun a milky sphere, a smudge, upon a horizon of intractable grey.

———————

NOW THEY ARE SAILS MERELY, DWINDLING DOWN THE Thames.

———————

THAT'S IT, THEN.

My father is at the rail, small ambiguous figure, a hieroglyph above the waves. Harry Owen stands beside him.

That's it, my father says, as if some doubt about the reality of the matter has been dispelled by the sudden rush of water beneath their bows.

He nods with a strange, slow gravity, a serious question having been answered, then turning gently away from his companion, bends stiffly at the waist, as if bowing to the river—offering it his best regards—and vomits, violently, over the side.

As he does, a voice rings out:

Papa, look! Mr. Dell'oro is sick already—and we haven't even reached the sea! We're only in the river! Is it not terrible, Papa? Will he not suffer horribly when we really do reach the sea? I fear he will be very miserable, Papa, will he not?

I cannot fault my mother on her timing, it is impeccable; for, of course, it is she, who else? Dressed in a thick shawl of blue and gold, with her hands plunged deep into a furry muff, cheeks reddened by the raw wind off the river, blond hair disarranged, she looks, as she approaches, like a picturesque detail from a Scandinavian mural: *Ice Skaters on the River Lule*, or something like that.

At the sight of her my father blanches again, offers himself once more to the Thames, and once again is sick.

Such an inauspicious beginning.

Felix Girard, more ursine than ever in his greatcoat with the collar raised up stiff around the back of his neck, like hackles, seeing Leo Dell'oro curled up against the rail, growls, *He is a poor creature, Tildy! A poor weak-chested creature! A creature like this will take some time to develop sea legs, petite! Have patience! Be merciful! You must not poke fun!*

Yes, Papa. I'm terribly sorry, Papa.

She's brilliant, is she not? And brilliantly unfair, because my father isn't seasick, he's hung over. Harry Owen knows it, of course, but is too much of a gentleman to say. He was there the night before, on the eve of the embarking, saw my father, drunk, wavering up the Embankment, heard the *rat-a-tat-tat* of his ill-fitting new shoes, Leo Dell'oro bobbing rapidly from one to the next sickly pool of lamplight, such an uncanny figure in that dapper dark suit, running from lamp to lamp with the herky-jerk movement, *like one of those automata of which the French are so fond*, until suddenly he pitched sideways, toward the oily water, and disappeared.

A dangerous business this. There are cutthroats and thieves among the bushes.

There he lay, limbs rigid, quivering slightly, bright eyes staring fixedly ahead at nothing—completely absent. Being a gentleman, Harry Owen has thought no more about what he saw: that husk of my father, essence missing. Carapace only. Impolitic among strangers. Even among friends. From this Harry Owen has averted his memory; and taking the little artist back to Half Moon Street to recover, was relieved to find the carapace retenanted in the morning, after a night in the spare bedroom. Having revived it further with strong coffee, he said nothing. It is unclear if my father remembers anything of this.

It's just as well, probably, that my mother knows nothing of it. The less material she has to work with, the better. And anyway, she's about to be distracted: Hugh Blackstone has just discovered her spinet, and is shouting at the top of his voice for his men to *Put the damnable object over the side—before I do it myself!*

This handsome instrument, long-legged rosewood gazelle, purchased for Clotilde by Felix Girard, in Paris, is very important to her; though it is true, perhaps, that the ocean is an improper place for a spinet. Nonetheless, the evening concerts in her stateroom will be much enjoyed. "Wär' ich so klein wie Schnecken," that is what she will sing, with considerable skill and grace, as the *Narcissus* bucks and rolls upon unquiet seas; and later, too, as it idles under the stars in that endlessly still, tropical night. There she will be, Felix Girard on the bench beside her, gently turning, with his great bearlike paw, the pages of her music—

But this not yet. Not yet.

Hugh Blackstone disapproves. Even as he attends those concerts (crouching, stiff backed, in the passage just outside her door, frowning)—even as he listens, almost, it seems, against his will—he will disapprove. And now four of his men (probably the same four my mother bribed to put the spinet on board) have got the instrument up, forelegs resting on the rail, ready to heave it over, even as Felix Girard, furiously shouting *Touch not the darling piano, Blackstone, you stinking bugger!*, makes his way furiously amidships, and rescues it.

This will buy my father some time, he'll be forgotten for a while, among the shouting, the tears; it won't be until much later, when they've all sat down to eat, that my mother will suddenly remember her other, unfinished work, and cry, *Are you quite thoroughly done being sick, Mr. Dell'oro? Mr. Dell'oro has suffered most horribly from mal de mer, has he not, Papa? And we are still only in the river!*

Eyes will be averted from this, focus placed instead on the uneasy cantering of the silver tureen from the center of the table to its edge and back, soup stirred by the waves. Only John McIntyre, the Scots ornithologist, will smirk, and even he only from behind his monocle; nonetheless, my father, with those few words, will be put completely off his meal.

. . .

Why does she do it? Who knows why anybody does anything. She doesn't know why herself.

I think it is simply, instinctively, her way of being in love. The equivalent, emotionally speaking, of the love bite of the lioness. Once he is in the teeth of it, she must tear him.

It's in her nature.

And there's something else, too. Something in that single-minded adoration of her Papa, Felix Girard, that fights to preserve itself despite whatever else she might feel.

She's a difficult woman, my mother. Delectable, but difficult.

Leo feels it, though he will pretend otherwise.

Here he is, below deck, tucked up in his narrow berth, in the dark down there with a fragment of candle stuck to the wall, writing. It's a letter, a letter home, to his sister, Anna, I think.

There are memories in this.

They two curled up together in the same bed in the narrow house on Henrietta Street, warm little animals, the two of them, smelling each other's smells, feeling each other's little movements, kicking, elbowing, jostling, fighting each other for everything in that poor house. Now he crouches alone over his paper and writes. She like a part of him, recently abstracted. Darker of the dark twins, indulgent goddess of seventeen, striding up the Scaur in a dismal early twilight. Spit of snow off the sea. Ancient monster undulating, darkly. Her hair flashing out behind her like wings as she walks, lustrous even in this dull light. What can he say? *Dear Anna.* I can't imagine this really. What, after all, is there to say about this, all this, his situation? *Dear Anna. I find myself at sea.* He pictures her back in Whitby, hanging out the washing. The cobbled yard there. The dingy smallclothes dangling from the wooden pegs. The slippery edge of the cesspit, acrid sweet smell of night soils, himself perched at the edge, about to heave the bucket in. *Hsst, Leo! Hsst!* And the workshop where his father carves jet. Him, too, once upon a time. Not so long ago. Dark things, black things, memento mori. These are home. The cliffs at Whitby are lined with dark things, entire forests embedded blackly in stone, and monsters, too, from another time. My father left there early in the morning, never said goodbye. He had his reasons, I suppose. The sea spread out before him as he descended Henrietta Street in the direction of the harbor. *Dear Anna. I never said good-bye.*

Dear Anna. She cuts me so, with those claws of hers.

No: he writes a great deal, but he would not write that. Some things he cannot confide.

Shortly Harry Owen comes down to make sure Clotilde's talk hasn't bothered Leo too much. *What? What did she say? I honestly didn't hear her, Harry, so of course I don't mind it, whatever it was*—blinking his luminous eyes, neck a pale stalk rising out of the stiff collar he insists on wearing even here as he sinks deeper into the berth, draws the thin, scratchy blanket up around him. Safe, in this shuddering, groaning cocoon.

Water rushing darkly just behind his head.

Mustn't think about that, though.

Think instead of earthier dreads, the small scutterings beneath, rattling insinuation of vermin. Thorax, wing, carapace, tail. Seek comfort in the quivering whisker. This is where the gnawing begins in earnest.

It is not unusual for a single word from my mother to unman him completely.

Waves without, waves within.

———————

IN TIME HE WILL CULTIVATE OTHER SAFE PLACES. UP in the crow's nest, or on the mainmast, on fair days. Down below, in the laboratories, where the specimens are stored. He will spend hours there, organizing the sarcophagus, sketching its contents. And time, too, beneath the tarp, or in the smallboat stored amidships—that is safe. Or crouching among the ill-fated charges of the cook, finding refuge among their warm, sweet, doomed breaths and the manure that repels Clotilde's fastidious boot. As things progress he will grow fond of the railings aft, where, every night at midnight, once they have reached the warm latitudes, he will stand quietly watching Harry Owen smoke, both of them observing the miraculous phosphorescence of the million small floating animals plowed up astern by the rudder—the brilliant green sparks that come and go, rise up out of nowhere in a milky-green froth, then subside again, whirling away into watery oblivion.

. . .

Time is heavy on their hands. It's an object that must be carried through one day, into the next, into the next. In all directions ocean, that terrible monotonous beauty. Even the birds disappear. Then they are really alone, at sea.

That will be me, too, soon enough.

They met at sea, they were at sea, they parted by sea.

No. I'm getting ahead of myself again. In retrospect there is such a sense of inevitability. But they don't know that.

And so: even the birds disappear, and then they are really alone, at sea. Floating in all that vastness like a smut in a saucer. Someone wise has said, an ocean voyage consists of nothing more and nothing less than hours of tedium, punctuated by moments of terror, and this, it seems, is true. For every moment they spend with their hearts in their mouths—surrounded by crashing crockery, tumbling luggage, a chaos of spilled beakers and rolling funnels and shattering vials, science itself upended, papers loosed from beneath their weights, whirling like moths—and themselves as well, whirled around, whirled around, as the *Narcissus* hops and bucks and spins upon the waves—they will spend a hundred more languishing idly in their berths, perishing of boredom, pressed close by the rushing blackness of the sea.

It is very close, that sea. It is just there, on the other side of that wooden hull, which, after all, is a membrane merely, a flimsy man-made thing, a floating illusion, porous as a sieve. Why else are Blackstone's men constantly below, manning the pumps? So as to stop them slipping through, into all that cold, black water.

Harry and Leo sleep poorly in the cabin they share, inches away from all that cold blackness and the million unseen, uncomprehended lives lived within it. They lie awake for hours sometimes, the two of them, not speaking, each assuming the other is asleep, listening to the chuckling rush of the water— then Harry Owen looks up, sees, in the shifting gloom, the tiny luminescence of Leo Dell'oro's candle, suddenly lit in the opposite berth. *What's that noise, Harry? Did you hear it? That noise— that's it—that one, there!* But there are so many noises. The *Narcissus* is never quiet. There is a constant groaning, rending, wood upon wood, bone upon bone, strange thuds, thumps; it vibrates, deeply—shudders—from deep within the fragile shell separating them, just barely, from the sea.

'Twas just the timbers settling. That was the night watch, throwing down a rope. It's just the rain on the quarterdeck—

They paddle desperately, together, trying to keep the flimsy illusion afloat.

It's easier, for some. John McIntyre and Felix Girard, for example, are seasoned travelers, drawn violently together by the magnetism of a strong mutual dislike. It is not unusual to find them, in the saloon, at any time of day or night, regardless the weather, angrily disputing the nomenclature of the *Satyridae*, while all around them plates and saucers are borne floorward by the violence of the waves. My mother, in the same weather, may be found on deck, hugging her shawl around her, trying to tease the sailors into teaching her how to tie a granny knot, or a carrick bend, or a Matthew Walker. *Under—around—and up—!*

For she is fearless, mother mine.

But others are suffering. Linus Starling, Felix Girard's new assistant, becomes, from the moment of departure, a strange, enigmatic beast, remaining below deck, working at who knows what in Girard's laboratory, perhaps at nothing at all. Here he is: see the glint of his glasses in the swaying lamplight as he staggers along the dim, rocking passage between the cabins and the scientific workrooms. There is a sudden buckling heave; all at once he is thrown violently against Harry Owen, who is creeping along uncertainly in the opposite direction in that narrow, pungent space; lapels gripped for support, obsequious smile a pale, smudged, rat's grimace in the briny darkness, his *Begging your pardon, professor*, a pathetic squeak, neatly swallowed up by the ferocity of the gale. Then quickly they separate, the dance has ended, Starling moves past with a strange, unnerving, crabbed motion, clinging once again to the walls: he is maddened by mal de mer, and will not be seen above deck until the *Narcissus* reaches the calmer waters of the tropics.

There is something unsavory about this fellow. My father dislikes and distrusts him, though without knowing why. In this, the restless ocean, the cat's paw, not now at play but in earnest, is his ally. Containing that which is best contained. Though this cannot last forever. Eventually, hidden things emerge.

My father has proven a tolerable sailor. Somehow his small, compact form is an advantage at sea: lower center of gravity. There is, though, so little for him to do, during the long hours of rotten weather. He is unoccupied, but then, they all are. And so he sketches, furtively. What is he drawing? This I cannot say. I can see him, though, hunched over the pad of paper that is his constant companion, the gentle, self-referential movement of the pencil, this is how he comforts himself: a bulwark against all that blue and green and grey. He combats infinity with a pencil point. Or tries to. At a table in the workroom, or maybe in the saloon. Approach and he pulls the sketch pad close, into his body, or leans over, shields it in the crook of his arm. Such a furtive creature. What has he got to hide? He is nineteen at most, perhaps twenty. Too young yet to have a history. When the others talk he is quiet. He comes from Whitby, he has told them that much. The city that stinks of rendered blubber. Carved out of it. Ships in the harbor heavy with paper and ambergris, cramped little whitewashed houses creeping tenaciously up their crack in the cliff, up toward the wrecked medieval abbey that reigns over all. The breakwater with its two lights. And the Scaur, which passes there for a shore, a bed rather of stone and wrack, the grim spine of the earth exposed— laid bare, like bone at the stroke of a cleaver, by the sudden ebbing of the tide. My father broke his boots on it as a boy, on that humped black spine of rock in which fossils are embedded, ammonites in pyrite, garnet, amethyst. Snake-stones, they call them: St. Hilda's work. Old things, interesting things, things that have been lost; buried things, pushing up like unstoppable rebellion from beneath cracked and compromised ribs of bedrock. A repository of the living and the dead.

Its breath the ancient stinking breath of the sea.

My father loved to inhale it, standing in his boots on the humped rock in spite or perhaps even because of his mother's aversion and her fear.

That would be Gentilessa, my grandmother. The fearful one. I picture her in the small house on Henrietta Street, shivering in a woolen wrap. She is always cold; cannot adjust to this cold place. Her hands are red and sore, cracked. This is from the cold to which she cannot become accustomed and from constant scrubbing. The house on Henrietta Street is always clean, spotlessly clean. Gentilessa scrubs, scours, sweeps, fumigates. Drags the mattresses out into the sun when there is sun to drag them into. Scalds the wash, then wrings it, then smokes it to rid it of bedbugs. This, at least, she can do.

How she hates it there!

They came from Italy, from a place on the Adriatic, a place of green and blue and gold, to this place of black stone. To this place of surreptitious Catholicism, where even in a creeping minority redoubt they are a minority. *Crazy filthy furriners. Crawthumpers. Pikeys.* To break a living out of the rock, form it into obsequious memorials, brooches, earrings, lockets, mourningwear. Emilio Dell'oro is very good at that. He is an artist, a craftsman, a slyly obsequious salesman who succeeds, despite all, and prospers, in this place of bitter rains and hard rock and cold, unyielding unacceptance.

My other grandfather, that would be. The one with the little, round spectacles, the rather severe manner. I'll never meet him either.

My father, though, is having none of this. He has chosen the sea instead. He has his reasons.

And does everything he can to avoid her.

It's a wonder I'll ever be born, at this rate. Such ineptitude on his part. Also on hers.

Yet, of course, it's inevitable, it's going to happen. For am I not here, at the edge of the world, getting ready to jump off it, the whole ginger length and breadth of me? My father feels this inevitability, he senses it, feels me, perhaps, readying my leap, and hunches all the more tightly over his pad of paper, clutches tight to his pencil, as if this will make him safe, and me, too.

Mr. Dell'oro, what is that you are drawing? Is it a portrait of me? Or is it a porcupine fish? I'm sure you are a very talented artist, Mr. Dell'oro! Won't you let me see?

He won't.

Her laughter is like an object in itself.

He clutches tight, very tight, until she has passed by. Repulsion and attraction, attraction and repulsion. It's as if he can see the future, and he doesn't like it. That stink of inevitability.

For, in fact, she's right: he *is* drawing portraits of her. It's all her. How does she know? She can smell it, that's how: his adoration, his fear, it's in the air, and something else, too. She senses it, fears it herself, without knowing what she fears. Of course she's used to the rest, the admiration, the desire, the hand that longs to touch, repressed: stilled. That's nothing new, to her. But for him. It makes him feel naked. Exposed. Flayed. Vulnerable. A poor soft creature, unshelled. And then the drawings: Clotilde at the taffrail. Clotilde at the spinet. Clotilde bending over to button her boot. She mustn't see those. But there's no denying it's all her to him, as far as he is concerned, the blue of the sea her eyes, the gold sun her hair, the thrilling, vertiginous swell of the waves her breasts and belly, even the sea in its darker moments, its rages, yes, all her, already he is lost, lost, already sinking, he with his pale stalk of a neck, his awkward, ill-fitting suit, with all around him filth, discomfort, danger, bad food, foul companions, the whole wobbling scientific contraption, the career he might or might not make of it, the home he left, none of that matters, it's all Clotilde, all around, to him.

He doesn't want her to know.

Everything swollen, stinging with brine.

As for her, she is interested in her Papa only. He is in his workroom, studying the *Proceedings*. Or hunched over a map book, latitude and longitude laid out before him in wedges, exotic fruit that he longs to devour. Is devouring, with every mile of progress. *Papa will not leave me. Papa will never leave his Clotilde again.*

My father, though, is not neglected. In the half life they occupy beneath the billowing canvas, he, too, is pursued, though not by

her. What need has she to chase that which comes to her naturally, inevitably, like an act of homage? Rather, Harry Owen is
on his trail. The scientific gentleman, momentarily lacking in
objects of study, studies my father instead. *In the Mayfair of my
existence I've never met anyone like him.* So he writes in the jour-
nal he keeps of this voyage. That familiar, precise handwriting.
Soothing it is. Soothing. They each have their methods. Here it
is on my desk. *In the Mayfair of my existence.* And: *He is a study
indeed.* And: *Today, walking into our cabin, I found Dell'oro,
motioning over his shoulder and muttering some weird incantation,
thus: Black black bear-away, don't come down by here-away. Twice
he said it. Then seeing me behind him, commenced to look thoroughly
ashamed.*

Harry Owen makes of my father a scientific undertaking.
A meal of sorts, and a disappointing one, evidently:

He speaks little, despite my best efforts to draw him out.

In the end, though, the sea itself will assist.

They are in the workroom. How many weeks in? Three
weeks. Harry Owen has pressed Leo Dell'oro into assisting
him. In the liquid half-light of down below they are seated
together on stools, uncomfortably (but then, when, since the
pressing off, have they been comfortable?—never), shelves
around them bristling with beakers and vials, microscopes,
wads of cotton, jars of ether, scalpels, the tools of the trade, all
the necessities of capture, subdue, disembowel, preserve, these
are not symbol but fact. The ship beneath and around them
shuddering. Outside the porthole: wet, grey. Horizon indistinct,

uncertain. They do not look out. Afraid, perhaps, to see an eye looking back? No. They are too busy; they are hard at work making a surface net. Harry Owen has designed it himself, and will use it, when they reach calmer, tropical waters, to catch tiny pelagic creatures, helpless floating things aflame with the green fire of the sea, wandering spirals and crystallines, minute plants like snowflakes, tiny dragons fierce and bristling, these really the larvae of starfish and whelks and lobsters; phosphorescent fishes, medusae with blue translucent disks, minute pulsing tentacles; spawn, goo; dream objects. The net to be lowered over the side of the quarterdeck when the sea is calm, blue, in a yielding mood. Disinclined to notice. Open to plunder.

There is so much in her, she won't miss what we take.

All in the interest of science, of course. Hoping to discover one that will be named after him.

In this he will be successful. See: *Porpita minusculus owenii.*

So it is not all in vain after all.

My father perched on his stool, sewing transverse hoops into Harry Owen's net, doing his best to assist in the plunder. He works with severe concentration, despite the juddering of the ship, the juddering of his heart. He has seen my mother up above; therefore is hiding. Unwitting of his impending capture.

Waves within, waves without.

Then the sudden heave. Leo Dell'oro, upended, unceremoniously flung, sent sprawling beneath the worktable, arms and legs akimbo, this is so undignified, tangled in the toils of the net he has lately been sewing, hopelessly raveled; and at the same time—accompanying clatter—a small object, liberated from somewhere about his person by the vehemence of the wave, careens onto the floor, bounces, slithers, is lost.

He rights himself and within moments is crawling around on his knees, feeling around in all the convolutions of the net, searching for whatever it is he has dropped. *Aha!* Here it is, in the corner, underneath the worktable. A lunge and it is in his hand. Safe there. But he does not immediately emerge. Kneels instead, oh eccentric father, makes a short, sharp, thrusting backward motion with his arm and hand, as if intending to throw something over his shoulder that he does not in fact throw, chanting, *Black black bear-away, don't come down by here-away!*

It's the same mysterious doggerel Harry Owen heard before, in the cabin. Only this time he won't let it pass. He's got a strong spirit of scientific endeavor, actually takes my father by the wrist this time. Refrains though, from the cotton wool and the ether.

What have you?

It's n-nothing—

The nervous stammer coming out now. I wonder does Harry Owen remember Leo Dell'oro passed out in the bushes off the Embankment, that hollow vacancy, the tremor, the horrible, empty staring. The carapace.

Or is he too much of a gentleman to remember?

Purposeful pretense, that.

Show me. Severely, as if speaking to a child.

Sulky-eyed, like a child, Leo Dell'oro opens his fist, reveals, at the center of his small, pale palm, the tiny black figure of a horse, which Harry Owen quickly acquires, hefts, feeling the strange, porous lightness of this object, which is both and neither: wood and stone, wood nor stone. Feels the warmth of it, which is like the warmth of a living thing, though it is a borrowed warmth. Stolen.

This was made by a master carver, says Owen admiringly, all his tweeds and whiskers bristling with desire for the object, the smooth glistening blackness of it, the flared nostril, the shapely hoof, the veins beneath the polished skin, which have not been neglected by the evidently obsessive maker, these seeming to throb almost with life, though, of course, this is impossible, it is so tiny, simulacra merely, tempting simulacra, it longs to leap into his gaping pocket, to nestle there, that is what Harry Owen thinks, or rather feels.

Says Leo Dell'oro grudgingly, *My father made it—*

But this is excruciating, this blushing, the rubbing of the heel of the right hand against the left wrist, he can admit nothing, concede nothing, and always in the background the shadow of the small, severe man with round glasses, his posture stiff, upright, trudging up Church Street, in Whitby, in the rain. Carrying, in his pocket, a small box, tied up with a black ribbon. *Requiescat in Pace.*

Intaglio in jet of a child's face, oh, those pin curls, and the initials in seed pearl around the border.

How ashamed he was, my father, accompanying his father up Church Street, in the rain.

It is always raining there, in Whitby. Summer and winter both.

. . .

Your father is a great artisan.

Yes. Bitterly. *He's a very great carver. He's a better carver than he is a man!*

It is a question, whether Harry Owen will return the coveted object, or add it to his collection. I can feel him hesitating, running his greedy thumb over the lustrous skin that is not skin, that is neither wood nor stone, neither animal nor vegetable nor mineral but some other substance in between; and as for Leo Dell'oro's evident discomfort, well, never mind that. There is a shelf in a room in Half Moon Street that has an empty space. Or a cabinet, with a glass front, and a cunning inscrutable latch.

Once locked it will not open easily.

He made it for me when I was sick once. When I was a boy. This horse, Lath, stood by my bedside, and kept watch til I was well again. I almost died—

Afterward if ever I dropped it, I said the rhyme, to ward off bad luck.

There is petulance in this. Now Harry Owen must concede. There takes place a regretful separation, at the conclusion of which the small horse made of jet slides back into my father's pocket. Safe now.

Come! Now you must tell me! What has this father of yours done to deserve such harsh words? Have you always felt so? Did he punish you, perhaps, too harshly? Too often got drunk? Partook overselfishly of the roast? I am interested in this issue of fathers and sons, what keeps them together, what drives them apart—

Is that what separates you from your father? That he "partook too selfishly of the roast"?

Here it is again, that bitterness of Dell'oro by which Harry Owen remains unperturbed, into which he thrusts a doleful and lengthy scientific silence, sharply punctuated by a disappointed stiffening of the whiskers, until at last Dell'oro, compelled, must speak again.

As a child I admired and loved him. I wanted to be a master carver, like him. It wasn't until later—and anyway, it's not what he did to me, but something I learned about him. He's a rascal—a rascal and a sneak—and he doesn't even know that I know it.

Is that why you're here, then? To get away from the rascal?

I'm here because Professor Girard invited me.

And because it suits you.

Yes, it suits me. What of it? You're no different. Pugnacious outjutting of chin.

The tweed withdraws slightly, pleased or not with the perspicacity of its research subject, but must concede.

You're right. I don't like my father either, and I wouldn't follow him into the clove trade, though he's gotten rich by it. He's a true vulgarian—nothing but buying and selling, selling and buying— and eating, a great deal of eating. Gluttony alone, a continual gorging, on people, things, food, money—whatever he could get hold of—without even pretending to anything more. And why should he pretend? Certainly not to please me.

Certainly not.

And certainly I've lived well off it. Off him.
Certainly.

They hover together, cross-purposed in the watery light, the liquid creeping of the porthole reflected across ceiling, floor, the bristling scientific apparatus, their two faces, the whiskers of Owen, bright, dark eyes of Dell'oro, aqueously lit, burbling, sea-shuddering, unbalanced.

With stink in the background. Of fish, of tar, of wet woolens, of too many men in too small a space. And of that, too, of course: of fear.

The sea-shudders are deeply felt, and not just in the wooden membrane that separates them from it. Deeper yet. Each wave is a vibration in the body itself. Entering through the legs, exiting the stomach, the mouth, the eyes. Top of the head.

Whether he will tell it or not, that is the question. Small-footed creature that he is. Whether he will dig, unearth, expose. Lay bare.

The moment tautens, then at last he decides.

I learned that he was disloyal to my mother. He did not love us; he preferred someone else. My mother doesn't know it. All those years he deceived her—deceived us all. I couldn't be around him anymore, and k-keep his secret—so I left.

Thinks, *I didn't say good-bye.*

That ocean spread out before him. Forgetfulness there, in the blue infinity. Or so he hoped.

Behind the drawn shade the sister still sleeping. Dark head recumbent on white pillow. Now as far as he is concerned her innocence will last forever, she is suspended in that final moment of undisturbed dreaming. This is a gift he tried to give her.

His anger and his bitterness are like a window, closing. Harry Owen desists, returns to untangling what he hopes will be a more successful net. *I did not feel comfortable saying further about it.*

Such turning away, in my father. He is like his own father, in that. Emilio Dell'oro's is a nature that repels questions; by his very austerity, which allows no grasp, no lever, no fingerhold to be placed upon him, he forestalls from even being asked those questions that he will by no means answer. He is like a fish that slips away, elusive, glimmering, between waving fronds of eelgrass, completely self-contained in his silence.

My father will tell Harry Owen nothing but he will think about it again, later, when he is below, in the safety of his berth. There in the dark. Remembering. Himself at sixteen, pale, indwelling worm of a boy. What he saw when he unlocked it— his father's rolltop desk. This an act of petty larceny. What does he keep here? The desk is always locked, has been locked forever. Forever as defined by sixteen. Tedious account books, old envelopes, receipts, crumbling packing slips, crusted-over jars of ink, mucilage, frayed twine, pedestrian bits of brown wrapping paper, all the accrued business detritus of the Dell'oro Jet

Works, this seems a shame, hardly a just reward for the light-fingered pilfering of the small brass key, so many drawers, mysterious cubbyholes, nooks and crannies, latch and hinge, imagine the possibilities, spring mounts, false-bottomed drawers, so much potential wasted on ink and rubber bands and mucilage.

And then he finds them, wrapped up in a handkerchief. Tiny carvings in coral, some in jet, of a woman's face, her body. The same face, the same body, over and over. The warm, milky pinks of the coral very like flesh. So like that he must repress a fascination of his own in order to wrap these up, put them away in the cubbyhole where they have been hidden. He will revisit these, they burn in him, but, of course, he can say nothing. What can he say? He is a voyeur. He has seen what he should not see. The reward being silence, suspicion that can be neither placed nor dismissed nor spoken aloud as he watches now his cool, austere father filing jet in his workshop, or in the dining room, ladling out the stew. The father a stranger now, the beautiful small works, beautiful corallines, unexplained. Objects of desire. Warming to the touch with borrowed warmth. Emilio's creations.

For a year he carries the secret inside him. It is a raw place, an irritation that can be neither nacred over, nor expelled and forgotten.

In the end it is his father's cousin Giorgio who tells him, a visitor from the foreign homeland of which he knows nothing. For Emilio has told him nothing. *Did he never tell you why he came here, why he left Italy to come to this place that is nothing but two rocks above the sea? In Ascoli Piceno he was a successful man, a very successful goldsmith. He was very talented. He loved to work with colored stones, the most beautiful he could find, but in the simplest of cradles, so that the stone was all. He worked very hard, was always there, at his wheel, at his bench, cutting, polishing. Emilio was as he is now, very steady, very methodical. But then he made a mistake—he got carried away. That is how we are, we Dell'oro! But your father, Emilio, thought that he was different.*

But he was no different. For he began despite all a secret project. It seemed harmless at first; but then, so do they all. He had begun to work with corals, and these are most different from other gems, the hard, faceted gems with which he was accustomed to work. For corals, like jet, are porous, they breathe, like jet they are not alive but are the remains of living things. Maybe that is why, in his exile, he has chosen to work with jet, because it reminds him of the other, which he so loved.

He was fascinated by this new material, for by polishing it he could bring out all sorts of colors, all sorts of rich pinks and reds, which, it one day occurred to him, were like the pinks and reds of life itself, of the living flesh. Perhaps this is where the danger began, in this one simple realization. For soon he could not resist, he began carving figures, figures so tiny they could be set on a ring, or in a pendant, or on a brooch. To see these in the glass case in his shop was to wish to touch them—for they looked as if they might be warm to the touch, even though they were without life. Some might argue that they did live, in a way; a very particular kind of life—

He worked, at first, on traditional and religious subjects: the three Marys, the Christ Child, the thieves on their crosses—

Being beautiful, his things became very popular. Soon he began to receive special requests, some of which he would not like to share with your mother; for the special little corallines became very popular with a certain sort of gentleman, who liked to have them as secret watch fobs, carved in the likeness of the woman, pink, naked, and warm, whom he dreamed of loving . . .

And into it all the Dell'oro disease, all unseen, had already begun to creep.

Emilio found himself carving, for his own pleasure, again and again, the face and figure of the same woman, a woman of fantasy, a figment of his imagination, whom he regarded, because she was not real, as being of no real consequence. This despite the fact that he was spending a great deal of time with her, was even, indeed, a little bit in love with what he had created; but harmlessly so.

But then one day, as he was passing through the town square, he saw her: there she was, the woman whom he had carved, emerging from the lace shop, with a child, a little girl, by her side. Emilio could not help himself, but followed her, as far as he could, through the narrow, winding streets of our capital city, remaining always far enough behind so that she would not see him, until finally she made a turning, and he lost her.

It was a loss he could not accept.

Of course he was amazed, even horrified. How had this happened? He was haunted by what he had done, and made endless conjectures about it. Certainly there was a rational explanation. He had seen her before, in the street, perhaps, or glimpsed her profile in passing, in a window somewhere; noticed her, without noticing, at the park or the promenade; and her image stayed with him; or else it was just chance. But also it was strange, and with this Emilio was not comfortable; and I think he even believed, at the back of his mind, that he had created her, conjured her himself, coral made flesh, though this, of course, was impossible. And then it tormented him in another way, too, because he had already fallen more than a little in love with his coralline, his creation.

From this it was a very short step to thinking he must see her again, if only to prove to himself that he was mistaken. So he began to look for her, to search, in the squares, in the avenues, on the boulevards, in the gardens and the coffee shops . . . and when he found her again—as he was bound to do—again he followed her—each time he came upon her, in the shops, in the boulevards, he followed, for as long as he could keep her in sight. One day she noticed, and ran from him. She was his Daphne, and so he carved her, with coral branches for her hair, the arms and legs transformed, the beautiful Daphne turning, as she fled, into a tree all made from coral.

It was then that Emilio decided to leave Ascoli Piceno. He knew enough for this, that he could not stay. He was like a man who stands on shore and sees the wave coming, large and black, filled with terrible things, which will dash before it all that he holds dear. Gentilessa was still ignorant, busy with the baby, Anna, but for how long? And so he packed up before anybody could say anything, and took your Mama and the baby here, to this ugly place of two rocks by the sea . . . He gave up his goldsmithing; and in his perpetual mourning for she whom he has lost, now carves in honor of her memory these gruesome memento mori; and other things, too, perhaps, that you do not know of—

The cousin has more, family stories, the Dell'oro ancestor who carved jewels engraved with enigmatic runes and symbols, the remains of ancient languages only the jeweler understood, which were believed to foretell the fortune of the wearer; another who made a woman entirely of gold, so lifelike that she was believed to speak, saying *Help me*—in a voice peculiarly low, throaty, more like the painful gyration of an unoiled hinge on a rusty gate; another who created automata, beasts of the field, so realistic they could not be told from the real thing, until the slaughterer's knife revealed what was inside, the perfect coiled springs, the gears, the ingenious, jeweled mechanism; this was not life but something else, as Giorgio might have put it, a very particular kind of life.

There was obsession in it. A tendency to obsession. *La tendenza.* These things are rumors. Distortions. Monstrosities. It is these that my father thinks about there in his berth, down in the sloshing belly. And of course: of Clotilde at the taffrail. Clotilde at the spinet. Clotilde bending over to button her boot. *But I'm not like them.* Amended. Him. *I'm not like him. I hate him—and I'll never go back—*

AND THEN THEY PASS, MANWOMANBOYANDSPINET, INTO the heat of the subtropics. It is as if my father's anger at his father, once allowed expression, has dispersed, forming now a climate through which they will all be obliged to sail.

NOW BEGINS THEIR TRUE JOURNEY, TO WHICH ALL ELSE has been the prelude.

Many things, previously hidden, will now be revealed: my

mother's heat-bared shoulder; the wan, unshaven cheek and wild, staring eye of mal de mer–tormented Linus Starling, as he emerges from below deck for the first time in weeks, pale as a moth, as a mushroom, as the belly of a toad. Then, too, there is the monocle of John McIntyre, glinting ferociously in the light of that unrelenting sun, shooting sparks, divots of light.

For there are no ambiguities in the tropics. The sun shines mercilessly upon all; reveals all, mercilessly. It is a time of sharp contrasts, and sharp conflicts: of air and cloud and water against hull and sail, each battling the other, begrudging any progress; of pale skins turned painfully red, then gratefully brown; of stark, relentless blues and dense, dark, weighted shadows—for the shadows here, at the latitude 25 degrees north, possess the solidity, the authority, of objects. In a strange equatorial inversion, the occupants of the *Narcissus* find themselves rendered blind by an opulence of light, they fracture their vision on shadows each day as they pass from the burning brightness of outdoors into the ship's unbearable, stifling, stinking darkness. Imagine them (as do I), traveling, dazzled and blinking, from shipside to workroom, workroom to shipside, laden with buckets full of that imperturbably smiling ocean, brimming with all she has yielded and will not miss, firm in pursuit of their science yet made fools of by sun and shade, stumbling against each other blindly, spilling water, tripping over coils of rope, staggering among the piglets that run wild upon the deck with the cook in hot pursuit, his cleaver's flash as brilliant and as merciless as the sun.

Merciless. Yes, that is the word. It is all brightly, gaily, grandly merciless.

And my mother: the brightest, gayest, most merciless of all.

It's her turn now.

Now, during the hot, brilliant days and warm, languid nights, my mother begins the series of concerts in her stateroom. *Like a little snail I shrink/Into my painted shell*, that is what she sings, beneath a midnight sky alight with stars, the entire Milky Way, or so it seems, whirling away above them into a space infinite, black, and dizzying, while the *Narcissus* plows its own Milky Way, equally luminous, in the dark, fetid ocean, a galaxy of living creatures that twirl and spark for an instant, then spiral away again into depthless obscurity.

What a liar she is, my mother.

Because she does not shrink, she blossoms. In the hothouse tropic atmosphere she darkens with the influence of the sun, and also lightens, golden hair falling softly over tanned brow, teeth like pearls against berry-dark lips, her blue eyes more luminous than ever. In the somnolence of those short nights, when all on board are drunk with the heat, when the ocean, slackened, and relaxed, as if the moon, turning away its face, has released all from its influence, my mother exudes an unmistakable life force all her own, a pull as powerful as the moon's, and a perfume as intoxicating as any put forth by the orchids in Felix Girard's collection.

Wär' ich so klein wie Schnecken, indeed.

They're all there, at her concerts: the insufferable McIntyre, his mouth shut for once, Linus Starling, so pale and sinister, Hugh Blackstone, grudging but present, Harry Owen, calf eyed, my father, still in his suit that he will by no means shed, all there. The moon may have abandoned them, and the tides, but my mother holds them fast in her orbit on those still evenings, when their sighs, it seems, are the only breath upon the sails. A prefiguration in this of what is to come, but all in ignorance still, in their bliss, they are one and all in love with her: not just my father, but all. Though he most of all, sick with it, and sick with the hiding of it. He has been successful in this, the hiding, with everyone but her.

He shrinks from what he loves. Attraction and repulsion. Fortunately he has hidden the things he really cares about, the things my too-perceptive mother must by no means see.

And his other work, his official work, as ship's artist, his work sketching those ephemeral creatures brought up in the brimming buckets or captured in Harry Owen's surface net, goes brilliantly well. Night after night they two haul the net, invert it into their jars and vials of water, releasing a cloud of thrashing, scuttering things, soft, struggling ambiguities that wink, pulse, glow, retort, subside. At the height of it, my father is up all night, drawing by candlelight, his dark head bent over the paper, the pencils, despite Harry Owen's assertion that he must stop for the night and *Go to bed, Leo.* No: he will not. This is his obsession.

His other obsession.

What does he see, when he looks at them?

Soft, translucent bodies, electrical sparks, fiery snowflakes, palpitating stars. Ephemera. They will be gone by morning: gone, as if they never existed at all.

Thus his rush, to draw them as they fall. The brief bright shower, fiery descent.

For Harry Owen's creatures, his captives, do not thrive. Some disappear almost immediately, sinking down and away into those vials filled with seawater; others last a few days, throbbing, flailing, floating, dying. Some last a week. A week at most.

None are brought back alive. Though some will return in formaldehyde. Others, those solid enough, packed in cotton wool. But what will return are mere shadows of the living creatures, simulacra, gestures toward. In a drawer in the museum now, gathering dust. Unrecognizable things, giving rise to distortions, misunderstandings, mistakes in the science, fantasies.

The ocean has so many. It will not miss a few.

In my father's drawings, that is where they really live now.

He is almost happy, absorbed in the work that progresses, if not to his satisfaction—for this is impossible, he is never satisfied, though he is prevented, by the brief alighting of his subjects, from his usual picking and scratching, doing and re-doing—then, at least, well enough.

Their brevity aids his contentment.

It is my father's favorite time, late at night, in the silence and the starlight. The small, guttering flame of Harry Owen's cigar. Night watch on the booms. Hugh Blackstone at the helm. Sails bellying soundlessly in a night breeze, soft *slip-slop* beneath the bows the only sound. The dark water a solid thing, viscous membrane. There is a sense of breath held, of anticipation, an immanence, as of something unknown that is about to happen: a planet, rising on the dark horizon, out of the sea, it seems, Venus it is, bright as a flame.

That's it, that's what it was—

Except it isn't.

At Harry Owen's elbow there comes, not a touch, but the warm, familiar insinuation of a touch.

Dr. Owen, my mother says, *I have come to see what it is you are always tangling up in this mysterious net of yours.*

Her golden hair seen in darkness shines like a bright, submerged thing, half seen, rising in a rush to surface in dark waters.

And what about you, Mr. Dell'oro? What have you caught tonight?

N-nothing. We haven't h-hauled the net yet.

There is fearfulness in him, at her approach. She feels it, draws closer.

Excellent! That means I can watch. I have always watched my Papa at his work, you know. I have helped him with it, too. He tells me I am his only real collaborator—his scientific amanuensis.

Turning from them she leans against the rail, then leans over it toward the water; gazes at the place where the towline disappears. It is a thin, shining gossamer, a spider's web.

Well—ain't you going to take up your net?

Commanded, they cannot disobey. Together Leo and Harry take hold of the line, pull. Then pull again.

The net, though, will not come.

I can imagine my mother's laugh, high and clear and faintly derisive, in the watery darkness.

A further effort on their part, dark pantings at the line. And then it comes, all at once, furiously, dripping black with weed, green with foam, and falls, writhing madly, onto the deck. From among the coils there resonates a fierce, hollow, chopping sound, like the fall of a mallet on a block.

Small things scatter everywhere, shrimps, fishes, snails, angry squids, crabs clinging desperately to knots of bladder as the net twists and thrashes, contorts into a hundred wild figures, writing an alphabet from a dream.

Oh, how my mother enjoys it! She shrieks with laughter, she is filled with delight. And she is the brave one, she the delicate, the golden haired, she with the shawl cascading like foam from around her shoulders bends forward, while Harry Owen and Leo Dell'oro draw back. Bends forward, and reaches down her hand.

Don't.

This is Hugh Blackstone. His cool, severe observing eye has taken them in and judged them incompetent to cope.

Fetch the oar.

They, though, are paralyzed as at their feet the net turns upon itself in a last violent peristalsis, then disgorges: a great green eel, four or five feet long, jaws snapping, this is the sound they heard, the hollow chop of a mallet on a block.

Fetch the oar.

Still nobody can move but then at last my father does. He runs off up the deck, a glimmering, small figure, they see him struggle with the tarp on the smallboat, trying to lift it up to get at the oars. The eel, though, is quicker; it turns over once, a single sinuous contortion, slides over the side, falls back, there is hardly a splash, it is gone.

In the silence that follows, Harry Owen begins to pick sadly at the remains of his net.

My dear Dr. Owen, was it not magnificent?

My mother is still laughing, flashing her brilliant feathers in the starlight.

Blackstone turns the yellow glare of his bird-eye upon her.

That, madam, could easily have removed your hand.

Then there is that cold, unpleasant smile. It is admirable, is it not, the cold severity of this Hugh Blackstone? I wonder is he imagining my mother's hand in the eel's jaws, and smiling at that? Those pale white fingers, the delicate, pink pearlescent nails. Otherwise, at what does he smile? It doesn't matter, I suppose. My mother has her hand; and in a moment Hugh Blackstone will be back on the bridge, consulting his sextant as if nothing has happened.

Now at last my father returns exultant with the oar. But my mother, spanked, seeks immediately to spank in turn.

Mr. Dell'oro, she cries, *it appears you are an oar short!*

The air comes out of him at that, humiliated he slackens visibly, the oar held triumphantly upright makes a quick descent toward the deck and in that same moment something else happens, there is a kind of shift, a beat skipped, it is as if the air has gone out of everything, yes, that is it exactly, the air goes out of everything, not just him but everything, in the sails, too, the breeze has died completely, all the bellying white folds fall slack, something somewhere breathing has died, and its breath will not resume.

Hugh Blackstone, on the bridge, utters a soft oath.

My mother, as if conscious of what she has done, runs away then, my father and Harry Owen stand helpless watching the curl of her shawl glimmering in the dark, lessening and lessening like the crest of a wave that breaks and slips back into the sea. In a few minutes they will hear a few notes of the spinet, rising from down below.

But they're done now. They're finished. They've entered the Trough of Leo's Despair. A trough that will be deepened, almost before they really realize they're in it, by a shout from the mainmast the next morning:

Land, Captain! To the south, sir!

There it is, after all those weeks, the sought-after object, land: purple, wavering slightly, miragelike, insubstantial as smoke, seeming, like smoke, to float just above the water, rather than to rest upon or arise from it.

But they are becalmed. Stuck, in the Trough of Leo's Despair.

Best not make too much of this, nobody's mood controls the weather, not really.

A cheer rises up from around the ship, there is a sudden flurry of activity, trunks being packed, scientific instruments readied, gear stowed or unstowed (depending), piglets chased into their pen, breeches laundered, hair combed, faces washed, gloves buttoned, for the first time in seven-odd weeks.

It's a long time to float like a smut in a saucer. Grime builds up, a certain amount of filth that may be ignored while at sea, but must be removed before progressing onto land. Even onto such a land as Punta Yalkubul is likely to be.

There is a shimmer of anticipatory dread, thinking about that. Quickly buried, though, as the decks are scraped with holystone: scoured once, twice, three times, and the barnacles chipped off the hull, in preparation for a landing.

But they will not be landing. The sails will hang slack throughout this very hot day, and through an entire sultry night as well. Nonetheless, optimism runs high. It isn't until the end of a second day that the truth of the matter is suspected; and even then it doesn't win wide acceptance. The gloom isn't widespread until the end of the fourth day.

Hugh Blackstone, of course, is the exception. He's been scowling consistently since he uttered that oath.

Then begins the murmur. That's when, on the fourth day.

It arises, first, in the lower parts of the *Narcissus*, those areas which, lying under water, are perpetually dark—beneath the cabins and the workrooms, beneath the space where the men hang their hammocks and stow their trunks, down beneath, where supplies are kept: the casks of water, the biscuit, the salt beef and cornmeal, the bread and the raisins, the peas and molasses, the sacks of dried apples and of rice, of potatoes, cocoa, tea, the barrels of pickles, butter, beer and onions—and lower yet, down below the ballast, in the bilges, where the pumps are manned continuously, day and night (though night from day cannot be distinguished there, and the lantern burns all the time).

That is where the murmur begins. Indistinctly, at first.

At least, on the fourth day it is indistinct. Also on the fifth day, as the sails hang slack, and the viscous, blue-green membrane of the sea clings around the ship, determined to hold her fast. Things are said—indistinct things—in the hold, in the berths, in the cabins; in the companionway, in the galley, in the saloon; on the forecastle, amidships, and astern; up in the rigging, in the crow's nest, on the mainmast; around the mizzen, and over the boom.

My mother's name is being mentioned. The eel, too. Bad luck is mentioned, as is ill omen, mermaid's curse, the mop over the side, the bucket likewise, the tossed stone, the ginger-haired man, the wrong foot forward, the three gulls flying, the mysterious whistle, the trimmed beard, the pared nail, the parson's collar, the flag through the ladder, the dog at the tackle.

What my father hears he's never sure he's heard correctly.

Someone's got the cat under the basket.

What? What?

It's nothing, a whisper around a hatchway. When he looks at them they avert their eyes.

The cat's under the basket all right.

Someone's put it there, for sure.
But what does it mean?

Him with that ginger hair. And her.
 It's her that brought the beast out of the sea. But he's bad, too. That hair's a sign, for them as has eyes to see it.
 You bet it is.
 Launch with the devil, sail with the devil, that's what they say. Ginger hair's the devil's hair.

They cross themselves, duck furtively along the passages. They know my father's heard them, but they don't want to meet his glance.

And that sea, indifferent as a cat, smiling its noncommittal cat's smile, barely flicking its cat's paw in the pitch of a wave: it lies like a cat, languorously, stretching itself without effort in the unbearable heat of the afternoons, through the starlit torpor of the nights; with land just there on the horizon, teasingly beyond reach, insubstantial as smoke. It will make no effort on their behalf, that indolent, smiling sea.

A cormorant, black as pitch, flies above the bows: the men cross themselves; from somewhere down deep the murmur rises—

.   .   .

At last Hugh Blackstone must say what it means. *The men believe the ship's been cursed—a sea witch has stolen their wind. They blame you, Miss Girard. A woman on board is bad luck, in their eyes. If anything goes wrong she's bound to be blamed. They're a superstitious lot, these sailors—and stupid besides. Toss a pebble overboard and they believe it'll drag the whole ship down with it. It makes no sense. There's no logic in it. But once they get these ideas, they never let 'em go.*

The explanation itself falls like a stone. There is nothing to do but wait.

My father bears up poorly in the heat. Eventually he concedes to remove his dark jacket and yellow waistcoat, to appear on deck in his shirtsleeves. But he keeps faith with his formerly proper, formerly starched collar and cuffs, he will not remove these, though they wilt sadly around his neck and wrists in the overwhelming humidity. He would not want *her* to see him without them— such a sweating, suffering fool. She does nothing but laugh at this, he in cuffs and collar, stifling in a tropical heat that demands, above all else, a sacrificial progress toward gleaming nakedness.

A progress that she makes gladly, and much to his unease.

Then, too, the sailors affect him. He dislikes being in close proximity to their superstitions, which, after all, are so similar to his own. I imagine him staring at the lifeless sails when nobody else is looking, muttering *Black black bear-away, don't come down by here-away!* or some other savage nonsense, as if this might lift the curse. Hours and hours he spends, perched on the taffrail as the *Narcissus* lists, first one way, then the other. What is he doing? Brooding upon the traitorous stillness of the sea. Muttering his incantations.

Dark shapes move beneath those waters. He comes away from the taffrail hollow eyed, subdued. Who knows what he is thinking.

But then who knows what any of them may be thinking— floating there, under the weight of the unrelenting sunlight, with land, the merest puff of it—a sliver, a rind, a crust, a peeling like the skin off an orange—stretched out, completely unobtainable, on the far, purpling horizon.

It is a weight in itself, an internal weight, this land that can be seen but not touched, which itself seems not to touch the waves, buoyed above them, rather, by some peculiar alchemy of water and light.

There's an equation for that.

It floats but does not wander, is tight upon its tether, always there, to the south. Tantalizingly.

But it is not for them. Water is for them. Plenty of that. Water and murmur. Water and murmur and malaise.

.   .   .

It's inevitable, I suppose, that arguments should begin, under circumstances like these. Have I mentioned that my grandfather, Felix Girard, is of a choleric temperament?

Ginger hair is the devil's hair. Or so they say.

He is a man addicted to movement, forced now to be still. In tedious times he remembers his old operating theater in l'Hôtel-Dieu, misses it, that hated place, the gleaming sharps, even the sickly, sweet smell, this, too, is a memory. The Saint Jerome Ward, there beneath the shadow of the cathedral. The dutiful Sisters of Bon Secours with their sallow horse-faces, their bound-up hair, their disapproving looks. All that dingy linen.

He flexes his hands, feels the old longing. To cut. *Me next, doctor. Help me.* Three, four, six to a bed they were in that filthy place. They bled them into buckets on the floor. Most could not be helped. He cut, regardless.

Sister—the blade!

He has strong decisive hands, my grandfather. Butcher's hands. Now idle.

Well. It's hard on everyone.

If he could cut anything in the current circumstances I think it would be John McIntyre he'd cut. Excise him like a tumor from the otherwise healthy flesh of this expedition. The hatred between them is of long standing, based in professional jealousy. Each having something means neither can have all. This, of course, is unforgivable. And McIntyre is Harry Ellis's appointment here. A functionary of the museum. Hence: a snitch, a rat, a spy. He with that greasy monocle of his. And the clipped, arrogant *I see.*

This is a real irritation.

They bicker together, in the long, hot waste of the days. I wish I could say they didn't mean it. But they do.

What are they arguing about? Classification of the *Psittaciformes* of British Guiana, in particular the Guianian sun parrot, John McIntyre's particular discovery. My grandfather, it seems, has found McIntyre's monograph unconvincing.

Admit it, McIntyre—you have never seen the thing! And why? Because it does not exist! Come, come now, confess! You identify this bird by the cry only, is it not so? By the characteristic mee-hoo! mee-hoo! *Why, it is not a bird at all, it is a cat; and a domestic cat at that, that came to Guiana in an Englishwoman's stocking! Of course you have never seen it—admit it, McIntyre, come clean!*

He is very serious, my grandfather, not just serious, he's livid; his face is as red as his hair, he is shouting, he is laughing, I wish he did not have this side to his character but he does and now he must show it.

And McIntyre, too, is furious, he must, of course, strike back, this he does by questioning the origin and accuracy of certain passages in my grandfather's book, *Felix Girard's Ghosts of Bain Dzak.*

One passage that I particularly enjoy is in question, the one that describes a particular sandstone formation in the desert, southeast of Dalanzadgad, at Bayan Ovoo. My grandfather writes that the rock there *had been peculiarly deformed by the wind, coming to resemble, over vast eons of time, the traveling sledge of the legendary Altan Khan; upon close examination there may be discerned, carved upon the rock, whether by human hand or divine, the words "By the will of the Eternal Blue Heaven" (Köke Möngke Tngri). This object is worshipped by the local peoples, who leave upon it each evening offerings of food, coins, bells, sheepskins, walking sticks, even empty bottles of usquebaugh.*

My mother always liked that passage, too, because my grandfather was in Bain Dzak when she was born, and used to read aloud to her from this book, when she was a child, as if, in this way, to explain his absence, of which her mother, Marie-Louise Girard, used bitterly to complain.

But John McIntyre holds that there is no such object. *It's lies, all lies, a fabric of fatuous fibs. You are a fraud, sir; you have never been to Bayan Ovoo, to Dalanzadgad, or to Bain Dzak—why, if you've been a step farther east than Chicksand Street, I'll eat my hat!*

Why must they do it? Are they not hot enough? Now everyone's dinner is ruined, and then my mother's performance of the "Der Vogelfänger" aria is interrupted, my grandfather punctuating the amusing refrain, *"der Vogelfänger bin ich ja, Stets lustig, tra la la!,"* with his imitation of the characteristic but disputed *mee-hoo! mee-hoo!* of the Guianian sun parrot, to everyone's dismay. Now the concert is over; and McIntyre, monocle blazing with fury, has stomped off somewhere—and all the time there's that ocean, that implacable, winking object, duplicitous in delft blue; and land, Punta Yalkubul, there to the south, resembling, sometimes, a wisp of fog, pearly grey in color, at other times a ribbon that has fallen loose from my mother's hair, deeply violet, reclining—

And my father, nervously rubbing the heel of his right hand against his left wrist, poor sweating fool, the sailors make him uneasy. They are doing something peculiar down below; they are making faces at him behind his back—

Malaise and murmur, murmur and malaise.

And water. Never a shortage of that.

Something has to happen eventually. They can't go on like this forever, all this floating, it has to end sometime.

Maybe now.

Harry Owen, unable to sleep, rises at 3:00 A.M.; sees, by the light of a gibbous moon, as he stands on deck with his cigar, Punta Yalkubul on the horizon, dense, blue grey as smoke, slightly lighter, in color, than either sea or sky; sees it from starboard, instead of the usual larboard; thinks it looks nearer than before; then, disoriented, thinks that he is dreaming, or else that they have drifted, though there is no wind by which to account for this, and hardly any waves. A dream then. A dream wind has moved them. Who dreamed it, this wind? He has, Harry Owen has; Leo Dell'oro has; Clotilde has; they have done it, all of them, together, it is a collective dream, a collective sigh, a wished-for exhalation. This is satisfactory. Now Harry Owen can sleep. Morning, though, reveals him to have been mistaken: this is no dream; nor have they moved. A thick bank of cloud has drawn up, and approaches the *Narcissus* from the north. This is what Harry Owen saw, and mistook for land. It was gathering, even then; gathering, while they dreamed. Hugh Blackstone, tight-lipped, regards this object through his glass, then begins shouting, *Haul the jib! Take in the fore! Furl the mizzen topgallant! Clew up the main topgallant!* Suddenly the *Narcissus* awakes from its torpor, the men spring up into the rigging. Certainly something will happen now.

But no.

Now it is still, with a stillness unlike any they have known before, a stillness so utter and so complete that the sound of my mother dropping a single hairpin as she completes her morning toilet could carry throughout the entire ship—a stillness of men and nature both, as if somebody, pulling a celestial plug somewhere, has suddenly let all the *murmur* in the world run out a drain.

Hugh Blackstone, unpleasant over breakfast, will only say *Now we will have some weather*—

Who knows what this might mean. Only that it is eerily still, that the bank of cloud grows closer, mounts the horizon, a great, grey-green fist of a cloud, shot through at the top with vivid green bursts of light. Here it is, hanging over them like judgment; but beneath the cloud is stillness, dead calm, a tepid sea, no wind, the air hot and sweet and rotten. It is unhealthy air; but breathe it they must, and so they do, cautiously, in shallow gasps, through handkerchiefs if possible. It is crackling, that air—saturated. And they are saturated. The electricity enters them upward, through the timbers of the ship, downward, through that air, the heaviness of which makes everything difficult, walking, speaking, raising to the lips a fork or a cup of tea; better to paddle through it, that would seem natural. Except that nothing is natural, least of all they, crackling with the static of the cloud.

Surely, now it will happen.

Instead they eat lunch.

Now it is coming. There is a spark, a flash of monocle, John McIntyre has begun again upon Felix Girard, calling him *fraud, fake, charlatan, swindler*. This over an unfortunate fish stew. *The entire expedition is a fraud—a trick to bilk money out of Harry Ellis—there was no intention of ever arriving in Punta Yalkubul— him at the helm is in on it, too—all of you together—crooks—cheats— thieves—confidence tricksters—!* McIntyre pulls a piece of paper out of his pocket, begins waving it around, a tiny, square ghost, brilliant white and incorporeal in the sickly grey-green light. *Here it is, a letter from your partner in crime, Arthur Petrook, laying out the entire scheme!*

Now my grandfather, always fiery, turns brick red, the veins in his temples bulge as he cries out fiercely, *It is lies, all lies! I will show you, McIntyre, you scoundrel! I will show you, you rotten arse- kisser! You monster! You deformed abortion of a man! I will show you what is real science and what is bluff! Just wait!*

Yes, this is it: now it has happened. They are all appalled now, my mother near tears, my father shrunk down in his corner, Harry Owen dabbing nervously with a piece of bread, Linus

Starling hunching and ducking over his fish stew. And yet at the same time nothing has happened, this they are made to know by an outcry on deck, where something else is happening, something altogether bigger.

The great fist on the horizon has taken everything into its grasp. That is what has happened. The constriction has begun, the sky dark as ash, though with an eerie cast of yellow, all hands standing silent and staring—

(So lost are they who emerge from the saloon that they do not know where to look, what to see, looking therefore and seeing nothing but the pale, upturned faces until the mate takes pity on their confusion and points—)

—up into the rigging, where a dazzling, white-green light is sparking and spitting along the main topgallant masthead; bouncing down then onto the topgallant yard, twirling, it's like a top, if tops were made of fire, then down, further down it goes, bouncing onto the flying jib boom end, such a dance, a flamenco I believe, before it disappears for a moment—just a moment, leaving in its wake a black afterglow, a momentary blindness, before it reappears again, assuming a playful posture just above my father's head, his face is lit with it, lit green—

(Now they see it, even he sees it now, my father, Leo Dell'oro, as down it comes—)

—down, further down, onto his chest, onto that once-starched shirtfront that he refuses to take off, oh, how it sizzles there, it sings, it pops and hisses, it cavorts, such a performance, with his chest for a stage; a jig it dances, a clog dance, as the sky above and sea below turn blacker than black, and then with a crash it all splits open, the fist tightens and the flood comes down just as, with a soft sound, a sigh, a gentle letting out of air, Leo Dell'oro's legs fold up neatly beneath him, and he falls, too.

Such a pandemonium.

It's hard to imagine it almost, sailors running, and pigs, these squealing, and my mother, she squealing also as Felix Girard attempts to shield her with his shaggy bear's body, McIntyre groping like a blind man with his monocle transformed into a waterfall, and what of my father, lying there like that, at the bottom of it all.

Someone ought to help him.

Why have I done it, put him in such a position, he's out cold, helpless, but now Harry Owen has him by the armpits, and this other one, Linus Starling, takes him by the feet, this is unfortunate, that it had to be Linus Starling, why have I done this, my poor father, and together, with much effort, they carry him back into the saloon, lay him out on the table like the Christmas goose, he's at the center of it all now, and they're all there, crowded around, as many as can fit, seeking shelter from the deluge, soaked like rats the lot of them, trying to wring themselves out.

Look at him, says Linus Starling, *he's steaming.*

It's true. Steam is rising from my father's sopping clothes. He's unconscious of this, mercifully.

It's damned hot in here, says Harry Owen. *Better unbutton him.*

Unpack him's more like it, Starling says.

It's too bad Linus Starling has to be involved in this. My father never liked him. Yet all the same it's true, as they unbutton the proud shirtfront they find that Leo has a second skin, he's lined himself underneath with all sorts of stuff, letters, drawings, pages torn from magazines, bits of textile—

Hey, ho! says Linus Starling, *what's this?*

He holds up what appears to be a crumpled swatch of material, a bit of stuff that might (were it larger) be used to make a curtain, or upholster a chair.

It looks like one of Petrook's bits, says Harry Owen, remembering. *No doubt something Dell'oro picked up off a pile in Bury Place. He's a compulsive gatherer of the worst sort, you know.*

I remember, too, my father in that hot dark room in Bury Place, shoving something into his pocket. It's come back to haunt him now.

Hey, ho! says Starling, *it looks just like Madamoiselle Girard!*

Don't be a fool, Starling—

Harry Owen takes the bit of textile away from him, carefully spreads it out on a corner of the table where my father is not, sighs over it a little, what, after all, can he say? It is a woven exotic miniature my father has stolen, the image of a fair servant girl kneeling before a beautifully brocaded elephant, presenting to it a jewel, an emerald, perhaps, the image very small, yet it cannot be denied that Linus Starling is right, it bears a startling resemblance to my mother, who, standing just to the left of the table wringing out her hair, sees it, and gives a tiny gasp, that is all, just a gasp, and then turns away, pretending not to have seen. They all pretend—some things, after all, are better unseen—yet this cannot be avoided.

Hey, ho ho! Here's another—and another—

Continuing the unpacking, this Linus Starling has rolled my father over and found, pressed against his back, drawings of Clotilde. He's so exacting, my father. Here she is: Clotilde at the taffrail, Clotilde in the saloon, Clotilde bending over to button her boot—

Poor unconscious father, peeled like an onion to the vulnerable, milky-white core, all the secrets of his heart and body ignominiously exposed. They'll make a feast of him now for certain.

Poor silly fellow. He cannot help it. Who can defend against my beautiful Clotilde? Gentlemen, even I cannot. Certainly not a silly fellow like this. Owen, Starling, when the rain stops, take him below and put him to bed. And take all that stuff with you, eh? Put it away somewhere safe.

So my grandfather has rescued him, for now.

And my mother, what about her?

Now she's seen it. Now she knows. She's gazing at my father contemplatively. He's a pale, unshelled creature, laid out there on the table for her delectation, every bit of him, every scrap, every fragment of his poor disarticulated soul exposed. But she says nothing. Nothing. Only turns away.

That's not like her. Something has really happened, now.

. . .

When the rain has done its battering, they take him below. At seven he'll wake, confused, asking Harry Owen if he's dead. *No, by no means. It was nothing; just a corposant, St. Elmo's fire. A kind of electrical discharge brought about by the storm—quite harmless—*

Harry Owen can hardly bear to look at him now. He does everything not to look, his gaze averted, over my father's shoulder, or down, in the direction of his feet.

He is thinking about that night on the Embankment, the frightening absence. And this, the subsequent voiding. It is difficult to be a gentleman about this.

My father, though, sees nothing amiss, sleeps again, for him there's nothing but oblivion, despite the storm. Brief violent downpours, thunder and lightning that shake the ship, this continues until dawn. Probably nobody sleeps, except my father, who sleeps so poorly, in the best of times.

In the morning the sky is clear, it's as if nothing has happened, nor have they moved. Punta Yalkubul is once again a purple ribbon dropped by a careless girl, tapering away narrowly, like a ribbon, to nothing at the ends.

Lightning seldom strikes a ship at sea. But the saint's body is a different matter. That means bad luck. My father is a marked man now. But, still sleeping, he doesn't know it; and by the time he wakes, rather late, it won't matter anymore.

. . .

Hugh Blackstone, on the bridge, observes, with his glass, the horizon's edge. Land is there, lives being lived, though giving no sign: no lights at night, no sails by day, it is odd is it not, a mode of life difficult to imagine. As he stands one of his men approaches, speaking quickly, with a faint air of emergency. *One of the smallboats is missing. Gone, sir, and the oars, too, sir, gone without a trace.*

Gone? What do you mean?

The withering glance of Blackstone.

I don't know where it's gone, sir, but it's gone, and cook says a sack of his best salt fish is gone, too, an' one of potatoes, and a cask of water.

That's impossible. I suppose the fairies done it? The faint derisive smile, this is something to be avoided. Even if Doyle does think the fairies done it, he will not say so now; and as far as Hugh Blackstone is concerned, that is a good thing.

I don't know, sir.

Very well, Doyle. I'll deal with it.

Wisp of Doyle, running away.

Blackstone at the rail now, smiling still. Smiling. *Well, I'll be damned.* Training his glass at the edge of the earth.

By lunchtime it is confirmed that Felix Girard has gone. His bed has not been slept in; John McIntyre has found a note, pinned inside his *Compendium of American Psittaciformes*, which reads, *I will show you, McIntyre, you bastard! You puny man, now you will see!*

Clotilde is in tears. She can't find her dear Papa anywhere. And neither can anybody else. A search of the ship is fruitless, the import of the note clear: he has taken one of the smallboats and some supplies, and set out to row himself to Punta Yalkubul.

God help him, says Hugh Blackstone, laughing, *he's just mad enough to succeed!*

Everyone's looking at the horizon now. If the *Narcissus* is a smut in a saucer, then what is Felix Girard in a smallboat?

All that immensity.

And my father, sleeping. He doesn't even know. He's dreaming, maybe; of what, who can tell. Far distances, perhaps, or the opposite of that, the delicate pink whorl of one particular ear.

I've taken him this far. The rest is inevitable.

He won't be back, my grandfather. The search party, sent out despite Hugh Blackstone's reluctance, will run aground on what they think is Punta Yalkubul, finding there, instead, a small island, ten miles in circumference, consisting of an east-facing coral-sand beach and a west-facing red mangrove swamp crouched over a shallow lagoon formed by a coral reef. Sand flats extend prettily, at low tide, perhaps three quarters of a mile to the south. All that will be left here, of my grandfather, is the mark of his keel in the sand, and a plug of tobacco, left behind when he pulled his smallboat through the shrubbery, and rowed off the other side.

All the days they spent, staring out at this crust in the sea. We all have our illusions.

Though Felix Girard could not be produced, the search party brought back samples of what life there was. There were beauties there, in the place where my grandfather disappeared, the place where I, too, now, am bound: honeycombed corals, some growing in thin, perpendicular points, others forming thick, fawn-colored antlers, still others round, green knobs, some convoluted like brains; brittle, whip-legged starfish, delicate shrimps, minute, sparkling amphipods, alive, still, in the jars, before Harry Owen kills them; sea whips and sea fans; the sea cucumber, *Holothuriae*, in bright yellow and brown; sponges in every color, every shape; beautiful shells; and a diminutive sole, two inches long, marbled gold and black above, creamy white below—named, for the first time, by he who catalogued it, Owen's Darling Solenette, *Monochirus amatus Owenii*.

He would have loved this stuff, my grandfather, if he'd seen it.

There's solace here for some, for Harry Owen, for my father. He is interested in the smallest finds, in the sand that turns out, beneath the microscope, to contain shells, miniature in size but magnificent in architecture, glorious spires and intricately incised whorls, cathedrals, each one smaller than a grain of rice. I can imagine him, after the wind turned (because it did turn, finally), drawing these, spending many hours on that long journey home hunched by a candle, separating out, with a pin, these tiny beauties from among the dross, then sketching, sketching. I have seen what he found there: entire cities, miniature worlds, ancient and beautiful catacombs, mysterious curving passages leading to who-knows-what-or-where, glimmering opalescent walls signposted with the runes and hieroglyphs of the sea. I imagine he sees, within their pale pink or golden or creamy white curves, curves softer yet: of a certain cheek, the nape of a neck, of the closed and slightly trembling lid of a downcast eye—

For her there is no solace. There will be no miracle, no chance sighting, no encounter with another vessel that has picked up *a ginger-bearded Frenchman, floating*. No matter how many days she spends at the rail, gazing at that empty blue mirror of a sea, she will never find him. She finds nothing but herself reflected there. Felix Girard is lost, as quick and as sure as her blue shawl would be lost, if she flung it upon the water. He will not be retrieved.

You see we have so much in common, she and I.

I turn my face away from what comes next, her loneliness, his obsession, attraction overcoming repulsion, the edging toward and away and toward again, the first touch, then the second, the loss in her, desire in him, that's it: that they will be together is inevitable now. What else is there for her, after all? Rooms in Bury Place, dead things, and, down below, that vulture Petrook waiting, preening himself, sharpening his claws.

I wouldn't do that to her. I've done enough already.

In the brightness of the day I can see there's a hieroglyph outside my window, though I cannot read it: two halves of something brilliant that has been broken, and a gesture that says, *Carlotta, it's time to go.*

II.

———◆———

THE BIRDCAGE

It is hard to get in; harder yet to get out.

These are first two things my mother, orphaned now, cast ashore, learns about her new home in Whitby, on Bridge Street, above the River Esk. The house is called the Birdcage. Here it perches, above the river, here with my mother in it, the Birdcage, the narrow, whitewashed, pentagonal house where my parents begin their life together; the house with its two cramped, winding staircases, one designated for up, the other for down, since only with difficulty may two persons pass through either at once; with its thick stone walls and stubborn, low-jambed doors, none of which opens the first time—none willing—all must be pushed, pushed hard, with the shoulder, or, in my mother's case, because she is slight, pushed with the whole of the body. They must be pushed twice, at least, those doors, if they are to yield; and when they yield at last they do it grudgingly, the wood grating against the uneven flagstone floor up to the final sticking point beyond which it will not move at all, the point at which even my mother, small as she is, must turn sideways in order to slip through, whether into the next room or out into the raw cobblestoned outdoors.

Hard to get in, harder yet to get out.

Like everything else in the house, the doors are swollen with the damp. Rusty of hinge. Disinclined. The house shudders above the river as if it would prefer to rise up and run; but, held fast, it receives, reluctantly, through its foundation, through its floors, its walls, its windows, the rush and suck of the tumbling Esk as it carries toward the sea a malodorous cargo of grease and gut, fin and bone, pulp and tar, bitumen and slag, night soil and glue: the runoff of the blubber works, the fishing fleet, the boatyard, the knacker's yard, the jet works, the privies, the mines. My mother, in the house above the river, is puzzled, per-haps, after so many months at sea, to find that, though cast ashore, she still hears water rushing beneath her all the time; still smells it; still feels the damp of it everywhere, permeating everything, the furniture and food and clothes and bedding, the sheet music that she so seldom touches now, even herself, her skin, her hair, all rich and damp with the unwelcome oily scent of the river, the scent both of life and of death, which no amount of washing will ever remove. Through leaded windows that cry out upon rusty hinges of their own she observes when she so chooses, and also sometimes when she does not, the edge of the harbor, one arm of the breakwater, the cold North Sea beyond. These are dangerous objects—shards of glass upon which she may cut herself if she is not careful.

. . .

And my Papa?

Very often my mother turns her back upon the sea. She dislikes it in all its moods, its grey wintry indifference, its boiling infuriated white and green, its bright icy dissimulating blue. She cannot help but sense, no matter what is on the surface, the dark that lies beneath.

My Papa . . .

She cannot think about him. She cannot think about anything else. She cannot think.

His things, of course, are all around her—those, at least, that Petrook, ever calculating his profit and his loss, knew he could not sell. They are her inheritance and her dowry, shipped north from London in a series of packing crates and bundles, crowding now each of the five corners of each of the three rooms of the Birdcage, and rendering more precarious by their presence the screw-tight turning of the two staircases, both down and up. These are her old friends, her playmates, the splayed and grinning confidantes of her girlhood—the elephant's skull, the stuffed orang-utan, the snakeskins and skeletons, the gaily patterned venomous cone shells, the butterflies and moths askew on their pins, her father's prized *Morpho telemachus*, his *Attacus atlas*, his box of rotting silkworm pupae, the jar containing a mysterious object labeled "Mermaid's hand," the heads and arms, the broken-off chins and noses and fingers of stone idols neglected and fallen—even a single large crate containing nothing but the skins of birds Girard had been interrupted in the process of preserving, shedding now their feathers of crimson and violet and indigo, their delicate beaks shattered, packed in obvious haste, without care. Her father's hummingbirds arrived in a cage, all dead but one. The single survivor, emerald green above, ruby red beneath, batters itself all along the crooked ceilings, buzzes like a trapped fly in the casements, never resting. Hovering in place it drinks sugar water from a glass that my mother has set out for it, then darts away up the stairs, or tangles itself among the last, dying filaments, cold nipped, of Felix Girard's remaining orchids, or dodges between the rotting, rolled-up Turkish carpets leaning in the corners; or zooming downstairs makes Mary, the girl-of-all-work, scream aloud when its wing (moving so fast that it does not seem to move at all), grazes her cheek or her hair. For days at a time the hummingbird disappears completely, until some slight motion—a vibration among the white lace of a curtain, perhaps—reveals it; and then it is gone again, until next time.

Señor El Galliñazo is intact, though balder than before, it is true, and rests now upstairs in the bedroom, on top of the chest of drawers, along with a snaggletoothed cayman that used to perch on the shelf above my mother's bed in Bury Place. Her family gone, these corpses make Clotilde feel at home; she will not throw anything away. What does not fit inside the house is piled, still boxed, in the shed out back where Leopold struggles against the cold to make his studio in an ever-dwindling space, surrounded by curiosities.

Up to his neck in them.

But then the whole house is a collector's cabinet without the collector, except as he is reflected in his accumulation. My mother, stroking El Galliñazo's molting back, or thumbing through the *Conchylien-Cabinet* (from which Arthur Petrook has removed the best of the colored plates with the sharpest and subtlest of knives), or touching the leathery palm of the gorilla's hand that she keeps hidden in a drawer among her stockings, or arranging the heads of six terra-cotta goddesses along the fireplace mantel in the room that serves the Birdcage as sitting and dining room both, feels the collector's presence so vividly that she would not be surprised to hear him say: *Ah, Tildy! Why must you tease and torment your poor Papa so?—*

But she doesn't.

She doesn't hear him; yet his waistcoat, against which she sometimes rests her cheek, still smells like him, and his old watch in its silver case still bears the smooth spot where his thumb rubbed nervously against it, again and again, during the months he spent in her grandfather's attic, writing *Felix Girard's Ghosts of Bain Dzak*. If she holds the watch long enough in her palm, it grows warm, almost as if it has just emerged from his waistcoat pocket, warmed by his body, not hers.

Petite! Cannot you allow your poor Papa to write his book? Do not pull so on his whiskers! Let Papa work, my dear!

Inconsolable! Yes, that my mother is: inconsolable over the loss of he who returned from the deserts of Bain Dzak one day to stare at her in her cradle, a desert-stained stranger fingering the frizzy blond ringlets that had only lately exploded upon a blue-veined scalp as delicate as an eggshell. *Ah*, he had said, *there you are, Tildy. There you are. I've been looking for you everywhere.*

. . .

He with whom she had fallen in love, and searched for, in vain, ever since. He who was always leaving.

Gone now, again. She cannot bear to think where he might be. So she turns her back on the ocean, averts her eyes from windows where the blue is contained, in the sitting room, in the bedroom, in the turnings of the staircases both down and up. She catches a glimpse, sometimes, by mistake, in the mirror over the mantel, above the heads of the goddesses, and then she feels something inside herself tighten ominously; she imagines a spring inside her, something mechanical, not human, a vise in her chest that constricts her heart, her lungs, her stomach, until the margins of her vision darken and she must sit down; or else she flies down the stairs into the kitchen, shouting at the girl-of-all-work, *You slattern, you slut, the beef was bad, the dishes were dirty, the bedbugs are back* . . . thus releasing, for a moment, temporarily, the tension in the spring.

It is winter. The darkness, coming in midafternoon now, relieves her of the burden of vision. The black outside the windows presses close for a while, then Mary draws the shades, ignites the fire, sparking smoking anthracite. My mother sits, her face and breasts and thighs directed toward the dazzle of heat and light and flame. Behind her, shadows gather. Her back is cold. Outside, carts pulled by stolid ponies, their breaths hot upon the air, rumble over icy cobblestones, the lamplighter makes his progress up Bridge Street, gas jets flare in shopwindows, beneath the house the Esk rushes, the vibration is carried up, through the stone foundation, the walls, the floor . . . into my mother's body, her chest, her spine, her heart.

In the distant steppe, the camels stride . . .

Holding her father's book on her lap makes her feel better. But she does not read it; holds it, merely. It is her amulet, her talisman. Her hands are idle, her eyes half closed; she resides in a firelight dream. Suddenly a sharp, whirring buzz rouses her; jumping up, she urgently shoos the hummingbird, its gemlike feathers flashing, away from the flames. For this purpose, and this only, does she move.

In the distant steppe, the camels . . .

It is half past three. She will not stir, even to prod the coals when the fire dies. Her face is unwashed, her hair in disarray, the house dirty, the supper uncooked, Leopold's socks unmended. When he comes in, he will find her sitting, just like this, face forward toward the hearth, hands resting, palms down and open, upon a dog-eared copy of *Felix Girard's Ghosts of Bain Dzak.*

I went there with him, you know. I helped him to write this book. My Papa took me with him everywhere . . . to Bain Dzak . . . to Khartoum . . . to Sfax . . . to Morocco . . . to Patmos . . . to Peru . . . Why do you not take me anywhere, Leopold?

She turns upon him blue eyes puzzled, sad, reproachful. *If you loved me you would take me somewhere,* those eyes seem to say; or, perhaps, *Why has my Papa gone away, and left me here, in this terrible place, with you?*

Madame Marie-Louise Girard, confronted similarly ten or more years before, responded with indifference, and reached for another slice of bread. This Leopold cannot do. He loves Clotilde . . . loves her to distraction. In the shed in the back garden where, in the cold and dark, surrounded by boxes from Bury Place, he is building his studio, he keeps every drawing of her that he made while on board the *Narcissus*: Clotilde at the taffrail, Clotilde in the saloon, Clotilde at the spinet, Clotilde bending over to button her boot. He still keeps, always, in his breast pocket, the piece of soft textile bearing the woven image of the fair servant girl reaching to place an emerald upon the head of the sultan's elephant, because the girl looks so very much like Clotilde. He knew it even then, when he stole it: *she is his fate.* And so what can he do? He is not indifferent to her suffering.

I . . . I . . . I will t-take you e-everywhere. . . .

He promises; he means it. But he is still nervous when in her presence. He stutters. Familiarity has not diminished his fear. If anything he is *more* nervous, now that he has seen and touched her luminous white body, her body that seems always to recede before him, no matter how tightly he holds her. Even in the entanglement of the bedsheets she torments him—especially there.

My Papa—

In her grief for Felix Girard she seeks, it seems, something lost that Leopold cannot replace—that he never will replace, no matter how hard he tries. And he knows it.

I used to stand on my Papa's feet, and we would walk together in the garden . . . Dash was there . . . Where is he now, I wonder? Leo, where is Dash now? Is he with my Papa, do you think?

Leo cannot answer; he hardly knew Dash; Dash, to him, is a dark figure, silent, receding into the jungles of memory.

I d-don't know—

Her disappointed gaze settles upon him for a moment, then wanders away, searching around all the five fire-lit corners of the pentagonal room, along the walls where her father's orchids hang dying of the cold; probes the tops of the curtains where sometimes a hummingbird hovers; circles six terra-cotta goddess heads on the mantel; then settles back into the hearth.

My Papa will come for me . . . You'll see. He would not leave his Clotilde . . . My Papa always comes back.

It is true, Leopold thinks, that sometimes people come back. Himself, for example. He did not intend to come back to Whitby, and yet he has come back. And then, having once come back—having contradicted himself the one time—he had sworn he would not return to the Dell'oro Jet Works, and yet he has done that, too. For one entire afternoon he has stood in Henrietta Street, slightly up and around the corner from his father's house, pressed into the alley between the millinery and the joiner's, watching the pony carts laden with stone rumbling into his father's cobbled courtyard, then rumbling out again, emptied (the ponies, unburdened, tossing with relief their lathered necks, slavering, their hot breaths white on the cold, damp air). He has seen, from a distance, the men with whom he'd grown up, with whom he'd sorted jet and carved it, and one more, a man he doesn't know, a short, squat, red-faced, scowling figure, directing the carts into and out of the yard with sharp, impatient gestures of his thick hands—Matty Mohun, the man to whom, one day, in the absence of my father's interest, the jet works shall eventually belong. He has seen Gentilessa emerge carrying a basket, a kerchief tied around her head, obscuring her face; heard Emilio, in the yard, shouting at the men. But he has not seen Anna.

That is who he is looking for. That is who he must find.

He has followed the path of her usual errands, through narrow streets and alleys upon the turnings of which the harbor may be seen, to the market, to the bake house, to the fishmonger's; but her familiar silhouette, the longed-for figure of his sister, dark hair flying out behind her, eludes him. She is not in the yard; she is not in the streets. From the corner where he stands, he can see, in the window of the bedroom they once shared, the shade drawn firmly down. It is well past her time for rising. Certainly she is not there.

He thinks, *She never answered any of my letters.* All those hours, writing. Hiding from Clotilde. Hiding from his fate.

In his distress he does not know whom to ask, *Where is my sister?* He will not ask anyone at all until one evening, by accident, in the rain, he runs into Jamie Humber in Sandgate Street, neighbor of his childhood but a different Jamie Humber, hunched beneath the weight of jetty's tools, his eyes older than they used to be; and then without even the preamble of a decent greeting he will blurt it out, *Where is Anna? Hast seen her?*— falling, in his anxiety, into the old, childish way of talking; and Jamie Humber will look at him and want to move on; his face will be streaked with dirt because he has been out on the Scaur all day; he is tired, the rain edged with ice stings both of them as they stand awkwardly together beneath the awning of

Edward Corner's, the butcher's shop. A half dozen slaughtered piglets and a dead goose, hanging in the window, peer over their shoulders, listening eagerly. Leo, too hasty, impatient: *Hast seen her?* Jamie Humber, soft voiced, gentle as ever—*I ain't seen nowt, Leo. Nowt.* And then Jamie will do what he wants to do, will shrug and move on, in the dark and rain, into the crowd in Market Square and then up the cliff, toward Henrietta Street, and home.

Nowt. I ain't seen nowt.

Shrugging indifferently, as if it were not he who, as a boy, once scrambled desperately behind her up the twilit Scaur, calling her name, begging her to wait, longing for her indulgent mercy, mercy received and forgotten.

Yes, my father thinks. Sometimes people come back. Sometimes they don't.

Outside, in the cold, in the shed, where he is attempting to make himself a studio, he wonders where his sister can be. Beneath his preoccupied gaze the penciled lines of his own drawings come together and fall apart, transform into runes, maps, a palimpsest, which, if only he can read it rightly, will reveal the answer. But the answer is not there. There is only Clotilde at the taffrail, Clotilde in the saloon, Clotilde at the spinet, Clotilde bending over to button her boot; Harry Owen with his cigar; Felix Girard, hat over his face, sleeping in the smallboat; and specimens—endless specimens, drawn in exacting detail. My father, while recognizing the skill with which he has worked, nonetheless regards all these with despair. *Where*, he thinks, *is Anna?* He had hoped for her indulgent mercy himself; and finds himself, now that he is unable to claim that mercy, suddenly bereft. It has been brought home to him that he and Clotilde are utterly alone. With the remains of his stipend as *Narcissus* ship's artist, with Clotilde's small inheritance (mostly the last proceeds of *Felix's Girard's Ghosts of Bain Dzak*), and by selling the few saleable objects from Bury Place that held neither sentimental value for Clotilde nor sufficient worldly value to interest Petrook, they have rented this five-sided, shuddering house above the river, the Birdcage, for one year. Beyond that: the abyss. Sitting by the fire with his bewildered young wife, feeling the house shiver and shake beneath them, Leopold feels their future, too, shuddering and shaking, ready to sink, to slide, to fall, to drown, to be carried, along with the rest of the offal in the River Esk, out into the cold North Sea.

He must work. He does not know what to do. He will not carve jet again, not ever. He will never step foot inside the Dell'oro Jet Works.

But then what?

In the cold, dark, sleeting afternoons he rounds the streets, as if, looking into windows, he will find the solution—will, perhaps, peer into a grocer's or shoemaker's or a smithy and see himself looking out, staring back through time from the vantage of some happier and better-ordered future. Round he goes, up Bridge Street past Horne and Richardson, Booksellers, to Grape Lane, skirting the entry of Walker, Hunt, and Simpson, Attnys-at-Law; he clings to rough-surfaced, whitewashed walls, guides himself where the lamps have not yet been lit, until he emerges around a corner into Church Street; then up past Jonathan Smallwood's smithy, Appleton's brewery, and Jim Watt the chemist's; past the My Infant Academy, Ann Davis, Proprietress; all the way up to the circle at Tate Hill, where, barely pausing to glance at the purpling line of horizon at the lip of the sea, he skirts the turning to Henrietta Street, makes his way instead down Sandgate Street, past Hugill's Hairdressers and the Victoria Inn, into the bustle of Market Square, where, pushing through a wooden door heavy at the hinges, he makes his way into the Bird in Hand, settles himself into a dark unnoticed corner, his drawing paper unfolded from within his coat and opened surreptitiously on the bench beside him. The place is filled with fug of smoke, wet steam rising off drying woolens, voices decrying the state of the weather, the state of the state, the state of the neighbors. *What a flirtigiggs she is*, a woman is saying, close to him, by the reeking fire. *She's browden on un, surely, the daft fool.* From farther off, by the counter: *It's cawd as hell. Better button up them gammashes, Robby.* And then, softly, a whisper almost, carried to him on an eddy in the conversation: *He'll rue it tomorrow. He'll rue it for sartain.*

In his corner my father does what he has always done when he seeks distraction: he draws; with quick absent strokes creates curve of cheek, curl of hair, plump, booted foot, shawl with fringe unraveling across a broad, matronly back. But he is not content; cannot remain absorbed; it itches at him. He cannot get quite right the mole upon the cheek, the angle of the hairpin, the knots in the yarn. This is painful; he turns away. And when he turns away, the twin anguishes from which he has sought

momentary escape come rushing back, like brutal jabs—*One!
two!*—of the butcher's knife.

Where is Anna?

What will we do?

Folding up his paper he emerges into the cold, turns left,
finally, back to Bridge Street and the acrid stink of the Esk.
Leaning above the water, he sees, in the semidark, shadowy
objects barely discernable and therefore dreadful, circling, quivering, trembling along the surface, then disappearing into the
swift, green-grey rush of the river.

Like us, he thinks.

What will we do?

All the time, of course, it is right there in front of him, although
he does not see it; or rather, perhaps, he sees it without seeing.
How many times, walking along Church Street, has he passed,
without a second glance, Argument's Glasswares, with its ambi-
tious glittering window, lighted from below by brilliant, jewel-
bright jets of gas? Or, if he happens to be walking on the
opposite side of the street, the somewhat darker but no less
crammed shop front of Argument's chief competitor-in-trade,
William Cloverdale? Perhaps the translucence of the glass has
allowed it to hide itself from him; perhaps that is why, passing
these windows, he has not looked inside, at and then *past* the
wares—the everyday glasses and plates, the wine goblets, the
candy dishes, the deep green and burgundy decanters, the vases
and goblets, the figurines, the paperweights, and other, more

fanciful creations—to see the glow of the ovens beyond, the flare of the fires, the white-hot, rotating globes and cylinders of glass, *the objects being made.*

What, after all, is my father, if not a maker of objects? A creator of things from nothing? Despite the lessons of his cousin, Giorgio Dell'oro, it seems clear that my father still does not, at this time, comprehend his own true nature. He is still searching.

In the end it is my mother who sees, and understands. On one of her few excursions outside the Birdcage, on the rare day cold but clear, strolling down Church Street in her blue shawl and fur muff, averting her eyes from views of the sea, Clotilde pauses, just for a moment, in front of a window, to rest; the window happens to belong to Argument's Glasswares. The name on the door, Thomas Argument, means nothing to her, although it would to my father, were he to notice it, since Thomas Argument is the son of Argument the knacker, whose yard Leopold walked past many times, as a boy, on his way from Henrietta Street down to the Scaur, and vice versa. The Arguments are an old Whitby family; Thomas is not the first to resent the family trade but he is the first to succeed in leaving it. He fought to leave it, tooth and claw; to remove himself from it and to remove it from himself, to eradicate, from his very being, even the faintest clinging molecule of the knacker's yard. He is a fiercely competitive man—the brightness of the gas lighting in his window being directly proportional to the nearness, in time, of the reek of rendered livestock, the rattle of disarticulated skeletons, in his past. Can the brightness of the light blind the passersby to the too-close proximity of corpses? Can pure white heat burn away the stink of death? Thomas Argument thinks so. He stakes his livelihood upon it. The gaslight in his window, in the evening, is dazzling white, dazzling hot, and it is reflected, magnified, ferociously, again and again, in a hundred faceted surfaces of glass.

But it is still early afternoon when Clotilde rests against Argument's window, so the gas jets aren't yet lit. All she sees in that vast and flawless pane is an unexpected and therefore unbearable reflection of the sea. It is because of this—to escape the sea—that she opens the door of Argument's Glasswares and ducks inside. As she does, a tiny bell jingles merrily above her head. Immediately she is absorbed into a world shadowless and clear, sharp and sharply articulated; she must blink several times, so intense is the winter sunlight refracted in shelf upon shelf (the shelves, extending from floor to ceiling, are much taller than my mother is) of Thomas Argument's pitchers and sugar bowls, his saltcellars, his magnifying glasses, his oil lamps, his hourglasses and pipes, his glazed boxes and dangling chandeliers, his millefiori paperweights and parti-colored perfume bottles, his sherry glasses and wine glasses and brandy snifters . . . and his mirrors.

In Whitby Thomas Argument is known for his mirrors. He makes them himself, casting the glass in his shop, painting the silver foil on the backs of the plates with his own brush. This is part of the competitiveness of Thomas Argument: his mirrors must contain no flaws, no warps, no blurs, no bubbles. His rival across the street, William Cloverdale, makes mirrors, too; once

Thomas Argument, who looks very closely into things, found a bubble in one of Cloverdale's mirrors, and this, for Argument, was a triumph. *A bubble in glass is a great misfortune, sir, a great misfortune, madam,* Argument has been known to tell his customers, *because a bubble, madam, is a flaw; and what is flawed is fragile; and what is fragile can break—never forget it.* Argument has certainly never let Cloverdale forget it, referring, whenever they meet, to the *misfortunate bubble.* Of course it is unpleasant, Thomas Argument is not always a pleasant man. But his mirrors are very good, this even William Cloverdale must concede. Argument makes mirrors that can turn a single, poor room into an endless suite, a dark claustrophobic hallway into a maze. Light, reflected in his mirrors, is more vivid; colors are brighter; shadows more dense; faces more beautiful; images are multiplied, fragmented, reduced, distorted . . . But my mother has not heard about Thomas Argument's mirrors, and, overwhelmed, she does not notice them, hanging along the back wall of the shop (the better to reflect, to magnify, to multiply Argument's wares, which are vast enough in any case), until it is too late—until she suddenly finds herself a hundred times reflected (a small woman, blond, pale, astonished), staring over her own shoulder, a hundred times, into the cold, unblinking blue eye of her enemy, the sea.

She gasps; cries out one or two words that she will not remember but that sound (Thomas Argument will tell her later) like *My Papa!* or, perhaps, more puzzlingly, the contradictory *Not my Papa!* Then she faints (her collapse reflected a hundred times in a hundred reflecting surfaces); sags against Argument's crowded shelves, but so gently that nothing falls, nothing breaks; there is just an ominous shiver, followed by the soft, high-pitched, troubled sighing of glass.

When she returns to herself (this strange expression implying she has lost herself somewhere—and perhaps she has—or perhaps she will) she finds she is no longer in the bright main room of the shop, with its relentless light and its vertiginous shelves of glass, but in another room, darker; the light here filtered through thick, drawn curtains, a vigorous fire burning on the hearth. It is warm—almost too warm. Someone has laid her on a couch thick with pillows and tapestries; someone (the same someone?) has removed from her feet the clever little black boots that her father bought her in France. Her skirts are disarranged, her stockings exposed, but nonetheless, in this close and thickly carpeted space, she feels cosseted, wrapped, strangely protected. She feels (for the first time, perhaps, since the day Felix Girard disappeared from the decks of the *Narcissus*): safe.

Madam, Thomas Argument says to her, *you frightened me.*

Clotilde starts. In the semidarkness she has been unaware of Thomas Argument, except as a mysterious rescuing presence, a cosseter-in-wraps, an unseen remover-of-boots; now, suddenly, she realizes he has been sitting behind her, in a low, leather chair, all along, watching. She does not know how long he has watched her, and the sudden consciousness that it may have been a very long time fills her with shame. She colors, and is briefly confused about everything: who she is, where she is, who Thomas Argument is. She is confused at being addressed as a married woman. In her faint she has momentarily forgotten about Leopold, about her marriage. *Who does he mean? Madam who?* But the ring is there on her finger—evidence, clearly. Clearly Thomas Argument has noticed it. He is a man who misses very little; and so, inevitably, he has noticed Clotilde's confusion, as brief as it is, as quickly disguised. Indeed, he enjoys her confusion, for he already perceives, better than she, everything that it contains. The only question remaining for Thomas Argument is what, if anything, he wants to do about it.

This he will decide in time.

Now he says again, gently, *You frightened me. Are you all right? Yes . . . I . . . it was so bright . . .*

Clotilde smiles placatingly in the direction of this man who is as yet an indistinct presence in the darkness; but she does not tell him the real reason why she fainted.

It is my fault, says Thomas Argument. *The shop is very bright. Sometimes my customers are overcome. Men as well as women. You'd be surprised. The gaslight in particular is too much for some of them . . . it is so new.*

And there are so many . . . reflections.

Yes, Argument says. *There are very many reflections. I apologize. Let me get you a brandy.*

Abruptly, before she can refuse, he unfolds himself from his chair and with a swift, spiderlike motion of his long legs, disappears through a door she hasn't noticed, into the inner recesses of the house.

By the time he returns she has risen, straightened herself, put on her boots and buttoned them, and circled the room twice. It is filled with books. At its rear is a large desk of some heavy,

dark wood—walnut, perhaps?—the surface of which is strewn
with papers and what can only be called "apparatus"—small,
smooth machines of ambiguous purpose. Clotilde has her fingertips upon one of these machines when Thomas Argument
returns with her brandy.

Ah! I see you have found my collection. A few toys with which I
amuse myself. Would you like to see?

Clotilde sips, grimaces slightly, nods. Argument parts the
curtains, filling the room with bright light in which motes of
dust dance and then settle, revealing that they stand, he and
she, in a typical gentleman's study decorated in burgundy and
green—or in the study of a man who aspires to be a gentleman;
and he reveals himself, also, as a gentleman or a man who aspires
to be a gentleman, it is not quite clear which: an unusually tall,
thin, aspiring gentleman, with small, hooded eyes and a high,
hooked nose, dark hair, long arms, long, delicate, spidery fingers. The overall impression is one of disjointedness rather than
of grace, yet as Clotilde watches, fascinated, those long, delicate
fingers probe with surprising precision among the disorder of
objects on the desk, finally selecting one by touch, it seems,
rather than by sight. He holds it out to her; taking it, she finds
that it is a small bronze disc, one side of which is elaborately
carved with the figures of animals—a snarling tiger, a dog on its
back in a posture of submission, a plunging stallion, a grinning
rat, a hen on its nest, a pig with its snout thrust deeply into the
earth, others—and with a finely detailed calligraphy that Clotilde cannot read. The other side of the disc is smooth, slightly
convex, polished—a mirror!

She catches the reflection of her own blue eye, stiffens unhappily.

You're making fun of me, she says, pouting.

I'm not, says Thomas Argument. *Take it to the window. Hold the surface to the light.*

Clotilde does as she is told, holds the mirror's reflecting surface up to the light; instantly the images on its back are cast in bright relief onto the wall behind her, the snarling tiger, the docile dog, the foraging pig, the stallion, the rat . . .

But how—

No one knows how, says Thomas Argument quickly. *It is a tou guang jian—a magical Chinese mirror. I obtained it from a fellow dealer in glass who obtained it, himself, in the Orient.*

Clotilde, whose Papa has traveled everywhere, is neither impressed nor intimidated by mention of the Orient. Thoughtfully she hands Thomas Argument his mirror.

What else have you?

You might like these, he says, smiling, and sets gilded spectacles on the bridge of her nose.

Oh! cries Clotilde, *they make me dizzy! I see six of your room . . . or eight . . . I am not sure how many . . .*

At this Thomas Argument laughs aloud. *Yes,* he says. *I am never sure myself how many of anything I see through these glasses . . . they are multiplying spectacles . . . the lenses are made from faceted rock crystal.*

If I were to wear them very often, says Clotilde, *equally often would I fall down, disgracing myself and all who know me. Have you anything more?*

More! Madam wants more? She is difficult to satisfy . . . this he
says more to himself than to her, and strokes his chin in pretend
perplexity.

My Papa sometimes said I was, says Clotilde.

Your Papa is a wise man, says Thomas Argument.

Yes, says Clotilde, very serious now, almost stern, almost
defiant, lower lip thrust out. *My Papa* is *a wise man!*

Argument registers this—the sudden seriousness, the defi-
ance, the stern self-correction, the emphasis, as if in reminder to
herself, on that present tense *is* . . . Registers it, and, being himself a shrewd man (if not a wise one), says nothing. Instead he
retreats into a corner, and brings forward, from behind the desk,
a polished cabinet, longer than it is wide, made up of six hinged
wooden panels, four long, two short, standing on a painted
wooden pedestal of Dutch design; he has picked this up, despite
its size, despite its awkwardness, and carried it forward, pedestal
and all, carefully—gracefully, even (with surprising grace, given
the disjointed appearance of his long, agile limbs)—before
finally setting it down at the center of the carpet, near Clotilde's
feet.

Madam, he says, *observe.*

Clotilde does observe, for a moment, in silence; then she
begins to laugh.

Why, it is just a silly box, she says, *with a window in it!*

It is, says Thomas Argument, not at all nettled, *my* theatre
catoptrique—*my splendid show-all. Look!*

He gestures toward the pentagonal peephole centered in one
of the shorter end-panels of the cabinet, and Clotilde, willing
despite her scorn, leans over to peer inside, pressing her eye,

unsteadily because she is still laughing, as close as she can to the glass.

Abruptly her laughter ceases.

Oh! she says. That is all. And then once again, rapturously: *Oh!*

She stands quite still, leaning forward, blond hair tumbling over her shoulders, unable to look away.

She sees an impossible paradox, a panorama inside a box, a vast desert stretching infinitely forward, sand dunes of red and gold undulating toward a distant horizon, mysterious stony obelisks, cliffs glittering with quartz, an endless ochre dome of sky; she hears—or thinks she hears—the familiar, the beloved voice—

In the distant steppe, the camels stride . . .

But, she cries, *how—?*

If you will allow me . . .

Thomas Argument gently draws a reluctant Clotilde away from the cabinet, smoothly turns a metal crank in its base. *Look now,* he commands.

She looks again, and finds herself, this time, in the midst of a snowy forest of dense pines through which stealthy figures glide, always just slightly out of sight—the white tip of a fox's tail retreating at the periphery of her vision—dark mountains beyond . . .

But—I don't understand!

I will show you.

With sensitive fingertips Thomas Argument probes the join where the cabinet's long top panel meets its side, folds it open upon its hinges to reveal a catacomb of mirrors—sixty small mirrors, at least, attached to five of the cabinet's six sides; on the sixth side, the bottom or floor, is arranged a minute scene, a cluster of miniature pine trees made from wax, painstakingly painted to achieve an admirable realism; on the left edge is a tiny cork fox with a brush made from real hair. He turns the crank; the bottom panel flips over, and here is Clotilde's desert, the dunes glued sand, the obelisks a scattered handful of stones, the cliffs tiny quartzes, the ochre sky a painted illusion . . .

Ingenious, is it not? These mirrors, you see, magnify the scene, these others multiply it, creating the appearance of infinite horizon . . . It was made in the seventeenth century, in Amsterdam, by a Jesuit named Kircher, a master of illusions. I purchased it there myself from a collector I know . . .

Oh.

Clotilde has turned pale; Argument helps her to sit down.

I am sorry, he says. *My mirrors have upset you again. I am being inconsiderate. You see, I am so fond of my toys, and so eager to share them . . . and I so seldom have visitors . . .*

It is just, Clotilde whispers, *I just thought . . .*

But what *does* she think? Uncertain, she falls silent. Before her mind's eye: deserts, dunes, cliffs of red sandstone, ancient bones turned to rock, to clay. *In the distant steppe, the camels stride.*

I should go.

He does not try to keep her—he is too shrewd for that. With one hand cupped protectively beneath her elbow, stooped, obsequious, a very tall man embarrassed by his height, he leads her into the passage that will take them from the house where he lives alone, with just a housekeeper, across the yard, and into the rear of his shop, passing en route first through the glassworks itself. Argument walks this passage very often, walks it automatically now, even at night, when he is alone—especially at night, especially when he is alone. He follows a habitual path. His limbs know it, follow it, almost without the active intervention of his will. But for Clotilde it is new. For her it is all revelation: the heat, the darkness, the fiery furnace with its sulfurous hiss, the colored rods of glass, the men with their blowing irons and shears and punties, the sight of Jack Rose, Argument's gaffer, swinging a black metal rod upon which a blossom of red-hot molten glass bursts, suddenly, to form the open bud of a drinking vessel. Men and boys seem to hurry everywhere, barefoot, barelegged, nets drawn over their faces, bearing red-hot fiery masses of glass. A boy runs past too close, flush with the heat, carrying, at the end of a pronged stick, a goblet shaped like a fish, mouth agape, ready to receive, to pour . . . *Pardon, madam! Pardon, sir!* The object quivers in the pincer's grip, flashes close beside Clotilde's muff, disappears into the crimson maw of the lehr.

Argument yanks her aside with a tug so sharp that for a moment—for a moment only—she falls against him, and then, laughing, he chides the boy, who has already disappeared. *You, sir! Take care! 'Tis hot!*

The boy is lucky. Because my mother is there, Thomas Argument will not strike him, not this time. Not while she is there.

It's like hell, that glasshouse. The heat. The stink. The fire. A revelation of hell.

Clotilde thinks of my father right away.

. . .

You make it here?

Now she has realized—now she has her idea. Argument feels her sudden small start of excitement. It puzzles him; he cannot understand it; nonetheless, he responds smoothly, as always.

Yes. We make most of our glass here, good English lead crystal, the best. Some I purchase abroad. Specialty items. Venetian pieces, ice glass, latticino, opaline . . . Inferior items, but ladies like them . . .

It is a small shop—a dozen men, four boys—but I have plans— expansion—a gas furnace—in time, a factory. There's a bit of land near Thirsk I've got my eye on—

If she can see or sense the smokestacks belching on the horizon of his words, Clotilde gives no sign. She says nothing, merely nods; yet Argument can still feel, through his cupped palm where it touches her elbow, the nervous throb, like an electrical impulse, of her quickened interest.

But she only says, *It is very hard to breathe—*

Yes. It is very hot.

He gently leads her out; yet even as they pass through the glasshouse and back into the shop he can still feel her excitement; and still he does not know what it means.

At the street door, just as she is about to leave, he hands her something—a small, smooth object, wrapped in paper.

Please accept this, he says, *as a token of my apology. I hope you will return, despite all.*

Clotilde, her eyes already averted, grants him a sweet, quick, evasive smile, tucks the gift into her muff, and steps out into the street. As she goes the bell tinkles cheerfully above her head.

It isn't until later, when she is back home again, seated in front of a tamer fire, that she recalls the package hidden in her muff and decides to open it. All afternoon the new idea, the revelation, has turned quietly in her mind like the gather of glass at the tip of Jack Rose's blowing iron. She cannot see what it will be quite yet, the idea is still vague, it troubles her, she cannot shape it, it resists form, but sensing its promise she cannot let it go; and then, quite suddenly, she remembers Argument's lagniappe and runs to retrieve it. She pulls at the twine with eager, agile fingers, tears away the brown paper, and finds, inside, a short, squat, polished, tapering wooden cylinder with glass at either end—an optical instrument of some kind; applying her eye to the narrower end, she sees a symmetrical mosaic composed of brilliantly colored bits of glass that fall together and apart as she turns the instrument, forming the images of, on the one hand, a circle of doves entwined in a garland of roses, and, alternately, crows in a holly bush, their fiercely gleaming beaks reaching to burst the blood-red berries. After contemplating these twin visions for a time, she slips the kaleidoscope (for that is what it is, although she has never seen one before, and does not know its name) into her pocket; and that evening, when my father comes in from his studio, she shows him Argument's gift, and tells him how and where she got it. Then she tells him that she knows what he must do.

He must learn to make glass.

．　．　．

Glass! Leopold resists it. He has never thought about glass before. He has walked past Argument's Glasswares, past the plaque for Wm. Cloverdale, Glass, a hundred times, at least, without noticing either. Surely that means something. He does not wish to make glass. Glass does not excite him; he feels no desire for it. It is purely utilitarian. It is uninteresting. Glass is tumblers and decanters and bowls. It is Gentilessa's sideboard. It does not challenge him. And yet . . . turning the kaleidoscope around in his hands, peering through the lens at the narrow end of that polished wooden rod, watching as the brightly colored splinters of glass fall together, then apart, he recognizes the potential. Knowing nothing, yet, of the mirrors housed inside the wooden tube, of how they work—of how the *illusion* works— because it is, of course, an illusion—he recognizes the potential. Of course! He *is* a Dell'oro, after all. He recognizes the potential, sees that it is unrealized, and immediately, at the back of his brain, feels the scrabbling, the scratching, the unbearable, itchy longing to reach for his paper and pencil. The family *tendenza*!

Yet he says, sulkily, resisting it for all he is worth:

But I don't know how *to make glass.*

To which my mother, in one of her better moments, replies:

So what? You'll learn.

My father sighs; sits, like an old man, with his chin on his chest, in front of the fire. He has to think about it. But his attention is piqued. Glass, the idea of it, has entered his awareness at last. It will be some time yet before he has worked with it, felt its dangerous heat, its malleable, deceiving lightness, the stringy, sticky, viscous liquidity hardening into a fragile perfection so different from the solidity of jet. It will be a long time yet. All that is in the future. For the moment, glass is still an abstraction. Nothing of what it will become for him exists yet. It all hangs in the balance of this moment, as my father, an old man of twenty, sits, before the fire, with his chin on his chest, like a much older man.

One thing is not abstract. One thing is not in the future. It is all too present, all too real: the expression on my mother's face—a mysterious, secretive *something* that plays fleetingly about her lips and her eyes as she slips Thomas Argument's kaleidoscope safely back into her pocket. It is ephemeral, yes, and quickly disguised; it is unclear whether she is even aware of it herself; my father will not, perhaps, ever see it again; but it is certainly not an abstraction.

In the end, perhaps it is this look, more than anything, that prompts him up Church Street, almost against his will, for a glimpse of the glittering window of Argument's Glasswares, and of the other, more circumspect, opposing window of William Cloverdale. He hesitates, crosses back and forth many times between the brilliant shop front, refulgent with commercial triumph, of Argument, and the humbler, perhaps already defeated window of Cloverdale. What does he see? Tumblers, decanters, doorknobs, sherry glasses, saltcellars, fairy globes, desk lamps with green shades: the essence of domesticity, of Gentilessa's sideboard, Emilio's desk. Leopold is not interested in glass. Not yet, at least. That will come. For now he is interested only in

Clotilde, and it is this that will prompt him, finally, to offer himself as glassmaker's apprentice to Thomas Argument, despite the fact that he feels more drawn to the unassuming window of William Cloverdale, if to any window at all. But it will take some time before it happens, this offering, this self-immolation; it will be a matter of weeks before he can bring himself to do it, and until then, my father will hang between the two windows, Argument's and Cloverdale's, moving first toward one, then toward the other; will inhabit his own studio like a ghost, drawing nothing, seeing only, in his mind's eye, the look that was on my mother's face when she slipped Argument's gift into her pocket. Is it less dangerous, that look, for being unconscious?

In retrospect, of course, it seems perverse for my father to offer himself as apprentice, therefore as underling, as servant, to the man of whom, already, without quite even knowing it, he is jealous. But it is not perverse that he should want my mother to gaze with similar desire upon some object that he has made— to gaze that way *upon himself.* Because she does not, he knows, gaze on him, now, in that way. Does he think he can change it by aligning himself with Thomas Argument? It seems unlikely that he would place himself in such a position, so much in the man's power, were he fully aware of already having, as it were, an argument with Argument. Is it less dangerous, my father's jealousy, for being unconscious?

On the surface, at least, the decision is purely practical. He applies to Argument out of need, and because Argument's prosperity—however gaudy, repellent, even downright offensive, in its display—seems the crystallized embodiment of much that my father desires—success, security, wealth, the admiration of women (or of just one woman), even, perhaps, were he to think in such terms, which he does not, of the future. Yes, in its own way Thomas Argument's window with its sparkling glass and brilliant jets of gaslight is the future, and my father is drawn inexorably toward its promise, ignoring, as he moves toward it, its inherent fragility. It is bright, it is bold, and what is more—my mother likes it, and my father, despite all, still likes my mother very, very much. Loves her, in fact, to distraction. Enough to sacrifice himself—to the furnace!

At least, that is how he thinks of it at the time. He goes begrudgingly . . . with relief, because of the money; but also begrudgingly. My father goes to Thomas Argument thinking to make, of himself, a burnt offering, for my mother's sake. I imagine him now, reluctantly stalking up Church Street in the rain, a small, severe figure in a black suit and waistcoat. I suppose he looks very much as his own father must have done, on a similar occasion, ten years earlier, although I have got, in this case, no photograph to prove it. This is how I imagine Leopold. Hunched against the rain. Slightly angry. This is clear from his frown, but also it is in his bearing, the tightness in his shoulders, the way he holds his arms, slightly raised, bent at the elbows, tensed against his waistcoat, fists unconsciously clenched. He is wearing the suit that Gentilessa bought him for his travels. Still the only suit he owns, it is rusty from exposure to sun and salt water; patched, but proper, or at least, the best that he can muster, given the circumstances. I picture my father's unwilling hand on Thomas Argument's doorknob. It costs him much to turn that knob; but he does turn it, and the door swings open. A bell tinkles above his head. He enters that heartless, glittering world. *I make of myself a sacrifice. For her.*

What, exactly, does my father think he is giving up?

His life as an artist, certainly—the potential of it, at least, since it does not yet exist in actuality. It is at present only an idea, an idea that cannot possibly come to fruition without Thomas Argument's furnace; but my father does not know this; this is an irony of which he is, at the moment, unaware. What he is aware of, at present, is the potential—lost potential, as he sees it. And something more. Something that has to do, specifically, with Thomas Argument, and with the look in my mother's eyes when she slipped the little kaleidoscope, given to her by Argument, into the pocket of her skirt.

Later, when the furnace has become my father's life, it will be less clear what—*who*—he has sacrificed. Or why.

So it begins. Slowly at first, not only because my father, feeling the pull of the family *tendenza*, remembering the old stories, balks against it; but also because Thomas Argument wills that it must be so. He will hire my father, but only as a taker-in. It is a boy's job. My father, at twenty, will be the boy who carries the hot pieces of finished glass to the lehr for annealing, who runs errands for the men, fetches beer and sandwiches. He will replace the boy who, while carrying a goblet in the shape of an open-mouthed fish, almost brushed against my mother, coming so close that she felt, for a moment, the radiant heat of the glass against her arm. She could have been singed; she was not; but that boy, for his near mischance, has been fired. Now my father will take his place. Now, in Thomas Argument's glasshouse, he will be called, at any hour of day or night, to complete shifts of ten hours or more, whenever the furnace is hot, the glass soft enough to work—the teazer arriving at his door and shouting *Dell'oro, all in!*—my father must get out of bed if he is in it, or up from a meal if he is eating it, or away from his paper if he is drawing, and run to Church Street, where he will sweep the glasshouse floors before the blowers arrive. He will carry goblets and vases and candy dishes at the end of a pincer, placing them carefully and slowly (very carefully, very slowly) into the oven, where, by stages, they will cool. My father will also turn the winch that moves the iron trays of finished glass on a belt through the vault of the smoking lehr, bit by bit, away from the furnace, toward the cooler air. It is a slow progression. Each time a tray is filled with finished pieces, my father turns the crank once; the trays inside the lehr move forward one station; my father inserts an empty tray, which he will fill, in time, before he turns the crank again. It takes an entire day, a full twenty-four hours, for Argument's wares, his decanters and carafes and finger cups, his trifle dishes and water jugs, his sugar basins, butter tubs, pickle glasses, cruets, salts and inkstands, his glasses for champagne, claret, hock, and wine, his jelly cups and custard cups, his fish globes and beer tumblers to make their full transit through the lehr. Minding the lehr is an important job even though it is a dull job, even though it is a boy's job. Objects allowed to pass through too quickly, although apparently beautiful, are flawed: unevenly cooled glass is unstable, liable to shatter, to fly apart unexpectedly with the slightest of stress. A single touch is all it takes. A touch upon the *sensitive place*. Of course, this does not happen right away. The touch upon the sensitive place is inevitable, it must come, but it takes time. It may take days, even weeks, before the glass reveals its flaw. But the flaws are always revealed, in the end. This Thomas Argument will not tolerate. *A bubble in glass is a flaw, sir; and what is flawed is fragile; and what is fragile can break—never forget it!*

My father does not forget it. If Argument's wares shatter without cause, if they are returned in pieces, if there are complaints, it will be my father's fault. The cost of inadequately cooled items will be deducted from his pay.

He is, of course, not permitted to polish items of glass once they have emerged, still warm, from annealing; that is for somebody else to do. Somebody skilled.

A boy's job, then. The heat, the stink, the humiliation, the danger. Always the hovering edge of blame, the hot edge of Thomas Argument's temper. Responsibility without reward.

For a year my father will create nothing in Thomas Argument's shop. Even in his own studio, he will very seldom draw. He will lack the energy; and, in the uncertainty of never knowing when the teazer will call him back to Church Street, he will lack the concentration. Everything will be subsumed into the glasshouse. Into the fire.

One thing, at least, is to the good. At the end of a year of being balked by Thomas Argument, Leopold will balk himself no longer. He will long to make glass. But still he will not be permitted. Instead, he will be promoted to the position of footmaker, which means that it will be his job to stand at the red-hot glory hole containing the molten glass, right beside Jack Rose, the gaffer, and, using a handle shear, to stretch a blob of the molten liquid to form the handle of a pitcher; or, with the steel forming tool, to press out the foot of a wine glass; or sometimes to hold a wooden paddle against the rim of a sugar bowl to make sure the edges are true, or use a pliers to bend the lip of a carafe. And he will help to set the pot—winching the new clay tub full of seething, white-hot glass into the furnace—the dirtiest, most dangerous job in the glasshouse.

By some strange freak of chance, my father is always called when it is time to set the pot.

He will return home with his face blackened, his eyebrows scorched, his hands cramped. He will have made the base of a wine glass, the handle of a pitcher, the lip of a bottle, the spout of a jug. Nothing more. He will have watched Jack Rose animate the molten glass with his own breath, filling it, shaping it, but will have been unable to do this himself.

Over time this denial, this frustration, will become, for my father, the equivalent of watching, impotently, another man kiss the woman he loves.

And coming home to the Birdcage, there above the foul-smelling River Esk—the Birdcage with its bent angles, its jambs askew, its ill-fitting doors, its windows that stick at the hinges, its staircases and closets and corners crammed with artifacts belonging to Felix Girard, he will find Clotilde in the bedroom, folding garments purchased for her by her father in Paris, or sitting before the fire, saying *Mr. Argument was with me today; he brought me the most cunning new toy!*

What will it be this time?

A delicate bird, made from yellow glass, with hinged wings, and a winding mechanism that makes a strange piping sound, very like, and yet at the same time eerily unlike, singing.

A diminutive lantern, made from bamboo and translucent paper upon which is painted a complex pattern of branches and leaves; inside it, silhouetted figures, cut from tin, circle upon a metal gyre around four candles, in the light of which they cast monstrous shadows upon the wall—a man with a stovepipe hat and an umbrella and a grotesquely hooked nose pursuing a fat policeman with a whistle pursuing a pig that runs upright on its rear trotters with an enormous French horn pressed to its porcine lips.

A silver compact in the shape of a scallop shell, containing a mirror in which my mother can see, behind the shoulder of her own reflection, the ghostly reflection of somebody else, who, when she turns around, is not there—

It is my Papa, look and see! she cries—

My father looks, sees his sister, Anna, standing behind him

in the mirror, declares it *a sneaky trick*, and throws it at the fire. When my mother retrieves it from the ashes, the mirror is shattered, reflects nothing, will never reflect anything again; but this is all right.

Mr. Argument will bring me another, she says.

And he does.

In fact, Thomas Argument has become a frequent visitor to the Birdcage. His long, angular figure slouches and slopes uncomfortably through the low, crooked doorways of the three whitewashed pentagonal rooms, makes its stiff and hampered way up and down the tortuous, narrowly turning stairs packed with Felix Girard's curiosities, folds itself awkwardly, yet surprisingly often, into a chair before the fire, after having brought forth from some pocket or other (very much as Felix Girard used to do), a gift, varyingly exotic, eccentric, or strange, for my mother. In this chair, which, perhaps, should have been my father's—except that my father, delayed at the glasshouse, working erratic journeys of ten hours on, twenty-four off, never the same ten, never the same twenty-four, typically arrives too late, too tired, and too dirty to claim it first—Argument shifts, stretches his long legs toward the hearth, then draws them back again, crosses and uncrosses, leans right and then left, then sits forward on his haunches, elbows propped on knees, fingertips pressed together to form a tense arch that he will shortly dismantle by leaning backward again and putting his hands behind his head. His discomfort is evident. Thomas Argument does not fit—not in the house, not in the chair. Perhaps not in my parents' lives. But he comes very often, and sometimes he stays very late.

And he talks.

My father, coming home at midnight, having just put the crimped rim around the top of a glass jar or the notch in the spout of a creamer, enters wearily upon these conversations-in-progress, finds Thomas Argument delivering to my mother a lecture upon the suitability of gas lighting for home use (*The depletion of oxygen, madam, is vastly overstated, as is the staining—and the explosions? Pah! Just rumor, my dear*); his dislike for French *cristal opaline* (*Fine glass should not look like blancmange. It should sparkle, madam, it should sparkle!*); or the wonders of the latest addition to his collection—a drinking cup inside which is nested a magical mirror (*The first time you look you will see yourself in it. Look again and you are gone! It is most amusing when drunk. I bought it in Greece, Madam Dell'oro, the last time I was there*). Sometimes, when he is excited, Argument reaches out with his silver-headed walking stick and prods the coal in the fireplace. *It is the wave of the future—the wave of the future!* he cries (whether the subject is gaslight, or electrical conduction, or the daguerreotype, my father is not sure) and—poke!—crimson sparks shoot up the flue. Clotilde in her own chair sits, smiles, gently caresses a yellow bird made from glass. If she winds its mechanism it will sing; it will sound almost like a real bird; but she does not wind it. Her glass bird, a gift, is silent. Above their heads a living bird flits, flashes its ruby breast, quickly is gone.

My father, coming in like a stranger upon these peculiar conversations in which Thomas Argument talks very much and very enthusiastically while Clotilde sits sphinxlike, inserting only the occasional and perhaps ironic comment (*Is that so, Mr.*

Argument? I think you are quite—wrong!—about that), never feels included. Perhaps he does not desire inclusion. Perhaps he has had enough of Thomas Argument at the glasshouse. This same Thomas Argument who arrives at the Birdcage with gifts in hand, Thomas Argument the charming enthusiast, my mother's friendly admirer, is a tyrant in his own house, a petty martinet who abuses the men, accuses them of sullying the batch, destroys entire trays of finished glass that do not meet his specifications after failing to say what the specifications are. Whole trays are returned to the furnace to be melted and made again: *This glass is blistered! That is seedy! It is uneven! It's poorly flattened!*

No one but Thomas Argument can see the flaws.

It is terrible, madam, Argument confides to my mother, *the master's appalling burden of—surveillance!*

Naturally his behavior gives rise to bitterness. There are even rumors about the batch, which Argument insists on mixing himself. He is protective of it, secretive. It is said, both inside the glasshouse and outside it, that he mixes it with ash of animal bones, and that this is why his glass is so dexterous, so translucent. Thomas Argument, it seems, cannot leave the knacker's yard behind; skeletons rattle in his angry gaze.

Not surprising, then, that my father might wish Thomas Argument would go home.

If indeed he does wish it. My silent father may have removed himself from Thomas Argument entirely—mentally, at least. Almost certainly by this time, during his second year working in the glasshouse, he has begun thinking like a Dell'oro.

Fretting like one. He wants to make; he is frustrated because he cannot. He has begun, secretively, sketching. Almost certainly he has received by now the first of many similar letters that will be sent to him, from London, by Harry Owen: *Despite my best attempts preservation has failed . . . Can you please send to me at your soonest convenience, your drawings of the Holothuriae, the Monochirus amatus Owenii, and the Aplysi, which remain, at present, the sole scientific record of these wonderful animals . . .*

My father reads these letters, and thinks about glass. He remembers, in felt memory, perhaps, more than in thought (because *making*, for him, increasingly resides in touch, not in thought), the handle he attached to a pitcher in the glasshouse this afternoon—the hot responsive twist of the molten glass. Like a living thing. The white-hot sensuous melting. He hears my mother saying to Thomas Argument—

Why Mr. Argument, that is so very . . . interesting!

Her soft insinuating laughter the sudden, barely detected spark that begins the conflagration.

In retrospect, of course, it seems inevitable; I already know what my father will do. But for him, sitting there, in front of the fire, like a stranger in his own house, exhausted, listening to Thomas Argument's glib pronouncements, then my mother's adulatory ejaculations in response—what can he have been feeling? I already know what he will do, so I am not surprised when, eventually, inevitably, he gets up and leaves the room (receiving, as he does it, barely a glance from either my mother or Thomas

Argument, so engrossed are they in their mutual game of *admire* and *be admired*). But what can my father be thinking, in that moment when he decides to leave my mother alone with Thomas Argument? What will he be thinking on all those afternoons, those evenings, yet to come, when he will do the same again? All those evenings when, returning home from his shift, entering the kitchen, and hearing Thomas Argument's excitable voice reverberating down the screw-turn stairwell, he will simply pass up the stairs to bed, or through the house and out, going straight to his studio, without even bothering to find out what is being discussed in the parlor above?

I know what he will do. In his studio, in the cold, in the wavering light of his oil lamp, my father will pour over his drawings from the voyage of the *Narcissus*; bringing out his pencils and paints, he will begin the painstaking process of copying and coloring each one. Some of the originals he will send to Harry Owen, in London. *Your drawings . . . which remain, at present, the sole scientific record . . .*

Others he will keep. These are his secrets.

And then he will do something else.

For each drawing, he will also begin to prepare accompanying sheets of additional sketches. He will detail each spine, each filament, each fin, each limb, each tentacle, every undulation, each swelling sinuosity of each creature, separately, from every possible angle, creating, as he does so, a map—yes, as near as he can come, with just his paper and pencils, to a three-dimensional map of each individual creature. And as he does it, he will be thinking about glass.

Of this I am quite certain.

What he thinks about my mother, I don't really know. Perhaps he avoids thinking of her. Perhaps, with his drawing, he seeks to replace her. This may be what he is really doing, out in his studio, in the cold, as he pulls his paper and his pencils close, surrounds himself, makes, for himself, a second skin of paper within which he shelters. Perhaps he grows ignorant, unknowing, sheds knowledge there, within a fortress of paper. His actions, in regard to her, make very little sense—become, at a certain level, uninterpretable. His intentions cannot be translated. I only know that he leaves her alone with Thomas Argument many times, that *that* is his choice. There is a certain inevitability about it, I suppose. Viewed in retrospect, as I view it. Of course my father cannot have viewed it so; and so I can suppose that he did not know what he was doing, that he did not see the danger that was there, before his eyes, plain to be seen, were he only willing to see it.

Although I think, perhaps, he did see it, and acted as he did, inevitably, in spite of what he saw.

Or so that he would not.

In retrospect, therefore, I ask myself the following:

Did my father Leopold love my mother, Clotilde?

And I respond:

Yes, certainly he did.

And then again I ask, in regard to her relationship with Thomas Argument, did my father act like a fool? And again: Yes, certainly. He did.

Of course I do not know what goes on in the Birdcage, those nights before the fire, when my father, rather than going upstairs, goes straight through the kitchen and out, taking away with him a cold slice of ham on bread, or some other scrap, some poor leftover rind of whatever those two, upstairs, have had for dinner. I am not sure, really, what my mother and Thomas Argument could talk about up there in the parlor, what they could possibly have in common. He is, after all, nearly twice her age. But he has his fads—his glass, his gas lighting, his gas furnaces, the excise tax (which he opposes, because, he says, it stifles innovation); the obnoxious behavior of the duty collectors, who hang around his shop on tax day, harassing the men; the union (which he also opposes, apparently because of the financial costs to him, but really, although he cannot say this aloud, even to my mother, because it makes him nervous to think of the men who work for him meeting together, grumbling, talking about him, complaining about him, making up stories, and especially, *telling tall tales about the batch*); the likelihood of communication by electrical cable (which he expects to happen soon, within the decade); or his latest trinket, obtained by him for his collection from—. It is always from a far-flung place, somewhere exotic.

He is not an attractive man. He is long, thin, spidery,

angular, uncomfortable, with long, thin, probing fingers like spider's legs, coarse, ill-cut black hair, and dense opaque black eyes, like Hyalith glass from the von Buquoy glassworks in Gratzen—reflecting much, expressing little, other than anger or impatience, neither of which he shows to my mother, not, at least, at this stage. He acts pleasantly, dresses well, is gentlemanlike. And yet there is, at the same time, something about his demeanor that is off-putting. An edge of something, carefully disguised.

He says, bitterly, it is the fault of the knacker's yard that he never found a wife. Nobody wants to marry into bones and corpses. Maybe it is true.

He admires my mother. This is certainly true.

He picked her up, after all, when she fainted, carried her, set her down on a couch covered with rugs and tapestries; first loosened, then removed her boots. Having lifted her in his arms, he knows how light she is, how fragile, how slender and pale her neck, her arms, her legs.

And he is a shrewd man. He has seen how easily he can drive my father into retreat. He is a calculating man, this Thomas Argument, and he has made his calculations.

As for my mother, she is a beautiful woman, young, sad, and lonely. She misses her Papa terribly. She spends her days alone in the Birdcage, listening to the River Esk rushing beneath her feet. She avoids the windows, so she will not have to see the sea.

She batters herself about, trying not to think of her Papa, the same way her Papa's last remaining hummingbird batters itself along the moldings at the tops of the walls, above the windows and doors, looking for a way out, even though what is outside is the cold, the killing cold. The hummingbird does not know what it is seeking; it merely acts and reacts, instinctively responds. My mother, alone in a room with Thomas Argument, noticing that my father comes in through the kitchen and goes directly out again, and missing her dear Papa so much, does the same. Acts and reacts. Responds.

As he produces a gift from a pocket, Argument's hand brushes hers. This, it is clear, is an accident. To this no response is necessary, other than the usual thank you, the usual teasing smile. She caresses the gift gratefully: this time, it is a lacquered music box from China, decorated with a pattern of swallows. She turns the delicate winding mechanism, listens with an attitude of appreciation. But when he reaches out, as they sit before the fire, to touch her, taking between his fingers a strand of her hair, or laying his palm upon her arm, all in the excitement of some discussion—about the inferiority of press molding versus cut glass, for example—this is not an accident, this requires a response. Perhaps not much of a response, but a response. My mother rises, moves away from Thomas Argument, stands with her back to one of the five corners of the pentagonal room or, going to the window, parts the curtains so that she can see my father's studio below, the hesitant pinprick of light in the inky darkness that is my father's lamp. What is Leopold doing out there? Why isn't he here? But my mother is all right. She has made a response, and she feels secure in it. She has moved away from Thomas Argument. This, certainly, is enough. Thomas Argument will not pursue her. He will lean forward in his chair before the fire, sit awkwardly, elbows on knees. He will not take offense. The black opacity of his eyes will remain undisturbed. For all I know, for all my mother knows, he, like my father, thinks of nothing but glass.

The inferiority of press molding. The inferiority of opaline. The inferiority of latticino. The sanctity of the batch.

In his studio, my father draws the clear concave bell of a medusa, the central peduncle, the dangling tentacles—forty-nine of them, exactly forty-nine, no more, no less. He is exacting, never having forgotten the boyhood sting of Felix Girard's *It is wrong here. And here. And here.* Around the margin of the bell, he adds slightly raised spots, blue-green bulbs; these would be phosphorescent, in a living animal, in an ocean thickened by night. *Dear Harry, I have received your letter and thank you for the kind words regarding my little sketches. Please find inclosed, copies, as many as I could complete, with more to come. Dear Harry, I work very slowly these days. The cold cramps my fingers and I do not want to make a mistake. Dear Harry, Since you have asked, Clotilde is very well except she misses her Papa. Too, the early darkness at this time of year can be so oppressive. Dear Harry, Another recent rockfall has exposed more petrifactions on the Scaur. I think they are worth exploring, despite the danger of further collapses. Dear Harry, Recently I have begun, by necessity, to work in glass, a medium difficult and unfamiliar to me, but filled, I think, with possibilities, could I only gain the opportunity to explore them. Dear Harry, Clotilde is very quiet, and unless I am mistaken, she thinks often of her "Darling Papa." I am sure it would cheer her immeasurably, and me too, if you could make a foray north . . .*

He draws an anemone, the thick, warty stem, the pale olive disk, the lobes of the mouth, the four surrounding rows of lilac tentacles. These are slender and tapering, like fingers. The soft, inner whorl of an oyster like the whorl of an ear, listening. He writes to Harry Owen in London. But he does not go into the Birdcage, and so he is not there on that particular night, that one out of the many nights, to stop Thomas Argument rising from his chair, following Clotilde to the window where she has sought shelter in her discomfort and anxiety. Argument stands close behind her as she looks down into the courtyard, seeking that wavering light, my father's light. He stands so close that she does not dare to turn around, lest she find herself closer still. Closer than she wants to be.

A single probing fingertip traces the edge of her lace collar. In response, a nervous vibration. She trembles. Perhaps from fear.

I am sure it would cheer her immeasurably, and me too, if you could make a foray north . . .

All this, of course, is speculation. I do not know what Thomas Argument did, or how my mother reacted. This is all a refraction of my fears, which are my father's fears, handed down to me through his diary. My mother wrote nothing, left nothing, except, of course, that charming enigma, her photograph. She is a sphinx, a cipher. We have projected upon her in turn, first my father, now me. We are making her, he in his way, I in mine. She is our creature, our creation. At the same time, she is not ours at all. She has slipped away from us. Our created Clotilde is a simulacrum, inserted by us into the space where she really used to be, the space we are always seeking, and always failing, to fill.

It was a warm space. Warm no longer.

I believe the process of her slipping away began that night, at the window, when Thomas Argument stood so close behind her that she could feel, without touch, the heat of his body on hers.

And then the touch.

Every night since, there has been less and less of her.

Does my father, out in his studio, feel her slipping away, feel the escaping molecules of her attachment to him? Is that why he begins work on the complicated sketch of a prawn—striped carapace, tail-fan, antennas, the legs with their complex joints, the blue pincers, the stalk-eyes? Is this when he begins it? So as not to feel it, this process that is taking place despite him, beyond his control? Or because he thinks he can keep her, through some mysterious alchemy, by working harder?

It is easy for me, in retrospect, to imagine that it is so. More likely, though, my father sees nothing but the drawing he must copy, feels nothing but anxiety lest he make a mistake that will undermine the scientific basis of his work, and Harry Owen's, and Felix Girard's. Indeed, he apparently feels so little concern on my mother's behalf that he returns to the house very late that night, later than usual. She is already in bed when he comes in. The light from his candle outlines the curve of her cheek against the curve of the pillow, the delicate half-moon of her closed eye, the featherlight, telltale quiver of gold lashes. Already she is an abstraction. My father does not pause to calculate the geometry of my mother's sleep or wakefulness; he is too busy thinking about sea creatures, and glass, and rockfalls, and science. In the morning she is unusually tired, still asleep when he leaves. In the evening, when he comes home, Thomas Argument is at the Birdcage already: my father feels himself preempted, but as usual he does nothing about it, retreating silently to his studio, as has become his habit.

And then he is made to work, at the glasshouse, several exhausting journeys in a row. My mother is always in bed when he gets home, and already out running her morning errands when he is awakened, at the teazer's call, and made to go back.

Several days will pass in this manner. And in the course of this dark passage, Leopold and Clotilde will barely talk with each other at all. Outside, it snows. Stinging grains of ice, cold-struck from anvil-shaped clouds, slick the brine-spackled streets, web the distant fields in a ghostly frozen caul.

When at last they do finally speak, the process begun that night at the window will have advanced—my mother seeming paler than usual, almost translucent, Nordic, cold in her beauty; gentle, yet distant; withdrawn.

Clotilde is very quiet, and unless I am mistaken, she thinks often of her "Darling Papa."

· · ·

He *is* mistaken. Clotilde works very hard not to think of her Darling Papa at all, finding, in this respect, the early darkness a relief because it spares her the watchful blue eye of the sea. She turns away; her head is lowered; she gazes at something, some object she caresses with pale fingers and slips quickly into her pocket at my father's approach. As she smiles and moves toward him, he feels, vertiginously, as if she is moving away. The closer she comes, the farther she has gone, her touch the inversion of a touch, an absence; her warmth, cold.

It is all very hard to understand. Leopold does not understand it. Willfully, perhaps. By an effort of will, he fails to understand, and, failing, he does the opposite of what he should. He pulls away. Perhaps, confused, disoriented, he has begun to think and to act and to feel in inversions. Farther is closer. Cold is warm. Absence is touch. Glass is flesh.

Glass is flesh.

Yes. This is when it started. Already it has begun.

As my mother grows more remote, Leopold thinks very much about glass. After working all day, then sometimes all night, in the glasshouse, he dreams of it: the heat of the ovens, the feel of the rough iron punty or the blowing rod in his hands, the molten core that remains inside, persistent as heartbeat, even after the glass has been removed from its source, the batch. The throb of it. He wakes to the persistent rhythm of the river, sees its myriad dark reflections scudding over the bedspread, up the curtains, across the ceiling. My mother is beside him, her back turned; shrouded in blankets, she is a curve, an ellipse, a mystery. He touches her and she moves away, murmurs a sleeping complaint. Her skin is cool, smooth. Already she has grown too distant for him to feel the inner fire.

In response to this new loneliness that he hardly understands, he sketches: obsessively, in his studio; surreptitiously, during spare moments in the glasshouse; myopically, while walking in the street; and, when murmurs and reflections will not allow him to sleep, in his bedroom, by the light of a thin and sulfurously smoking candle. What is he drawing? My mother does not know. Clotilde does not awaken. She has entered a place of deepest dreaming, from which she will not emerge.

They are dissections, my father's drawings: the many-rayed body of a sea star, its flat, orange spherical eye, the spiny, sandpaper hide, tubular feet; a heart cockle splayed open, stomach, genitals, egg sack, siphon, mantle, tentacles, eyes, all exposed. The roughened spot on the shell's interior where a grain of sand once entered between the delicate membranes. Bud of a pearl, thwarted. Dissections of himself as well, perhaps. During these long days when Clotilde seems so distant, so cool, so like a river, frozen over, which he can skate upon but never touch (all movement now hidden beneath the sparkling surface), does he imagine himself like his subjects: split open, splayed, exposed? Are these drawings what he hides behind, shields himself, *covers himself with?* And her. Dissections of her as well. *I can't get any closer than this.* Seeking the warm unreachable core.

Glass is flesh.

He makes them, then he copies them, then he sends them to Harry Owen in London. Having completed the cycle, finding himself suddenly idle, he is confronted again by that which he does not want to confront, again exposed, laid bare. And so he starts over. It is, in its way, a time of great productivity for him, during which Harry Owen receives, in a period of two months, two hundred copies of detailed sketches of specimens gathered during the voyage of the *Narcissus.*

Think how much time my father must spend with his paper and pencils and paints, to make two hundred copies in two months. This in addition to the many hours that he spends, Monday through Saturday, in Thomas Argument's glasshouse, bearing the stink and the heat of the ovens, the sting of Thomas Argument's ire, the frustration of being held back—always held back—from being allowed to make glass. And then there are the other drawings, the secret drawings, that are for his eyes only. I have no idea how many of those there were.

I have seen the drawings that my father made for Harry Owen during this time. The lines are neat and precise, the renderings detailed, his lettering, in the labels, small, rounded, self-contained. There is a sense of control. Nothing is extra, nothing superfluous. This is his disguise. He hides here. He is becoming, perhaps, much more like his own father, Emilio Dell'oro. A small precise man, tight-lipped, difficult to know.

I haven't seen the others. Those are my father's secret.

With my mother's distance begins my father's impenetrability.

With what he supposes is her betrayal.

Because that is what he does suppose. Although, if she has betrayed him, there is no real evidence of it. A whiff of scent in the glasswares shop. The trailing edge of a familiar skirt, disappearing behind a closing door in the High Street. The sound of a woman's laughter, familiar or perhaps not, stifled at his approach.

This is not evidence.

This is my father's imagination.

It torments him all the time. Even in the overwhelming black heat and stink of the furnace. When he eats. When he walks.

He is only free when he draws.

Your drawings . . . which remain, at present, the sole scientific record of these wonderful animals . . .

It is hard to know at what point, out in his studio, in the glasshouse, in the street, he rereads Harry Owen's letter and thinks, *If only I could make them in glass!*

At some point he does think it. Lying in bed, perhaps, contemplating my mother's turned back.

． ． ．

If only I could make them in glass!

I prefer to imagine it comes to him in a moment of creative fer-
ment, not in a moment of cuckoldry. I like to imagine him in
the street, his hands filled with papers, a disorganized flurry of
papers—his drawings, on the way to the post, perhaps—passing
the window of William Cloverdale, Argument's ever-bested
rival, chancing to look in at a display of glass eyes on a velvet
tray (*Just the kind of thing,* Thomas Argument would say, has
said, a hundred times, in my father's hearing, *that holds that fool
Cloverdale back!*) and thinking:

   I could make them in glass!

   But he cannot make them in glass. Not as long as he works
for Thomas Argument. And even if he could get access to the
batch, gain independent use of the tools . . . how could he do it?
The material is light and strong and supple, but the tools used in
Argument's glasshouse are coarse, and coarse tools create coarse
objects. What do Argument's heavy, cut-glass goblets and pre-
tentious lusters have in common with the delicate, questing tentacles, the soft mouth, of the rosy anemone?

   But those eyes in Cloverdale's window . . . the hazel irises
shot through with threads of gold, the deep browns, the fila-
mentous blues and greys . . . like living things. Living glass.

   Glass is flesh.

   There must be a way.

Or, perhaps more aptly:
There is *a way, but Thomas Argument doesn't know what it is.*

I imagine it would have been a turning point for my father—a small jubilation—the diminution of a hated (though as yet only barely consciously acknowledged) rival.

There is a way; Thomas Argument doesn't know what it is.
Nor does he care.

I imagine there must have grown, in my father, a certain disdain for Thomas Argument then. A relieving disdain. A diminishment of the fear inspired in him by those expressionless black eyes.

Of course this is all speculation. I don't know what happened, really. A process took place, and this is how I imagine it. I try to imagine it to my father's advantage. But the bare fact is that, after two and a half years in the employment of Thomas Argument, during which time he has advanced only from the position of taker-in, a boy's job, to footmaker, a better job, a man's job, but one allowing no creative independence, my father will transfer his allegiance directly across the street, to William Cloverdale, Argument's nearest competitor—into what Argument calls *That dingy little Cloverdale establishment.* In Cloverdale's shop, small as it is, dark as it is (lacking the brilliant gas jets that emblazon Argument's Glasswares, its more modest window must depend for its sparkle on sunlight, a scant resource in

Whitby in the winter), my father will work, for the first time, with the lamp.

Argument's Glasswares doesn't do lampwork, Thomas Argument seeing this kind of glassmaking as *backward-thinking practice, tawdry, fairground trickery, gypsy's trade*, suited for itinerant makers who set up stalls in the street where they make little glass animals, glass ships webbed with glass rigging, replicas of the abbey ruins, and other *mementos for the mantelpiece*, intended to amuse sentimental women, small children, summer tourists, and others who lack serious discernment in glass.

William Cloverdale, of course, can't afford to be finicky about lampwork, not with Argument's window, which some might describe as a fairground in itself, glaring at him, full wattage, from right across the street. William Cloverdale will make whatever people will buy.

Who is this man, Cloverdale, with whom my father has linked his fortunes?

He is Thomas Argument's opposite: fat where Argument is lean, short where Argument is tall, coarse where Argument is smooth, terse where Argument is talkative. He is a red-faced, squat, balding, muscular man, bullnecked, with thick arms like butcher's arms (shades of Felix Girard in this)—it is easy to imagine him wielding the cleaver, strongly, through meat and blood and bone, although, in fact, he wields the blowing iron, the punty, the pincer, and the wood jack, artfully as Thomas Argument does—more artfully. When he bears himself forth into the world, which is often, he does it gut-first, fearlessly, yet with a delicacy unexpected, unnerving even, in a man of his size. There is something surprisingly subtle about him, in word as well as deed. More than one customer has been startled, in the act of fingering a vase or a doorknob in Cloverdale's shop, to find the man looming suddenly at his elbow, so silent and light of foot is this vast, leather-aproned, flux-and-enamel stained figure, who frequents the Fox, where he drinks freely of bitter, ale, and beer; who is not a gentleman; who does not aspire to be a gentleman; and who thinks Venice is a term Thomas Argument invented in order to stimulate the sale of violet and blue latticino glass.

William Cloverdale is a devotee of the candle. He does not believe in gas lighting in shops or showrooms or bedrooms. He does not believe in electrical conduction, in foreign food, or in foreign travel. He is fairly certain the Far East does not exist. It isn't that he thinks progress is a dirty word; it just isn't a word he knows.

In his shop shiny objects grow dusty, and are allowed to remain so.

Glass eyes are his specialty. He enjoys making them, and he does it well.

It makes sense, of course. What better meeting place for the coarse delicacy, the delicate coarseness, of a William Cloverdale?

The perfectly blue-grey iris of a perfectly convex glass sphere made for shoving into a raw, empty socket in somebody's skull. Glass and flesh, together.

It's easy to understand why Thomas Argument would find this work of Cloverdale's repellent, even threatening: the shadow of the knacker's yard again, prosthesis as dismemberment, glass rendered flesh; flesh rendered glass (because what is the sand, the ash, the manganese, the arsenic Argument is melting in his furnace, if not flesh broken down into its constituent elements, flesh rendered earth rendered glass?). No wonder Thomas Argument shudders each time he passes Cloverdale's window and looks into all those staring glass eyes; no wonder he cries *Dingy! Tawdry! Backward-thinking! Fairground trickery!* Those eyes simultaneously remind and expose him: knacker's son!

My father, of course, has no such sensitivity. I like to imagine Leopold, in the street, with his drawings in hand (these bound for the post and London and Harry Owen), pausing at William Cloverdale's window, and having an epiphany.

Glass is flesh.

The apprenticeship with Cloverdale is a risky proposition. Leopold will be paid by the piece. If what he makes sells, he earns. If not, then not. Difficult terms, given his and my mother's impecunious state, his lack of experience with glass, and the marginal nature of Cloverdale's business. Yet my father accepts them, and there appears, in the *Whitby Gazette*, the following advertisement:

William Cloverdale, Glassmaker

Since 1824

Introduces *Signor* Leopoldo Dell'oro

Master Glassmaker Extraordinaire

Exclusive—from the Continent

Maker of Glass Eyes

Mineral Teeth

Porcelain Prostheses of All Kinds

· By Appointment Only ·

Lies, of course: Cloverdale's bid to outdo and annoy his neighbor and competitor. For as it will emerge, outchaffing Thomas Argument where he cannot outsell him is something the tight-lipped and subtle William Cloverdale enjoys. He has, perhaps, hired my inexperienced father on this basis alone. After all, the arrangement is risky for Cloverdale, too—he will invest his time, his space, and his materials on an untried novice, when he has little of any of those things to spare. Perhaps Leopold has shown Cloverdale some of his drawings, which demonstrate skill and artfulness, patience, and the kind of exactitude needed for the creation of "porcelain prostheses of all kinds."

Or perhaps William Cloverdale has simply seen an opportunity to get on Thomas Argument's nerves.

This is, after all, a realm within which Thomas Argument cannot fight back. He will not, cannot, ever, make glass eyes, mineral teeth, prostheses. The union of glass and flesh is a horror to Thomas Argument, a chimera unbearable to his temperament, which otherwise seeks out, actively, glasswork wonders and curiosities of all kinds.

No doubt he's put out, too, by the exoticism of this *Signor Leopoldo Dell'oro, Master Glassmaker Extraordinaire*, with its implications of Araby, of foreign soils and glasswork magic, all of which have, up to now, belonged to him exclusively: his Venetian latticino, his Parisian *cristal opaline*, his Bohemian marbled lithyalin and bright yellow pieces of *Annagelb*. The Count von Buquoy is his personal friend! Whereas William Cloverdale has never even left Whitby, except to visit his niece in Staithes.

Thomas Argument is annoyed. If chaffing Thomas Argument is his wish, William Cloverdale has almost certainly succeeded. This alone, to Cloverdale, may be worth the risk of hiring my father and paying him by the piece. My father's career: founded on a joke.

And so Leopold gives his resignation; Argument accepts it wordlessly, with a thin-lipped canny smile, handing over without protest my father's modest remaining pay, a small sum, and having paid it he is back at the Birdcage the very same evening, projecting onto the parlor wall, for my mother's amusement, with a magic lantern from his collection, the image of a forest burning—Leopold hears Clotilde's shriek of combined delight and fear as specular birds, fleeing the illusion of flame, emerge from among dark pines and seem to swoop out, into the room—

Oh, Mr. Argument! It is so real—!

—as he passes through the downstairs, out, again, into his studio.

In this regard, nothing, it seems, has changed.

But in another regard, everything has.

My father will use the lamp for the first time.

He will not work at a furnace (although William Cloverdale does have one of those—a small, outdated, soot-puffing old beehive that barely suffices to heat the batch). Rather, he will sit at a broad table, surrounded by rods of glass of various thick- nesses and colors, by containers of metal oxides, and by an array of fine-handled metal tools, wicked, gleaming sharps and hooks, pliers and pincers and shears, by delicate, soft-bristled brushes. The lamp itself, at which he will work, is just a tin cup containing a wick and paraffin, with a bellows beneath to fan the flame, controlled by the glassworker's—William Cloverdale's—now my father's—foot. There is a hot metal plate for keeping the glass pliable while it is worked, a crucible in which to cool it when it is finished. That is all.

He will work in a small room at the back of William Clover- dale's shop, surrounded by cabinets filled with drawers of glass rods and glass sticks and glass-eyes-in-progress; by completed

glass eyes awaiting fittings; and by glass eyes that have failed.
These fascinate Leopold most of all—the failures. Whether out
of perversity or a reluctance to waste his materials, Cloverdale
keeps a wooden box full of them—the eye with a pupil shaped
like a rabbit; the one with the impossibly beautiful, impossibly,
inhumanly violet iris; another with the white tinted green—a
case of too much iron in the batch (Leopold has already learned,
from Thomas Argument, that iron in the batch can be balanced
by manganese, the green tint eliminated, the white made pure
again; in the case of this eye, William Cloverdale hasn't bothered); the eye with the edges ground too sharp for any man to
tolerate; the eye that is too large, too long; and one that is very
small—a tiny bowl that fits the tip of Leopold's index finger,
with a diminutive grey-green iris—the eye of a child . . . apparently perfect, unclaimed, in the box marked "Scrap." Whose eye
is this? My father turns it around on his fingertip, a small, staring cap of blue glass, a false interiority, disembodied embodiment, an enigma; shivers slightly as he feels himself caught in
its sightless gaze. Seen and not seen.

Cloverdale should have melted it down by now, melted all of
them down, returned them to the batch. And yet he has not.

It is a reluctance that my father understands.

(Glass is flesh . . .)

This is the beginning. Beyond doubt it started here. He
will always be surrounded by multiple gazes when he works in
this room, watched yet not watched; will grow accustomed to
knowing that when he is here, he is simultaneously always and
never alone. This doubledness is natural; it will become restful
in time; in time my father will relax beneath those watching

eyes, beneath their gaze he will shape more gazes like them, melting, first, in the slender, red-hot jet of his lamp, a white glass rod from which he will tease forth the form of the bulb or bowl that is the prosthesis itself, carefully measured; then the colored rod (made from smaller, intertwined rods of blue and black and grey, or green and copper, or brown and gold, that William Cloverdale has braided together himself at his furnace), a slice of which will form the iris; then the black flux, comprised of equal parts manganese and iron oxides, with which he will paint the pupil; and then the clear, curved dome of glass that overlays it, the delicate half bubble of faux cornea. When it is completed, he will place this object that is an eye and yet is not, this piece of glass that is and is not flesh, into the crucible for cooling.

There cannot be any flaws. What is inconvenient in a candy dish or a luster is critical here. A glass eye must not crack. Imagine the consequences! My father does, he sweats and grows anxious at the lamp, imagining. But in the crucible the glass eyes cool carefully, reliably, evenly. They gaze with calm indifference upon my father's puffing anxiety. He has caught it from Thomas Argument, this mania for flawlessness, and it serves him well in the making of William Cloverdale's glass eyes.

It is not, of course, the only mania that my father and Thomas Argument share. *She* rotates in his mind all the time, as he melts the glass in the flame, as he presses and manipulates it, caresses it with his metal sharps and tweezers, paints it with the fine-haired brush, anneals it. This living glass that is warm but not alive, that looks at him without seeing, gazes with the calm, cold indifference of flesh that is not flesh.

Her gaze, too, seems cold very often now, when it deigns to fall upon him.

She is against his leaving Thomas Argument although she will not say so. What, after all, can she say? She will not protest aloud, will not tell him. Instead he has to read it in the quality of her turning away from him, which is a new turning away, different somehow from all the other turnings. Her various averted profiles a series of runes for him to decipher. The averted face a palimpsest. And the body. Her face. Her body. Not glass but the actual body, actual flesh, which turns away from him, like pages turning, over and over again. Certainly she is flesh but in her silence she seems almost to become glass. She is so fair, so blond, so cool, so translucent. She glows from the inside, like glass when it is hot. Yet looking into her eyes he sees nothing. This is like glass, too. Glass looks back but it does not recognize. It may be inscribed but it does not read. Runes cannot read themselves. Nor can she.

It would be best, he'd feel better, if she'd shout angrily, nag him, yell about the money, at least, if nothing else, but she does not. This in itself is a warning, a sign. This indifference to her own fate, which is so closely, so dangerously, even, entwined with his. How can she be indifferent? She just is. She says, *Look what Mr. Argument brought me yesterday. Isn't it nice?* By which means he is made to know that despite his action, the visits continue. Inevitably.

He should forbid them but he doesn't. To forbid is to accuse, and of what, after all, can he accuse her? Of loneliness? Of boredom? Of missing her lost Papa, he who was everything to her? Is she not allowed to have friends?

Because as of yet it is all still in his imagination: the whiff of scent which may or may not be familiar; the skirt disappearing, perhaps or perhaps not, behind a door that closes, maybe abruptly, in the High Street; the woman's laughter that ceases, or so it seems, at his approach. This is all in him, not in or of or from her. And he knows enough to know it. Or, at least, he realizes he does not know what is real and what is imagined, and so, in his actions, he carefully assumes it is all imagined, assumes her innocence, does not accuse. Will never.

He doesn't want to make her life worse. That's not what he wants at all. On the contrary.

But in his head it is different. In the privacy there he tortures himself. The thoughts rotate constantly in his mind, the whiff of scent, the skirt, the laughter, as he melts glass in the flame of the lamp, pressing it, shaping it, manipulating it with his delicate tools; or as he turns round and round, on the tip of his index finger, a small glass eye in blue and grey, taken from a box marked "Scrap." *Whose eye is this?*

No doubt William Cloverdale knows, but Leopold never asks. He thinks of slipping it into his pocket, this small, living-but-not-alive object, as if he could hatch it there like an egg, or guard it, just make sure it is safe; but he doesn't do that either. He always puts it back in the box, but he revisits it often.

For whom is this intended?

Glass is clear, and yet my father cannot find clarity. Flesh and glass, intention and action, seem strangely obscured and without boundary. He thinks: *I am a ridiculous figure, my future is based on a joke, my present a tragedy, my past a series of random shufflings across distant and near cities and moors and oceans. My sister is gone. Where?*

He is also not unaware that, had her dear, dear Papa not vanished, Clotilde probably would not have married him.

This is what *he* turns away from. She is not the only one who can turn away. When he remembers *this*, he immediately thinks of something else.

If only I could make them in glass!
    He is closer now, of course. He is learning what he needs to know. And he almost realizes it. He is aware. It is there in front of him: his life's work, founded on a joke. On a tragedy.

I would be alone.
    If a crazy man, an impetuous man, a *great* man, a stupid one—had not been foolish enough to get into a boat and lose himself at sea. Leaving *her* alone.
    (Why would he want to leave her alone? It doesn't make sense, offends all that seems right and rational . . .)

· · ·

My father, aware that his fate has been decided by the inscrutable act of a madman, cannot know where he might have been, what he might have been doing now, had Felix Girard *not* disappeared. He'd be in London, perhaps, not Whitby, cataloging a collection in a museum instead of making glass eyes, illustrating a book, perhaps.

But she?

She would have been with her Papa, in their rooms on Bury Place. She would have been happier. She would not have noticed me, except to tease:

Papa! Who is that ridiculous boy?

Are you quite thoroughly done being sick, Mr. Dell'oro?

He has forgotten none of it. It revolves there, in the painful and private place inside his head, as he carefully paints a red enamel web of capillaries on the otherwise startling white of a glass eye destined to slip into an empty socket in the head of a man named Sherman. Sherman, of Scarborough.

Sherman of Scarborough has come a goodly distance for this. Scarborough is a city in its own right, with glassmakers of its own. It is a fact, one that would be galling to Thomas Argument if Argument knew it: Sherman of Scarborough has been drawn in by William Cloverdale's ridiculous advertisement. *Signor Leopoldo Dell'oro, Master Glassmaker Extraordinaire, Exclusive—from the Continent!* And Sherman isn't the only one.

They are tricked! They come! It seems almost unbelievable, but they do. Because of this—out of a sense of guilt and obligation, trying to give something extra to those who have been fooled— my father has begun the innovation of painting enamel capillaries to make his glass eyes look more realistic. It is a process that makes his job more difficult, forces him to work more slowly, to use more materials. Because he paints capillaries, my father makes fewer pieces and, therefore, makes less money. Yet it is not for this reason that he finds his work unsatisfactory.

The eyes don't look alive enough.

They don't glisten. It isn't just the expression in them, or the lack thereof, that my father can't, at present, and probably shouldn't, control. It's that they don't *look wet*. They don't look alive. Something is lacking. The vital membrane, slipped. This makes my father uneasy.

He doesn't know how to remedy it. He tries different methods, various fluxes, enamels, blendings of glass. Nothing works. He discards pieces, wastes money, gets no results.

Why does he do it? He doesn't know. Only that it is the seed of something.

Nobody complains of course. The eyes he makes are beautiful, and because they are beautiful, nobody expects more, nobody notices what is missing, even conceives that anything is missing, except him; and he only thinks of it because he is a Dell'oro, because of the family *tendenza*: nothing can ever be good enough.

If only I could make them in glass!

But he can't do it yet. They won't look alive, those creatures of Harry Owen's, any more than the glass eyes look alive. My father longs to create a chimera, a melding of glass and flesh, but lacks the formula for this particular feat of alchemy. *Is* there a formula?

If there is one, William Cloverdale doesn't know it. The large man, approaching softly from behind, as is his habit, finds my father contemplative at his table, turning round and round on the tip of his finger (where it fits perfectly, like a cap), the diminutive blue eye once intended for a child.

It's a beauty, that, Cloverdale says, a regretful sigh (*the best I ever made, spurned*) working its way out from among the ruddy complexity of his butcher's jowls. He blinks slowly, deliberately, as if it is an effort to gaze across the broad, red tumbled vastness of his person; but the quick perception is there, too, as always.

Too dry, says my father. *It don't look real.*

Cloverdale purses his lips, begins to whistle. Between thick fingers he bears a sheaf of papers: orders for the master glassmaker. Jotted on each sheet in Cloverdale's meaty hand are requirements of measure, of color, of time. Sometimes there is an old prosthesis to work from, in which case my father will copy, trying, though, in each instance, to add some improvement, something of his own.

Now handing over the sheaf Cloverdale says to him, *That's all right, Mister Dell'oro. Because it ain't real. And everybody knows it.*

. . .

Even when they are alone he insists on calling my father *Mister*, a weird incongruity between master and man to which Leopold cannot adjust himself, wondering always if it is another of Cloverdale's deeply buried jokes. But this time as ever he can detect no mockery, and his employer, still whistling, recedes bulkily into the dimness of the shop, that place of perpetual evening through which one swims as if through a murk of clouded vitreous fluid, past shelves of dimly viewed, dust-occluded glass objects, at last toward the filthy windows, where can be glimpsed the street and, directly across it, the inescapable, perfect, shining front of Argument's Glasswares.

It ain't real. And everybody knows it.

Thus Cloverdale, in a moment's quick and bloody-minded butchery, exposes the hard, intractable knot at the heart of my father's obsession, the one thing he can't ever and will never get past.

Glass is not flesh.

How easily it flies apart, once the flaw is touched upon!

My father is haunted for a time. He thinks about the impossibilities in Cloverdale's box, the pupil shaped like a rabbit, the violet iris, the eye that is too large, the eye that is too small, and suddenly understanding them, wishes to create depredations of his own, depredations too subtle to be noticed by anyone other than himself—a series of purposeful failures that will succeed and be joined to flesh in the revolting intimacy of prosthesis and socket. The desire grips him like a fever that is fanned ever hotter by the indifference of my mother's turned back. And so he does it: one day he places, among the intricate black and grey and white filaments of a grey iris, a very tiny black letter C. The glass eye goes to its owner with my father's mark unnoticed, and, encouraged by his success to a greater outrage, he plants in a hazel eye the golden initials CG. When this, too, remains undetected, he goes further yet: in a blue iris, in white, just above the pupil, the letters CGD'O, entwined among the strands in a slice from one of Cloverdale's braided rods of colored glass.

But these tricks, a form of vandalism against his own work, do not satisfy my father's restlessness for very long, nor in the end do they even amuse him, leaving as they do, like something sour at the back of his throat that he can neither spit out nor swallow, the thought—*And nobody noticed! Nobody noticed this, either!* It is an invitation to a cynicism that has been, up until now, foreign to his nature; and indeed he cannot stop himself from painting in enamel capillaries to make his glass eyes look more real, and experimenting with methods for making them look wet, while at the same time, surreptitiously, he continues to implant in each prosthesis the cancellation of that realism in the form of my mother's initials, CGD'O, formed of the very tiniest granules of colored glass that he can manipulate, hidden in the webbed core of the iris. From this time forward all his work in glass will embody not just *the thing* but also its *contradiction,* the acknowledgment of the frustrated artificer that nature has defeated him once again. *It ain't real. And everybody knows it.* CGD'O.

Now he's started. If only in a small way.

It amuses me to imagine my mother's initials, stealthily placed in the glass eye of a farmer from Thirsk, or a tailor from Thornaby-on-Tees, or in one lost by accident at sea by a fisherman pursuing mackerel somewhere east of Spurn Head. No doubt my father was amused, too. It is difficult to know whether this series of degradations of his own work by use of her name was an homage or a joke, a self-abnegation or something else entirely, an expression, perhaps, of the anger he must feel, but will not voice, when, on return to the Birdcage, he finds her caressing yet one more thoughtful lagniappe from his rival, the ubiquitous Thomas Argument.

He must be angry. How can it be otherwise? It would be unnatural were my father, coming home after twelve hours with William Cloverdale, Glassmaker, not to grow angry at finding my mother by the hearth, in hushed colloquy with Argument, their two heads bent closely together, hers golden, graceful, his dark, awkward, vaguely oblong, her soft laughter ceasing as my father enters the room.

Oh, Leo! Look what Mr. Argument has brought me this time!

Angry. Yes, it would be natural for my father to be angry— at himself more than at her, perhaps. Because he cannot make it stop.

Argument at this point has virtually ceased speaking to my father, as if the bonds of employment, now severed, were all that ever held civility in place. If they pass on the stairs, as sometimes happens, Argument ducking and stooping in cramped quarters, my father forced to press himself against the banister between an elephant's foot and a shuddering stack of collector's trays containing butterflies pinned to cork so as to let the interloper pass, Argument does not even acknowledge that my father is there. To him my father is an indistinct ghost that lurks in the turning of that stair, or a specimen indistinguishable from all the other rubbish collected by Felix Girard (for to Thomas Argument, with his mania for the made, Girard's collections from nature, his preserved flesh—despite being Clotilde's beloved patrimony, her memories—are indeed all rubbish, although he hasn't told *her* that he thinks so—at least, not yet).

If Argument and my father meet while my mother is present, then Argument nods—a terse, stiff, barely detectable motion of chin above shirt collar, nothing friendly in it, as if to say, *Yes, it's me. I'm here again.* At times it seems to convey, in a specific, slight jutting forward of the lower jaw, the pugnacious corollary: *What are you going to do about it?*

That's all.

What little he does, clearly, he does for her sake. If he meets my father alone in the street—as sometimes happens on Church Street, there at the junction of their mutual glassworld—he cuts my father completely.

My mother seems to see nothing wrong with this, or else maybe she simply doesn't see it, because she is too remote—too remote to see, too remote to respond. She is like a glacier, retreating, trailing behind her, as she goes, a brilliant, unnavigable train of ice. She observes my father as if from a great distance, even if it is just the distance across a pillow. The pillow might as well be the Mongolian steppe, she might see very tiny camels striding across it, attempting—and failing—to bridge the gap that has grown between them.

In short, no matter what Thomas Argument does, she will not interfere on my father's behalf.

Of course it is possible that Argument, in addition to whatever designs or desires he may harbor in regard to Clotilde, is, above all, angry, just as my father is angry, jealous, just as my father is jealous, and equally unwilling to admit any of it. He cannot be angry openly, jealous openly—not yet. So he resorts to demonstrating his feelings in the angle of his chin.

Naturally he has noticed the increase in foot traffic at Cloverdale's shop, not to mention the large, galling new sign, CLOVERDALE & DELL'ORO, MASTER GLASSMAKERS, that has lately replaced the small tarnished plaque above the doorbell that for many years read, in the cheapest available lettering, just, WM. CLOVERDALE, GLASS.

Not so long ago, my father was a footmaker, unqualified to work independently with glass. He could press the foot of a wine glass with the forming tool, bend forward the lip of a decanter with a pliers, use a wooden paddle to smooth the rim of a jar, stretch a blob of molten glass to make a handle attach to the side of a pitcher. Now, suddenly, he is a master glassmaker? Thomas Argument need not waste his time harboring deep suspicions—he *knows*, as well as my father does, that it is all lies: the new sign, the newspaper advertisements, *Master Glassmaker, Direct from the Continent!*, all of it. All gibes, all taunts, from William Cloverdale. As a master glassmaker himself, Argument is angry about this. He feels his profession reduced by the inclusion, even the sham inclusion, of my father within its ranks.

Perhaps also, though, Thomas Argument is afraid. Perhaps he senses a truth that he seeks to avoid:

William Cloverdale is teaching my father.

My father is learning.

This possibility makes Thomas Argument angrier. In the place inside him where my mother resides—where he fears my father will overtake, will surpass, him—he is angry.

Thomas Argument is a man who does not like to be bested. It is only a matter of time, therefore, before he must respond to the provocation across Church Street.

It comes quickly. One morning my father, approaching Cloverdale's shop, with, as usual, his mind elsewhere (he has had another letter from Harry Owen, containing a request for further drawings), finds himself entangled on the sidewalk in front

of Argument's window with a crowd of admirers who have
gathered to read a poster plastered up on the glass:

View of Naples
Eruption of Vesuvius!
and Destruction of Herculaneum and Pompeii!

In the year 79 *(by Argument)*

THE ERUPTION OF VESUVIUS!
THIS PICTURE

Represents as accurately as can be done, the

GREAT ERUPTION IN THE YEAR 79,
WHEN THE DESTRUCTION OF
HERCULANEUM AND POMPEII
TOOK PLACE

The practical observation and experience

of *Mr. Argument*

Has enabled him to produce effects

never before attempted.

Argument has obtained the new double magic lantern of
Negretti and Zambra, and will use it, on alternate Wednesdays,
to show, in dissolving view, glass slides he has created himself,

using a new and secretive process of etching and enameling: Vesuvius erupting by moonlight, image dissolving into a lurid, rubble-strewn Pompeian dawn; the Great Fire of London gradually reducing St. Paul's Cathedral to ashes; the flood of the Huskar Pit overwhelming the child laborers of Silkstone . . . fade to a particularly affecting view of the seven mass graves in bright July sunlight . . .

There is nothing William Cloverdale can do about this—his customers sucked, every Wednesday week, into the inexhaustible maw of Thomas Argument, Showman; into the voyeuristic thrill of all that plummeting, scorching, drowning, exsanguinating humanity, projected onto a neutral wall in a glasshouse; all those thrilling, glowing, palpitating fades, enhanced by rolling voile screens or shades of fine muslin; and later, when the more sensational subjects have begun to pall, those that settle more gently beneath the banner of education and enrichment: sunrise over Tintern Abbey, or, Napoleon, at sunset, facing his men.

My father's glass eyes, even those containing, in secret, my mother's initials, are no competition for this. This is the full emanation, after all, of Thomas Argument's mania, his passion, and his anger. All that flame and hot lava! The raging floods! The secret unveilings! From behind Cloverdale's grimy windows my father watches, surreptitiously, the crowds that gather across the street.

.   .   .

He is looking for *her.*

She isn't there, of course. All showings, for her, are private.

Cloverdale is watching, too, although for different reasons. He gazes narrowly, disapprovingly, upon the ebb and flow of Argument's public. William Cloverdale dislikes the magic lantern in principle, just as he dislikes kaleidoscopes, stereoscopes, praxinoscopes, thaumatropes, dioramas, panoramas, spectacles in particular and entertainments in general—all of it, in William Cloverdale's opinion, goes beyond the bounds, just as the idea that there is a place called Venice where latticino glass is made goes beyond the bounds. Such things, for Cloverdale, enter rapidly into the realm of the not possible. *We can't have this, Mister Dell'oro,* Cloverdale's grey glance, cast over, above, and across the mountainous bulk of himself, coming at last to rest upon my father, seems to say. *Mister Dell'oro, something must be done!*

It is almost as if he knows—*He knows!*—that it is all Leopold's fault, as if he knows—*He knows!*—that Clotilde Dell'oro is at the root of it. Leopold must do something—must mend it. Customers, drawn to Church Street by William Cloverdale's *Gazette* advertisements—*Master Glassmaker! Exclusive—from the Continent!*—are being diverted by Thomas Argument's poster. They come, they see the poster, they are drawn in. They enter Argument's Glasswares and they never return. And it is Leopold's fault. He must do something. But what can he do?

There is nothing. Nothing he can do. He is helpless. This he knows.

My father, beneath the presumed accusation of Cloverdale's glance, begins sweating, runs his finger nervously around and around inside the too-tight collar of the dress shirt—the one dress shirt he owns, the one Gentilessa bought him, which he wears regardless the state of the weather because it is all he has and what's more, because he feels safest that way. All buttoned up, my father, just like his father before him. All buttoned up at the lamp, at the oven, at the window, regardless the heat. All buttoned up so as to prevent—?

Cloverdale shakes his beefy head and saunters away, whistling. *Those that got holes in their heads will always need glass eyes, no matter what, Mister Dell'oro,* he says. That is what he says.

The only accusation my father's, against himself.

Against her.

Or perhaps there is an accusation of a sort. *Those that got holes in their heads will always need glass eyes.*

Leopold reluctantly departs his station at the window, returns to his lamp, to the creation of a hazel eye for a farmer's wife who lost hers in an accident in the fields. Thresher threw a stone. That is how it happens. The thrown stone, the shattering glass, the slip of the knife, the splash of acid, the fall downstairs, the punch in the face. Diseases. Or some are born that way. The gap. The lack. The fissure.

The missing piece.

Those that got holes in their heads will always need glass eyes.

As he works, my father thinks about the people on the sidewalk in front of Argument's Glasswares. He pictures *her* among them, until the image in his mind becomes so real that he believes it. He can feel her there. It is a strong feeling, palpable as a touch. It mounts in him until he is almost crazy with belief.

Were he to look, though, she would not be there. She is at home, in the Birdcage.

He resists. He longs to look, but he resists. This time.

He diverts a strand of honey-colored glass to form the initials CGD'O.

Sometimes my father also thinks or imagines that William Cloverdale has noticed these small acts of simultaneous self-destruction and homage. Sometimes Cloverdale smiles in a manner that suggests it—a sly, confidential smile. A wink. But Cloverdale never says so—just fishes the finished piece out of the crucible, measures with his calipers, looks at the color, checks it against his slips of paper, nods. *Very pretty, Mister Dell'oro. A good fit. Once again.*

And smacks his lips.

Cloverdale does not know.

He knows nothing about Clotilde, about Argument, about the state of Leopold's marriage. There is no secret wink.

It is in my father's mind, all of it.

The most recent letter from Harry Owen, though, is not in his mind. *My Dear Leo, having received from Hornsby of the British*

Museum, Zoological Divisions, a commission . . . am very pleased to be able to ask of you further drawings, and to offer this small remittance for your considerable labors; and also to request further information in re: your suggestion, of the possibility of reproducing, in glass . . .

Here is a place for my father to disappear into, when he finds himself thinking too much about my mother, or about the volcanic emanations of Thomas Argument. A bolt-hole.

He is finally positioned to try it. He has the lamp, the rods of glass. William Cloverdale has taught, and my father has learned. He is timid though. His collar is still buttoned up tight.

Hornsby is skeptical but will pay . . .

Emerging into Church Street, into Thomas Argument's crowd, my father feels something quicken inside him. *Eruption of Vesuvius! Destruction of Herculaneum and Pompeii!*

The crowd shifts and murmurs in front of Thomas Argument's window. They are buying tickets, already, for Wednesday next. Leopold threads his way through and between and among, feels the anxiety, the indrawn breath of the waiting, the shift and surge and ebb of it, the hoping for a seat at Argument's spectacle.

She is not there.

Perhaps it would be better if she were. If it were for her, too, a public thing, a matter of tickets, of crowds, of waiting on sidewalks. But she is at home, in the Birdcage. Thomas Argument may be there as well.

. . .

It is a goad.

Dear Harry, while the materials are somewhat lacking . . .

Leopold is tepid. He is timid.

Dear Harry, though the materials are somewhat lacking and the tools imperfect . . .

Where does it come from, this fearfulness of my father's? The timidity, the hesitation, the acquiescence plus qualifier? The materials are lacking, the tools imperfect. And so, too, the maker. This, I believe, is what my father is thinking. But will not say. He remembers Felix Girard's *It is wrong here. And here.* He would rather hide than expose himself in an error. He does hide, feels himself hiding as he pushes through the crowd in front of Argument's Glasswares. Head down. Shoulders hunched. If he doesn't see them then maybe they can't see him. But of course he sees them, feels them, strikes against them, collides, no matter how small he tries to make himself he cannot be small enough, in this crowd: shoulder jostling shoulder, elbow prodding waistcoat, fingers brushing silk, brushing velvet, brushing serge. The ubiquity of ladies' hats, his face menaced by bristling feathers plucked with savagery from the New World. The intimate and inescapable intrusion of their perfume.

GREAT ERUPTION IN THE YEAR 79! DESTRUCTION
OF HERCULANEUM AND POMPEII! It is another cold
day, spit of rain and stink of sea, the sky above him a ceiling,
pressing down. He feels himself constrained, in his collar, in his
coat, in this town. Making his way, once again, home to the
Birdcage where he will find—what?

*Dear Harry, though the materials are lacking and the tools imperfect,
I will attempt the experiment, making no guarantee as to the
outcome . . .*

He is earlier than usual (a trick? a trap?), but he finds her alone.
Of Thomas Argument there is no sign, beyond the growing
profusion of gifts, which have edged in among the beloved
mementos of Felix Girard. No *immediate* sign, then, of the hated
rival, though the proximate signs remain to provoke my father.
And they do provoke him. The house is chilly, damp, the old
stones wet with the rushing of the river, and yet there is no fire.
Leopold, adding enamel capillaries to glass eyes, subtracts from
Clotilde's coal. This, perhaps, is part of his anger, but if so, then
he does not know it himself. My mother knows it. Of course.

I had a letter from Harry, he says.

She pinks with excitement.

News of my Papa?

No—n-no news. He asked me to make—he sent m-money—

He holds out the coin to show her.

But it is no use, already she has subsided, she barely listens, news of her Papa is all she wants to hear. She holds in her lap Thomas Argument's yellow glass bird, strokes it as if it is a real bird, the imaginary plumage soft and warm beneath her palm. Her own hummingbird, the one that belonged to her Papa, has disappeared somewhere among the curtain rods; she has not seen it for several days, but she continues putting out sugar water for it regardless, and the water is drunk, which seems, under the circumstances, enough.

If he hoped to impress her with the news of his commission, to overwhelm and blot out with his new money the drama of Argument's Vesuvius, he has failed. Clotilde, it seems, no longer cares about money, at least not about his money. What *does* my mother care about? It would be difficult, at this moment, for Leopold to say. He senses that a new quality has entered into her typical reserve, a quality of concealment as determined as it is fragile. She is herself and is not herself, simultaneously. It seems to him as though she has a secret that she holds fast. She would rather break than reveal it, that is what he thinks, even though the act of holding back might, in itself, shatter her into a thousand pieces.

Yet she does not break. She will not. She is determined. She is stronger than my father thinks. Her secret is not what he thinks it is.

Of course he has imagined what she must be hiding. There has been that whiff of scent, the stifled laughter, the trailing familiar edge of skirt behind the closing door, thoughts that torture him. My father's imagination (on this subject) is, in the end, an impoverished one, rushing to the obvious conclusions.

. . .

I w-will have to work m-more, he says. *But it will mean m-more money.*

My mother barely glances up at this statement, the towering irony of it. The icy pallor has returned. She does nod, though, and her mute acceptance seems to him another indication of that which he has already accepted as true, as inevitable.

She does not care what he does. If he works more, so much the better for her. His absence will be to her advantage. That is what my father, lacking in imagination, assumes she thinks.

And so he will begin.

He is surreptitious at first. In spite of what he has told Clotilde— that there will be more money—at first, in fact, there will be *less*: he takes what glass he needs, surreptitiously, from that which William Cloverdale has supplied for the creation of the pros- thetic eyes. As he is paid by the piece, fewer pieces from more supply means greater cost to Cloverdale, therefore less money not more: less coal, fewer petticoats, scanter food, no tea, this being, perhaps, one expression of my father's anger at my mother, although he does not think so. He does not tell her what he is doing. Simply, it happens that there is less. Nor does he tell William Cloverdale what he is doing. Instead, each day, he sets aside, surreptitiously, a few rods of glass, in various colors. This he will do, each day, until he has enough. It is clear that there will be problems. As he has said to Harry Owen, *materials are lacking.* There are severe limitations of color, and, what's more, he can only steal so much. This is, after all, what he is doing—stealing—although he does not think of it that way. He has other ways to think of it. He thinks, for example, that it is all a matter of expediency, a temporary arrangement, until he can find a better. He is merely conducting an experiment, and when the experiment is completed, he will cease to borrow (this is the word my father uses, in his mind) from William Cloverdale. He practically expects his experiment to end in failure, in which case there will be no further need for borrowing anyway. The situation is, by definition, short term. And so forth. So he thinks.

This is what anger, and Thomas Argument, have made of him.

The Dell'oros are not, by nature, sneaky people. It is just that the family *tendenza* sometimes drives us to commit acts that appear, for want of a better word, sneaky.

And so my stiff, anxiety-ridden father, with his shirt collar buttoned up tight, hoards rods of glass beneath William Cloverdale's unsuspecting nose, stuffing them in drawers, secreting them in bins, burying them at the bottom of the box marked "Scrap." He trembles a little each time Cloverdale, soft footed, whistling, comes near to one of these stashes, as a squirrel may tremble for the safety of its supply of wintertime nuts. But he is lucky; he is never discovered. If Cloverdale notices a slight diminishment in his stock of glass rods, he says nothing, assuming, perhaps, that my father is creating some new innovation for the betterment of the glass eye and, hence, for the wallet of William Cloverdale. If my father feels any qualms at this betrayal of trust, he does not indicate it by any diminishment of his "borrowing"; indeed, if anything, he hoards more, driven, it seems, by a larcenous rapture previously unknown to him. In the rapture's grip he even takes up Cloverdale's habit of whistling, identifying, in this way, with the man whom he defrauds.

As for creating the circumstances under which he can be alone with what he has stolen, this, too, is easy enough—the orders mount up, my father falls behind, he will remain into the night to complete his work; Cloverdale, shuttering up the shop, thinks profit is the motive—profit, and the desire to aggravate Thomas Argument by keeping the night fires burning late— and he is pleased. He sheds his leather apron, shambles off to the Fox, and will not think about Leopoldo Dell'oro again, until he returns early to find his master glassmaker asleep at the workbench, surrounded by bits and pieces of castaway glass, the lamp still on, burning low and dangerously close to the top of Leo's tangle-haired, unconscious head.

Hey, you, Mister Dell'oro! Wake up there! Get up! Come on now! Here all night again? Ye're a madman, all right! Get out of that now

and clean yoursef up! Shop's open, man, quick, quick! No foolin'! Cus-
tomers comin'! Customers comin'! What can that young bride of yours
think, eh? You out all night like this. Bet she wishes now that she'd
married an Englishman . . . A nice, normal Englishman . . . Not a
crazy furriner like you . . . Out all night, and that lovely young
woman home all by hersef . . . Ought to be ashamed of yoursef, y'
should . . .

The large man moves back now from the workroom out into
the shop, taking down the shutters, letting the first watery light
of morning filter through the smudged tumblers and fruit bowls
and creamers, the dust-blurred decanters, the higgledy-piggledy
piles of doorknobs and buttons, the ornate lusters greasy with
fingerprints. He whistles as he does it, his first tune of the day.
He has looked into the crucible. He knows how much work was
done overnight. Despite all his huffing and scolding, William
Cloverdale is happy.

He does not know that he has been robbed.

My father has used three rods of William Cloverdale's green
glass in a botched attempt to create the model of a sea anemone
for Harry Owen; the sad, mutilated result lies now in pieces in
the bottom drawer, left, in the cabinet behind the master glassmaker's workbench.

My father, rudely awakened, has only just remembered this
himself.

He meant to remove the evidence. Now he cannot.

He has used a certain amount of enamel, too, in an effort to replicate the delicate shading of the tentacles, deep mauve at the base, lightening to rosy pink at the tips.

This was also a failure. And a robbery.

A tremor of anxiety passes through my father as he thinks of the evidence lying in the bottom drawer, left, along with some yellowed packing slips, disused tools, and a very old leather apron, folded, cracking along the seams. Flakes of leather like black moths broke free and scattered when he tried to unfold the apron to wrap what he had made, to hide the aborted remains. Black moths still lie on the floor, the fortunately filthy floor. He meant to sweep them up, but he didn't. Black moths that are really flakes of skin. Instead he fell asleep, there beneath the gaze of the glass eyes in their cases. They watch him still.

This makes him tremble.

Though they are silent. Of course.

The robbed man—the victim—William Cloverdale—will not notice, or, if he does, will think it is a tremor of awakening. *Crazy filthy furriner.*

That is one of the advantages. Filthy. Crazy. Foreign. Therefore unaccountable. Bound to behave unaccountably. The unexpected, expected.

All day, as Leopold labors, deprived of sleep, over his glass eyes, he will think about his failures of the night before. The color was wrong. The shapes. The pieces cracked and crazed. And the overarching problem: *it did not look alive.*

It was a dead thing. An abortion. He should have returned it to the batch, but he didn't. Instead he put it in the drawer, and then he fell asleep. Now it will be in the drawer all day, all day he will worry about it, will tremble when William Cloverdale comes near, sigh with relief when he goes away on his wide, silent feet. That particular drawer is seldom used, it is forgotten, but still, it is dangerous. This and the falling asleep with the lamp still lit. And the reluctance (because there was reluctance) to return his failure, his mess, to the batch. To consign it to the fiery pit. *I will do it later.* But then there was no later.

It is dangerous.

The thievery could be detected.

My father, when he began his experiment, half expected to fail. But he did not expect to have feelings about his failure, to want to keep his failure, to study it. He has surprised himself. In this, he is unaccountable to himself.

Now, because of his failure and his falling asleep, which was careless, he will have to stay late another night, if only to melt down and thus repatriate that which he has stolen. Expunge the theft. The guilt. Perhaps, too (so he hopes), the failure.

This is what my father does. He stays another night. And another. Thomas Argument, from across the street, sees the glow of fire from between the slats of William Cloverdale's shutters, and feels himself goaded. But goaded to what? He has no idea what is going on in Cloverdale's glasshouse. Because he does not know, he will work longer, and later, himself. Just in case. So as not to be surprised. So as not to be outdone.

Which makes one thing clear:

He isn't with my mother.

Thomas Argument and Leopold Dell'oro are both in Church

Street, working, while Clotilde Girard Dell'oro, CGD'O, is at the Birdcage, alone, listening to the river.

She has a secret that she is holding to herself, very tightly. She holds it tightly even when she is alone, as if she is afraid of revealing, to herself, something she already knows, yet does not want to know. During these long nights, though, when my father does not bother to come home at all, she sometimes lets go just a little—just enough to be able to hold the secret at a small distance from herself, at arm's length, as if it belongs to someone else, so that she can look at it, and think what it is that she ought to do.

Hers is a secret requiring action. That is what she thinks.

She just doesn't know which action.

In fact, she has very few choices. It makes her feel better, though, during the long nights alone, to imagine that she has many.

It is difficult for me to understand why, feeling as he does, my father leaves my mother alone on these nights. Even if he thinks she is already lost to him, why does he not stay there, fight? Or at the very least, watch? Guard? Observe? Forbid? It is foreign to his character to forbid, but ought he not do it, *in this case?*

And I don't understand Thomas Argument either—seeing the breach, why does he not step into it, if this is what he wants, has wanted, all along? Inexplicable.

My mother, though, is all too easy to understand. I know what she must be feeling, alone in the dark in the Birdcage with its crazy jims and jambs, the staircases crammed with preserved corpses, the stink and froth and rage of the river beneath her as it carries off to sea Whitby's whale grease and slag and excrement. Her Papa gone, lost. A perpetual torment of rushing water. This is all too easy to imagine.

She doesn't understand why they've left her alone. They've left her, all of them. Left her with her secret, trying, all alone, to decide what to do.

Sometimes it's hard for me to like my father. He is, as William Cloverdale would have it, foreign to me. Unaccountable. Lost in more ways than one. While Clotilde, who will run away, washing her hands of me completely, feels close.

Despite everything, we have a lot in common, she and I. Not that I like to admit it.

Like me, for instance, she, too, has a map of the place where her father disappeared. She found it among the odds and ends of her "inheritance," in a box also containing the preserved head of a lowland gorilla and a specimen tray labeled "miscellaneous pupae." The map itself was carelessly folded and stuck in between the lid of the tray and the pupae themselves, which, true to their label, were rolled about loose, slightly seedy, peeling, like the fossilized stubs of partially smoked cigars. The map was Felix Girard's own map, bearing the stains of Bury Place and home—it even smelled like home, when she first unfolded it, a rich mélange of preserving fluid, gazpacho, Beaujolais, and chocolate. It is marked by Felix Girard's soup, by his tea, by his pencil. There, on the map with which he planned his trip, is Punta Yalkubul, a green, ape's-brow bulge at the northernmost prominence of the Yucatán. And there, to the north, in the blue void of the Gulf of Mexico, marked in pencil in her Papa's beloved hand: *Isla Desterrada.*

My mother discovered this map by accident. She was not, initially, interested in the map at all, but rather exclusively in the pupae. She had even some notion that she would try to identify and label the pupae, as a completion of and testament to the work of her dear Papa. She thought she would feel close to him that way. The map, at first, she set aside and ignored. She surrounded herself instead with books belonging to her Papa, containing pictures of pupae, and tried her hand at identification. The pupae, though, proved unpromising. She realized she did not even know where they were from. Were they European pupae? North American? South American? Central Asian? From New Guinea? Malaya? Mongolia? Toronto? Clotilde did not know, could not begin to know. Instead of making her feel closer to her Papa, the pupae made her feel farther away. There was nothing, in them, of her Papa. Clearly he had found them uninteresting himself, or else he would have labeled them. He did label very many things, but not these. Already distracted, she could not concentrate. Then one afternoon, she opened the map. She opened it listlessly, without any conviction. That is when she noticed it—written in, in her father's hand.

Isla Desterrada. 22'49" N, 89'70" W.

She noticed, and then she quietly put the map away. She put it away without thinking. She also immediately lost what little interest remained for her in the pupae as well. She thought she would never look at them again, and the map, if she thought of it at all, was included in that.

It would take her a while to digest the implications. She even, for a time, forgot about the map, as if she had never seen it. She put it and the pupae back in the box with the gorilla's head and took the whole thing out, into the shed, and left it in my father's studio. Dropped it on the floor and walked away.

Then one day she suddenly thought:

He knew.

A huge realization.

And then:

He planned it.

An even huger.

And worse yet:

He knew, and he left me alone regardless.

No, that can't be right. It's impossible.

She went back out to the shed, into the box with the pupae and the gorilla's head, and retrieved the map, and looked at it again. Saw that it was, indeed, as she thought.

No wonder my mother is preoccupied during the long nights when my father and Thomas Argument, too, leave her alone.

There is, of course, a positive side to her discovery.

My Papa is alive!

That is what she begins to think, at first hesitantly, then with greater and greater conviction. Over time, as her discovery chafes at her—as she grows pale, and distant, and lies awake at night, watching the reflections of the river crawling up the wall—it becomes *all* she thinks. She succeeds, almost, in forgetting the other implications.

My Papa left me. He did not care.

Now, when she is alone, she brings out the map, and studies it, and runs her fingers over the pencil marks. If she shuts her eyes she can feel them. That is how hard her Papa bore down, when he marked *Isla Desterrada* on his map.

Even then, I think, she was already packing her suitcase. Mentally, at least.

Emotionally speaking, she had packed it already.

How many times, growing up, was she filled with despair at the sight of her Papa caressing a map? Now she does exactly as he did. Except no one sees her. There is no one to despair. There is no one to beg her to stay. No one will want to come with her. She is alone. That is what she thinks.

There is a freedom involved in no one caring. Also, in not caring oneself. There is a detachment in it, a knot unraveled, a detail set free from context. That is what my mother has learned. Not caring makes the limbs lighter. She caresses the map without worries. I doubt she thinks twice about Leopold. Thomas Argument, with all his toys and gifts, is not even on her horizon. It is her Papa that she thinks of.

He is alive! I must find him!

. . .

It is interesting, is it not, how we always think most about the one who has gone away and left us? And least about the one who has remained behind?

She imagines herself on the water, navigating by the stars.

She has forgotten other aspects of the journey. Such as the heat. The stink. The poisonous vapors. And the getting lost.

(But that, after all, was just part of the plan—Felix Girard's plan.)

Mary! Go out to the shed and fetch me my bags! The small one, with the buckle! And the big one, with the strap! Go on! Why are you lolling, you lazy creature! I've asked you to fetch me my bags—and my trunk—bring my trunk too, while you're at it, you lazy, creeping, good-for-nothing—!

The girl-of-all-work, cap askew, grumbling, makes her way reluctantly out into the yard and then more reluctantly still into the shed, where my mother's salt-stained luggage resides among the swaying dis-ease of stacked crates shipped from London and other "parts (and ports) unknown." Mary loathes the collected goods and chattels of Felix Girard, *Gives me the willies it does, that stuff, all kind of dead things rotting, a great rotting dead bird I found in one o' 'em boxes once, and a seal's flipper in another—that's right—just the flipper—it had fingernails an' all just like we do—* *appallin' I tell you!—and I thought, well, what's next—the hind end* *of a giraffe?—a camel's pizzle?! And pah! What a stink!* But she goes into the shed; what choice has she got? If she needs her job (and she does), she must go. And there she will find, in addition to my mother's small bag with the buckle, large bag with the strap, and water-warped old trunk, the grinning stone head of a Persian *div—Staring straight at me it was, right out of the box,* *sticking out its tongue, very familiar and all, as if it knew me!*

Maybe it does know you, Mary, her sister Susan will say; *Yeah,* *and maybe I ought to quit that job,* Mary will say, *and that house* *full of evil things*; and someday she will; but not today. Instead, with much grunting and groaning and panting, she will drag the trunk and the two bags upstairs, while my mother sits on the sofa, dreaming over her Papa's map: *Idling her day away as* *usual, and me like a dog, around and around and up and down them* *stairs with milady's boxes and bundles and bags* . . .

All right, you silly girl, you can leave them.

The bags drop at the center of the parlor rug.

Does madam wish to pack her things?

*No—*sharply this time—*I said to leave them.*

The girl, grumbling under her breath about the obscenely out-thrust tongue of the *div—evil things in this house, evil* *things!*—disappears back down the corkscrew stairs into the kitchen.

Of course my mother will not pack directly. She isn't ready yet. There is much that she will need—so much that she can hardly think of it all. Clothes. Shoes. Maps. A ship. Advisers. Money.

A very great deal of money.

She contemplates her suitcases.

It will take time. For the moment, it is just a dream. She has accomplished the easiest part of the dream, summoning the bags, then sliding them underneath the bed, where my father will not see them. There they will wait, like a promise. Sometimes a promise can be enough. My mother is aware of those bags, hyper-aware. There is not a moment that she spends on or in or around the bed that she is not conscious of the bags beneath it, waiting, patiently, until she is ready. Sometimes she wants to laugh, thinking about them; but she does not laugh.

Instead she grows very silent. She goes to Lars Kiersta's in Flowergate and has a dress made. It is the first of what she will need. My father curses when he receives the bill, thinking the worst. So little imagination! Because of my father's negative response, my mother has the next bill sent to Thomas Argument. He will pay for the next dress—*With pleasure*. And for the boots as well. His Vesuvius is making him rich. He can buy enough dresses to pack my mother's entire trunk. He will also buy, before my mother is done, corsets, camisoles, petticoats, cotton hose, and a dozen nice cambric handkerchiefs, all of which my mother will fold carefully, reverently even, into her suitcases. Thomas Argument has no idea why Clotilde wants so many clothes; he has less imagination even than my father. Women want new clothes, therefore she shall have them. It may occur to him, once or twice, to wonder why he never sees her wearing what he has bought; he supposes he has forgotten which ones he paid for, and which her dear Papa bought her in Paris, back before *the disappearance* (he assumes Leopold hasn't bought her any, which is very nearly true); but he never goes so far as to imagine those suitcases hidden beneath the bed.

Nor could he imagine that she has obtained the schedule for the steam packet *Emerald Isle* (departing the pier, Wednesdays to London, Mondays to Stockton; John Barritt, agent), which she has also folded up, and keeps among her underthings, along with her Papa's map, in her trunk.

She is such a delicate creature. Incapable of planning.

It is true she hasn't purchased her ticket yet.

She is waiting.

She already has a few coins tied up in one of those cambric handkerchiefs, and each week she will stealthily extract a single coin more from my father's pay packet and hide it within that tight cambric knot.

So she is a thief, too, in her own way, and with her own justification.

My Papa is alive!

But he must be in trouble, or else he would return to me. I have to find him. I have to help my dear beloved Papa.

It is not very likely that my mother will succeed. She knows, herself, how unlikely it is. Yet she manages to continue the dream, hiding it in a particular space in her mind, where it is safe. In this space, the dream can be real to her, and also not real, and both at the same time. She does not, must not, look too closely. It is in the background, in the periphery. She sees it out the corners of her eyes. It is a bright flash of color, a flash like the flash of a wing.

Look directly and it is gone.

She needs the dream very much. Therefore she slips, each week, another coin into the cambric handkerchief, and continues forward, straight ahead, looking neither left nor right.

It would be so easy for my father to stop her.

It will take her a long time to save that money. And in the meantime, there are obstacles that she will face. She will be slowed immeasurably by one inconvenience, then another. There will be many opportunities for Leopold to intervene. But he will not intervene.

The trouble is that he has no imagination.

He becomes aware, for example, that money is missing. It takes time, but he notices a stricture in the domestic budget, greater than that caused by his own waste of material and time at William Cloverdale's glasshouse. He notices, and quickly forms certain assumptions about what it is that Clotilde is doing with the money. Not long afterward he finds, because he looks for them, already assuming their existence, the suitcases underneath the bed, and this discovery bolsters his confidence in the assumptions he has already made.

.   .   .

He is too much of a gentleman to look inside the suitcases. He recoils from this—out of respect? Discretion? Fear? So he does not find the map on which Felix Girard has marked *Isla Desterrada: 22'49" N, 89'70" W.* Nor does he find the schedule for the steamer *Emerald Isle*. Left to his own devices, he cannot imagine these things. He imagines only the usual things, all of them distasteful, many of them involving his rival, Thomas Argument.

Missing money. Suitcases brought out of storage. And there are other things, other signs. For a period my mother's spirits seem to rise. She sends Mary out to the shed to search for her old sheet music, and when, despite the menacing *div*, it has been found, she sits, for the first time in a very long time, at her little spinet. It is hopelessly warped now and out of tune, this dear instrument bought for her by her Papa; but Clotilde persists in playing, and she does not complain of its poor sound. She plays as if oblivious, simply for the pleasure of touching the instrument that she has not touched in so many months.

My father thinks (because he cannot imagine the dream that has lifted her spirits, the fragile dream that balances, precariously, in a place inside her that is hidden from him), *She is leaving me for Thomas Argument. Therefore she is happy.*

So little imagination! And so wrongsighted.

Even Thomas Argument knows better than to imagine this.

Especially Thomas Argument. He is busy with his magic lantern—too dazzled by his own special effects to be planning any radical moves with my mother. Though he still comes to visit at the Birdcage, of course; and he still brings gifts—except now, he brings corsets instead of music boxes.

My poor mother. I feel sorry for her sometimes. So much looked at, gazed upon, devoured, even, by them both, yet so little seen. Transformed by them, always, into something other than herself. Her happiness, such as it is, so fragile. She is about to face the first, and greatest, obstacle to her dream.

Mary! she cries, *you're hurting me! Don't tie my corset so tight, you terrible creature!*

La! Blame me? It's not my fault, is it, that madam's got so fat—?

Shut up, you horrible, lazy, impudent girl! Leave it! Get away!

This is the beginning: my mother clinging to the bedpost, her gold curls loose and in disarray around her shoulders, Mary tugging bravely at the corset laces. She can tug no further. *La! It's not my fault, is it, that madam's got so fat?*

How unhappy it makes my mother, this remark of Mary's. She frowns, not with anger, but with a misery so profound that it frightens the servant, who runs quickly away.

. . .

Mary, help me move the mirror out of the closet.

It is the afternoon of the same day. My father, as usual, is not home.

Really, madam? Incredulously. *Mr. Argument's big mirror? Are you certain?*

It is the one gift of Thomas Argument's that my mother has banished: a large mirror in a gilt rococo frame on a cherrywood stand—the only full-length mirror she has ever owned.

Yes, you little fool, of course I'm certain. Why would I say I wanted it if I didn't?

Of course, madam. I'm sorry, madam.

It takes both of them, huffing and puffing mightily, to dislodge the mirror from the back of the closet where, together, they'd jammed it a year ago, wedging it between a stuffed anteater with great hooked foreclaws posed on a tree stump, and a lacquered incidental table inset with ebony, belonging to Marie-Louise Girard. Back then, a year ago, my mother couldn't bear the sight of the mirror; now she regards it coolly, evenly, like an enemy she means to face down.

It's very dusty, madam.

That's all right. Now get out.

Yes, madam.

The door shuts behind Mary's bustling and bowing skirts; my mother, left alone, stands quite still, at an oblique angle to the mirror, its unruffled silver depths outside her line of vision,

which rests, instead, on the bed with its white, nubbled bedspread. Beneath the bed, like stones beneath the sea, lie her
trunk and her travel cases, but she can see these no more than
she can see her own reflection.

She waits a moment, during which the only sounds are the
chiming of the clock, downstairs in the parlor, and, farther
away, muffled, here, on the third floor, the hollow, echoing
boom of the river, whose vibration carries up through the bones
of the house into the soles of my mother's feet.

Quickly, then, she begins to undress, removing, first, the
petite leather boots bought for her by her Papa in Paris; then,
unpinning it from the bodice, the navy blue skirt, which falls
around her feet; then the bodice itself, low necked, with tight,
short sleeves, is unhooked and cast aside; then the petticoats—
there are four—the long one with the flounce—the short white
one—the petticoat bodice, with its buttons, embroideries and
frills—then the ornamental petticoat, expensively laced; then she
rolls her black stockings down and off, kicking them aside; then
the white cotton camisole, tightly fitted at the waist; then the
corset, which she unhooks from the front before reaching around
behind to loosen the laces; and then at last, the heavy white che-
mise, which she slips up and off over her head, her arms tangling
in it for a moment before, bending forward sharply at the waist
in a gesture of impatience, she casts it, too, onto the floor.

Finally naked, she steps before the mirror.

She has never seen herself this way before, the entire pink
and white and gold of herself unclothed. She surveys herself
critically—wincing slightly as she cups her breasts in her hands,
weighing them, considering the dark flush of the aureoles, then

turning slowly sideways to look at herself in silhouette. She un-pins her hair, lets it fall. She is a beautiful woman; she has known this; now she sees it. She places her palm against her belly, just above the luxuriant blond bush of pubic hair. Behind her, in the mirror, she can see reflected the sea, grey blue, frothy with white-caps, protecting all its secrets, framed in her bedroom window.

She does not linger long. This new being, her naked self, is not, for her, an object of admiration or of desire. She dresses again, rapidly, twists her hair up into a thick, glossy coil, which she pins neatly into place. A few renegade curls hang loose at the nape of her neck.

I wonder, does she miss her own mother now? Or is it still her Papa she thinks of—Marie-Louise Girard nothing but a ghost: unsought, unwanted.

She tries and when she cannot move it herself, carefully covers the mirror with a sheet she unfolds from the linen chest at the foot of the bed, making certain that each flounce of the rococo frame is fully hidden.

Not long afterward she appears in the kitchen, adjusting her hat, pulling on her ice-blue shawl.

Mary, I'm going out.

Yes, madam. Will you be going to see Mr. Argument, then?

No, Mary. I won't be long.

Still there is no anger in my mother, despite her servant's impudence; just a deepening of the glacial reserve, and of that cast of unhappiness that arrived in the morning, which she can neither dispel nor disguise—it shows still, at the corners of her lips, and in her eyes—a seriousness that stifles even the girl-of-all-work, who lowers her head, suddenly embarrassed, and begins to scour the stove.

There is no rush for dinner, Mary. It will just be me tonight. Mr. Dell'oro won't be home.

Yes, madam.

My mother emerges onto Bridge Street in the lengthening afternoon. It is spring, still chilly, the sky greenish, gravid, but without rain. She is on her way to Skinner Street.

As there is no sun she casts no shadow.

It will be three hours before she returns. There will be a wait in Skinner Street. This is beyond her control.

On her way home she will pass, on the sidewalk, Thomas Argument, who will smile at her, and nod, and walk on, saying nothing.

He is a shrewd man, Thomas Argument. Although my mother doesn't know it yet, he won't visit her again. This, too, is beyond her control, as she will very soon discover, to her infinite, though disguised, distress.

. . .

What is my father doing while my mother is in Skinner Street? He is with William Cloverdale, of course, making a beautiful, honey-brown glass eye, the iris shot through with strands of gold, for a girl from Hull who lost hers after being violently punched in the face by her lover because she had been, or so he believed, unfaithful. In this glass eye my father places four tiny brown grains of glass forming the initials: CGD'O.

If looked at very closely, by use of a magnifying glass, for example, these initials will be discernible in the glass iris, just above and to the left of the pupil.

But to most people, gazing unaided into the eye of the assaulted woman, the initials will look like a darker brown fleck in a honey-brown iris, a tiny ripple, constituting not a flaw, but rather an attempt to capture, naturalistically as possible, the inconsistency of the living organ that, as everyone knows, always has its flaws, its mars, its blots, its idiosyncrasies.

Add them up correctly and they equal beauty.

As in this particular case: my father's joke, his inclusion of my mother's initials, CGD'O, makes the eye beautiful, although nobody who looks at it will understand why; it is a beautiful enigma.

Whether the glass eye is more beautiful than the original is debatable. Certainly my father hopes, thinks, intends that it should be.

I don't like my father sometimes. This is one of those times.

. . .

Not that I like my mother much either, at this moment:

It is the next morning, or maybe the next—they're all the same, now that my father has ceased to come home, now that Thomas Argument has ceased to visit. This is a new morning ritual, only somewhat different from the old. My mother clings to the bed-post, Mary tugs at the corset laces—

Pull, you little fool!

But I am pulling, madam—

Then pull harder!

But I can't pull no harder—if madam will pardon me sayin'—

Tighter, Mary! Tighter! It must be tight as you can make it! Or I'll find a stronger girl!

Yes, madam! I'll do my best, madam!

Mary needs her job, so what choice does she have? She laces the corset as tightly as she can, so tightly that my mother cannot breathe, so tightly that she will have welts from the whalebone stays, a bruise on her stomach from the busk. Her white and pink and gold body won't be beautiful now—but then, nobody's looking, except Mary; even the mirror's gone back into the closet. And while Mary might run from my mother's room crossing herself—grumbling *Evil things in this house, evil things*—she needs her job, so she won't tell anyone, not even her sister.

Not this. Because it is too real.

Tighter, Mary!

But I don't want to hurt madam—

That's all right, Mary. You let me worry about that.
Yes, madam.

It is the first blow in the battle between my mother and me.
Tighter, Mary! Tighter!

She is trying to crush me—to squeeze me out. We are already
enemies, she and I. In fact we have been enemies for some time
already. Even before she knew of me my mother knew of me:
the secret she holds close beneath her rib, that she would not
look at until forced to do so by Mary's indicting words—*It's not
my fault, is it, that madam's got so fat?*

She had to look at me then. That's when I became real—
summoned into existence by a girl-of-all-work, confirmed in
existence by Dr. George Hawson Holtby, Surgeon, of Skinner
Street. From whose office Thomas Argument saw Clotilde
departing, in tears.

At least he acknowledged her. Nodded. Smiled pleasantly. But
the minute he saw her, he knew what it meant. A shrewd man,
Thomas Argument. A man of the world.

He won't be back. There will be no further gifts from him.
No music boxes or toys, no mirrors, no dresses, no corsets, no
stockings.

He won't respond, even, when my mother writes him a letter,
and sends Mary off, at great risk, to deliver it in Church Street.

He will simply nod again, and smile, and say, *Thank Mrs. Dell'oro for her courtesy*, sending Mary away empty-handed.

I don't know what my mother put in that letter. Mary didn't even dare to read it. Some things a servant doesn't want to know.

She can't help knowing, of course, because she sees it, Thomas Argument's cold, cruel, thin-lipped smile when he says, *Thank Mrs. Dell'oro for her courtesy*. As if he has just received, by special messenger, an order for an expensive custom delivery of glass.

My father will have won, very abruptly, the battle of Vesuvius, without even knowing how. Won't even know that he's won it, actually. He'll go on competing with himself for a long time. He's not a man of the world, he's the antithesis of that. He won't even notice, or if he notices won't understand, the other battle taking place right under his nose—the one between my mother and me.

She's a very determined opponent. I am, after all, a huge obstacle to her dream. Nobody goes to Isla Desterrada with a big belly. Even my mother knows that. And although Dr. Holtby has told her it is already too late for him to intervene—even if he would—and he wouldn't—my mother, fierce in time of war, is certain she can still get rid of me herself.

The too-tight corset is only the beginning. If she cannot squeeze me out, she will find another way. She is willing to damage herself in the process: thus the ugly red welts from the whalebone, the purpling bruise on her stomach from the rigid wooden busk. These marks bother my mother very little—the pain not at all, the ugliness, the marring of her beauty, hardly. Where has her beauty gotten her, after all? And then, nobody is looking. Nobody will see. Only Mary sees, and Mary is nobody. What's more, Mary does not want to see, wills herself, practically, to see nothing. She is nobody seeing nothing. Morning after morning she will tighten my mother's corset in silence, pulling as hard and as tight as she can for one reason only, to preserve her job. She doesn't comment on the bruises, but looks away, biting her lip. What would Mary say, if she could? Does she disapprove, as she pulls tight the laces of my mother's corset, choking me, squeezing me—choking and squeezing my mother? Does she sympathize? And if so, with whom? With me? Or with my mother?

She has seen Thomas Argument's cruel smile. She knows that my father is never home. Mary is a woman, too, with a woman's ambivalence, a woman's understanding. She pulls the laces tight, grunting and straining as my mother clings to the bedpost.

My mother does other things, too, of course—things that are just between the two of us, between her and me.

There are, for example, the long and strenuous walks that we take together, she and I, throughout Whitby, into the market, up and down the Harbour Road, down the East Cliff, past the dockyards, even out onto the Scaur; yes, up and down the Scaur we walk, over that black, humped and twisted spine of rock that she hated even as a child, back when Felix Girard brought her here, during the exhumation of the Whitby Beast. We are exhaled upon, the two of us, by the cold, wet, antediluvian breath of the sea. Licked by the tongue of it. Then we return, soaked, exhausted, shivering, and Mary puts us to bed, with scoldings and cups of tea.

Madam must not strain herself—Madam will get ill—

Mary pours the cups of tea but my mother will not drink them; will not stay under the clean sheets and white, nubbled bedspread, kicks these off, will not, for that matter, even stay in the bed, but must get up immediately.

I'm fine, Mary—really fine—

Mary says nothing to this, there is a collusion between them, the wordless collusion of mistress and servant, the terms of which are that Mary will object, but only to a certain degree; will take care of my mother, but only to a certain degree; after which the objections cease, Mary bites her lip, and my mother is let to do whatever she pleases.

It is, after all, none of Mary's business.

The matter is strictly between my mother and myself.

In our mutual struggle I am, thus far, mostly silent, but rooted. I have gotten hold of my mother, have anchored myself, have sunk my fibrous tethers deep into the deepest of her warm, soft, secret places. There I cling tenaciously, making her blood my blood, her oxygen my oxygen, her food my food, replicating, artfully, ceaselessly, the intertwining filaments, the spiraling that reads: CGD'O.LD'O.CGD'O.LD'O. I never rest from this, my life's work; I will continue infinitely: CGD'O.LD'O . . .

She cannot shake me loose. She cannot squeeze me out.

She cannot dislodge me by jumping off the chair in the parlor, no matter how many times she tries.

Nor by belly flops onto the mattress, even if she can feel the hard edge of her traveling trunk beneath each time she lands.

I am as determined as she is—maybe more so—even though I am nothing yet, just a bud, a floating branch, a wand, a thing without mind, without thought, without memory, without even, in the common parlance, a top or a bottom, limbs, digits, a head. I am nothing but pulse and root and will.

I got the will from her.

She has, in that regard, nobody but herself to blame.

Together we go down the cliff, she and I, down into the many-branching warren of streets piled with the whitewashed cottages of fishermen, and from a woman who lives there, my mother, in her most serious attempt on my life, purchases a small pouch of dried herbs—hellebore and juniper leaf—from which she will later make a tea that will make her very sick indeed, sick for a whole day and a night and another day, with only Mary to nurse her; my father, the entire time, is at William Cloverdale's shop guiltily perfecting his creatures by night, crafting fanatic numbers of glass eyes by day to make up for what he stole the night before, imagining—when he dares imagine anything—that she is in the arms of her lover. He doesn't imagine her vomiting into the slop pot, with frantic Mary holding her head, until there is nothing left to vomit; and then vomiting some more—deep dry heaves from the very bottom of her physical and spiritual self, yielding nothing but bile; though this is, in fact, what she is doing.

For a day and a night and a day.

And when she is done I am still there, my roots, if anything, dug deeper; still hard at my work, at my mindless replication: CGD'O.LD'O.CGD'O.LD'O.

There is starting to be something more to me now. From my single bud other buds have grown, though all of me, yet, is little more than potential. Pulse and root, will and potential. CGD'O.LD'O.

I have said I do not like my mother much, and that is true. But I don't blame her. I would have wanted to kill me, too, if I were she. For it is true that I have ruined, am ruining, will ruin her dream of going to find her Papa, the only person in the world she truly loves, the only one she can ever love, thanks to some strange, misshapen budding in herself, some small filament gone awry at the core in the making of Clotilde that no one now can ever change, not even me. What consternation she feels, sitting up in her bed after the tumult of the hellebore and juniper leaf, so weak that she must actually accept Mary's unwanted ministrations, the watery soup, the weak tea, the spoonfuls of mildly colored and tasteless porridge! Propped up on pillows, gazing impotently out to sea.

It's possible, of course, that she doesn't know what I am made of. This, though, I can't say for sure. I don't know, can never know, just what passed between my mother and that long-limbed, hyalith-eyed man, Thomas Argument. I can see, though, how it would bother her—not knowing, exactly, what it is that grows inside her, sapping her energy, generating, with its waterlogged backflips and somersaults, waves of gut-wrenching nausea and grief. CGD'O.TA—a monster in potential and in utero, a gangling, spidery creature with a calculating smile, wrapping itself around her innards, robbing her of her opportunity, making a mockery of her life . . .

I'd worry about that, too, if I were in her position. Giving birth to a monster. She dreams about that sometimes, in the long nights when my father isn't home.

A cruel-eyed monster. A monster with flippers. A monster without a head—just a bud with a gut, devouring her future.

It's voracious, in her dreams. It never stops eating.

She hasn't the comfort of knowing that it isn't a monster at all, cuddled there beneath the curve of her ribs; it's just me, twirling senselessly on my stem, inscribing, upon the placenta, in the amniotic fluid, on my own beautiful and rapidly multiplying fronds, a poem, composed of the only letters I know: CGD'O.LD'O.CGD'O.LD'O . . .

My mother is a stubborn woman. Even after the advent of the hellebore and juniper leaf tea, she refuses to call a truce. Instead, as soon as she is well enough to leave the house again, she purchases, from the chemist Jim Watt, a small, red tin containing "Widow Welch's Female Pills: A certain remedy for removing the obstructions to which Young Women are so frequently subject."

And when those don't work she also tries, in quick succession,

Hooper's Female Pills, then Trowbridge's Golden Pills of Life and Beauty, both without result.

None of these attractively packaged products lives up to its advertised claim to *resolve issues of female irregularity and obstruction.*

My mother's issues remain unresolved. She is still obstructed.

It is around this time, perhaps, that she begins to realize she is stuck with me—really stuck with me—or rather, that I am really stuck to her, that I have attached myself, that her heart is my heart, her lungs my lungs, her stomach my stomach, her liver my liver. We are, for all intents and purposes, one creature. She cannot shake or squeeze or press me out; she cannot poison me. The only way to get rid of me will be to get rid of herself. And my mother is much too conceited for that. A world without Clotilde is an inconceivable world.

She'll never be really, truly alone again. This will be her new torment and despair, also her new conceit and her new joy.

She is pursued. She must run. But not yet.

Her surrender, when at last it comes, is quick and complete.

Two more months have passed.

Tighter, Mary! Pull the laces tighter!

La! I canna do it, madam—it's impossible! You've grown too fat!

There is inexpressible weariness in my mother's reply.

Very well, Mary. Very well.

Clotilde relaxes her grip on the bedpost. Mary relaxes hers on the corset laces.

The servant is confused. She has never seen my mother give up—on this, or, for that matter, on anything. Except on Thomas Argument.

She had no choice but to give up on him. That was entirely beyond her control.

Does madam want to try again?

No, Mary. You can go.

Clotilde sinks down onto the bed. Beneath her thigh she can feel, through the thinness of the mattress, the sharp edge of her traveling trunk, half packed with dresses and corsets and camisoles and stockings and new cambric hankies.

This is it: it's the end. My mother has to accept, at last, the undeniable thickening of her waist, the engorgement of her breasts, their soreness, the darkening of the aureoles, the increased prominence of the nipples. The gorge that rises in her throat every morning, whether she's eaten breakfast or not. She knows what it all means:

I exist. I am coming. Whether or not I am a monster, I am coming. I am budding crazily now. I have a head. Limbs. Two cells rubbed together to form four, then sixteen, then two hundred and fifty six, and suddenly I have a brain, sparking, percolating with electricity, creating *thoughts*. All at once I have ideas of my own. Some of which are very definite ideas, about being born. I do not know there is a world, but I intend to enter it. I have begun to write something new, the limited letters of my

little alphabet, CGD'O.LD'O.CGD'O.LD'O, twining together
to form something new, the essence of me, the core of what will
be my self. CD'O.CD'O.CD'O . . .

   She can't stop me now.

Even as she accepts her fate, my mother won't give up, not entirely.
She doesn't know where she's going, or when, but she knows
she'll go somewhere, sometime, and she's got to be prepared. The
coins keep disappearing from my father's pay packet.

   As for him, he notices the coins going, but he doesn't notice
that my mother has stopped wearing her corset. He hasn't
noticed the bruises either, or all that jumping off chairs. He's
been home so little, he's unaware that Thomas Argument no
longer visits. It's true he hasn't seen any new presents from
Argument around the house. But then, that's been the case,
regardless, for quite a while. All the presents have been disappearing, along with those mysterious missing coins, into the
traveling trunk my father is too much a gentleman to open.

   What does he think is going to jump out at him if he does? A
Persian *div*, perhaps? A Persian *div* with a face like an Argument?

In fact he has no fixed ideas on that question. He has simply
averted his eyes. As long as he doesn't look, the trunk is empty.
It's a metaphysical proposition.

   He doesn't know that what is in that trunk is:
   Me.
   Because I'm bearing down on his life, too. Not just hers.

Bearing down like a steam engine. And I'm going to arrive, whether he opens his eyes or not.

At the moment, all my father really thinks about is glass. His thoughts are crystalline structures, chemical compositions, elastic solids, melting points. He thinks that he is thinking about my mother, too—and he does think about her, in a way, in a very specific way. He thinks not about my flesh-and-blood mother (who is throwing up, and throwing herself off chairs, and bouncing off beds, and tumbling desperately down staircases, and drinking toxic herb teas, all outside his notice), but rather about a Clotilde-in-his-head, she who exists in a vitreous rather than a fleshly state; malleable, it is true, if sufficiently heated, but mostly static, her molecules silent, slowed, suspended— glittering, like stars. Like a star she is distant, shiny, beautiful. Her movement is infinite yet indiscernible. As the flesh-and-blood Clotilde prepares to leave him for Thomas Argument, this other is drawing closer, one gleaming molecule at a time.

He does not see her yet. She is veiled still, just out of sight, a spark, balanced at the knife-edge of his perception.

Thomas Argument woos my real mother (so my father thinks), creating, with his magic lantern, spectacles writ large: Vesuvius. Pompeii. The Great Fire. While Leopold my father remakes her, suspends her in glass. His is a spectacle of the infinitely small, stopped in time: her initials entwined forever in the bud of a glass sea anemone. The rosy, pink tips of the tentacles, delicate as fingers. The engorged fronds of a nudibranch. Harry Owen's Darling Solenette, lavender freckled, tapering, thin as a coin at its thickest extremity, its underside a creamy, opalescent rainbow. Glass made flesh.

This is what my father is thinking about.

My mother, my real mother, hardly even impinges, though he thinks he is doing it all for her sake.

Honestly, he has no idea what he is doing.

Harry Owen's Darling Solenette, instead of my darling Clotilde.

During the months she has been simultaneously feeding me and fighting me with the very marrow of her bones, he has been gestating something of his own, too, wasting William Cloverdale's glass, but succeeding, at last, with these three models, the anemone, the nudibranch, and the Darling Solenette. There are flaws, certainly. Despite his efforts they still do not, for example, *look wet*.

He has made other things, too, instinctively, without knowing why, small, smooth objects of ambiguous design, which do not please him but which he cannot bear to throw away.

He averts his eyes from these. They are the secret he keeps from himself.

He has labored over his creation. The miscarriages now lie in the bottom drawer, left, in the cabinet behind the master glassmaker's workbench. My father does not melt down this carnage—cannot sever the umbilicus—he remains attached to his creatures, no matter how deformed, long enough attached, at least, to place them in this hiding place, his equivalent (although he does not think of it that way), of my mother's trunk. This Pandora's box, like the other, he also, very successfully, avoids. It is the lack, the gap, the missing piece, the lacunae in my father's attention. Although intending to study his mistakes, he never thinks about what is in this cabinet once he has placed it there, as if to look would actually cause him pain.

The wound exposed.

He has always been this way. An obsessive and a perfectionist, he dislikes looking at his own failures and secrets, even though he cannot let them go.

As if letting go would be admitting to something. Freeing it into the world.

But the successes—the successes are ready to be sent to Harry Owen, in London.

Really, Leo doesn't want to let his successes go either . . . he'd like to keep them all close, so that he can look at them again, rest his eye upon the good parts, pick with his thumbnail at the bad, contemplate further improvements, think about how he can make the next set of models better. He has already, it is true, kept his few, whole creatures longer than he should have— given that Harry Owen waits for them—given that Harry Owen has paid for them. My father has kept them in the drawer alongside their unsuccessful and ambiguous counterparts, perhaps for purposes of comparison, so that they rest together, side by side: a perfect solenette and a solenette without a head, another that curls peculiarly in upon itself as if somebody has tried to fry it in a pan, another with malformed fins, and so forth, an evolution, in glass, of Harry Owen's Darling Solenette.

My father only looks at his successes. That is what he is doing, at dawn, after another long night at Cloverdale's. It is a last look: he has decided that today he will send what he has made. And then he will wait—for Harry Owen's verdict. He will make no more until he has heard whether or not these will suit, whether they are sufficiently accurate for Harry Owen's purpose.

Very methodically, he wraps his creatures, watches them disappear beneath layers of tape and wadding, then into the box addressed to Owen at the British Museum.

He is exhausted. He has been up all night making glass eyes, trying to atone for a sin of theft that William Cloverdale doesn't even know he has committed. There lie, in his drawer, the failures on which he has wasted Cloverdale's glass. From these he must avert his eyes.

He will spend more time with my mother, now that he is done—while he waits for the verdict from London. He has, though, it seems, no feeling about this, no wondering, neither hope nor fear nor anger. It is as if the lack of sleep has left him hollow, lightened, emptied of content. He feels more about sending his models to Harry Owen than he does about my mother.

As he tucks the package under his arm and departs Cloverdale's shop, passing the still-dark premises of Argument's Glasswares with its posters touting Vesuvius plastered over the windows, he experiences: a feeling of accomplishment, as if he has completed something, at last, of which he may be proud.

. . .

As he approaches the post office at Old Market Place, having arrived much too early and finding it not yet open: impatience, as if this delay will last forever; anger, as if the postmaster has thwarted him on purpose.

Wandering down Harbour Road to kill the time, standing and looking out over the Scaur and the harbor, at the fishing boats scudding out between the protective arms of the breakwater into the open sea: a sense of how little he has done, how inadequate his efforts, how intimidating the immensity of this ocean, of the infinity of worlds beneath its surface, unknowable, ungraspable, and mysterious. How puny his skills in attempting to represent even a tiny fraction of this blue vastness.

When at last the post office has opened and he has handed his parcel across the counter and paid its fare to London: loss, a sense that something has been taken from him that he cannot replace. He fails, in the moment that the parcel disappears into the bin behind the counter, to connect this feeling with the loss of his sister, even though he looks for her every day, unconsciously now, though previously on purpose, fruitlessly, at the turning of every corner, in every shop, along the length and breadth of every street.

Nor does he think about my mother, she who recedes from him, molecule by gleaming molecule. He averts his eyes and thoughts from both my real mother, and from the other, she who has taken form, glitteringly, in his mind.

All the way back to Cloverdale's he is dogged by a sense of loss, a sense that haunts him all the more because he cannot quite place its point of origin, a place that seems to shift between several dimly perceived objects, none of which he really wants to think about.

At the twistings and turnings of the streets he sees the sea, blue emerging between and beyond the whitewashed walls, the black iron gates, the red-tiled roofs.

It is early still. The shopkeepers have just begun to open their shutters. Mostly he has the sidewalk to himself, the clamor of his heels on the cobblestones another kind of loss. Occasionally he passes an industrious enshawled housewife, or a servant all in black, clutching a basket, a loaf of bread, a chicken.

At Cloverdale's the shutters are up, morning light refracting uneasily through the bubbles, warps, and imperfections of a hundred glassy surfaces. The large man himself is in the back, a shape vague but vast, hunched over the master glassmaker's bench, humming. With a tweezer he retrieves glass eyes from the crucible, lays them carefully on the surface of the bench. My father paddles toward him through a multicolored shifting of light and shadow.

Mister Dell'oro. Cloverdale speaks softly, pleasantly. *Mister Dell'oro, there you are.*

Yes, says my father, *I'm here.*
Up all night again, Mister Dell'oro?
Yes. All night.
You work very hard, Mister Dell'oro.
Yes.

Then my father sees. He pauses. Cloverdale sees that he has seen.

What is this, Mister Dell'oro? What is this?

The bottom drawer on the left-hand side of the cabinet behind the workbench is open, and spread out on the bench itself, all of my father's abortions in glass. Cloverdale has found them, has laid them out carefully, tenderly even: a workbench of gently nurtured monstrosities. Of corpses.

Did you make these, Mister Dell'oro?

Cloverdale holds up, at the tip of a tweezer, something small, fleshlike, unnameable.

My father says nothing, nods; somehow the vibration of the nod is carried on the thickness of the air to William Cloverdale, who is not looking up, who looks down, rather, heavy lidded, terse lipped, at the mess upon the bench.

Using my stuff?
Yes.
And my tools?
Yes.

What are they, Mister Dell'oro?

My father cannot answer this question, not entirely. Silence the only solution.

So Cloverdale says, still pleasant: *It is disgraceful, Mister Dell'oro. I ought to have known. Crazy furriner.*

He looks at my father now. Or rather, he looks up, smiling, but his gaze is focused somewhere above and behind my father's head.

My father's response is inadequate.

I-I-I—

He cannot, of course, justify what he has done.

When Cloverdale finally speaks, he speaks calmly.

That's all right, Mister Dell'Oro. You can go now. I won't be needing you again.

The big man's disappointed gaze shifts back down into the crucible. He begins fishing around in it again, with the tweezer. There are no glass eyes left; he has already removed them all; but he fishes.

My father is dismissed. It takes him a minute to know it.

It is only when Cloverdale persists in refusing to look at him that he knows.

Dear Harry, said the letter my father placed in his package, *here are a few first efforts, inadequate I am sure, but I think promising . . .*

Returning home unexpectedly he finds the house in disarray, my mother in tears: she has found Felix Girard's last remaining hummingbird, missing for days, between the cushions on the sofa, holds it, now, cupped, like a sun, in the palm of her hand.

III.

———⋯———

THE GLASS OCEAN

I write these things in retrospect, from the vantage of a distant shore.

I write as if I know that they are true.

For example: In Whitby it is summer. At the twistings and turnings of the streets the sea may be seen: blue emerging behind and between whitewashed walls, black iron gates, roofs of tin or of red tile on which nets are spread. Rough fibers swollen with brine, set out to dry in the sun, which is high at this time of year; high, but sparse, brittle. There is a brittleness about everything, even the roses, of red, yellow, lavender, and white, which climb the walls of stucco and granite, pulling themselves, hand over hand, like jetties, up the trellises, the cornices, and the gutters; addressing, with their leaves and their thorns, the warped windows of the Birdcage. Gently they tap, lovingly, with their thorns, on the thick, bubbled glass, high above the River Esk.

．　．　．

I do not exist yet in this world, the old world, even though, in the new, I am addressed with various forms of desire. *Over here, Red. Walk my way, girlie! Oh, you're a biggun, ain't you? Come over here, Big Red!*

I am desired, therefore I exist. But also I do not.

In the old world, everything is about to begin.

My father, Leo Dell'oro, unyoked once again, spends his days watching his wife, Clotilde, expand. Despite the season, he does not confuse her burgeoning belly with the sun. He has not the imagination for that.

My mother lies naked in the heat. Her body, in past hidden scrupulously even from herself, has become a thing of opulent display: breasts, belly, thighs, glistening—tempting, untouchable fruit, openly on offer in the middle of the afternoon. She lies on the sofa, fans herself, turns immodestly from side to side, each revolution an eclipse as she tries, unself-consciously and without success, to balance her discomfort on the worn cushions.

She need not be modest. Modesty is no longer required. There is nobody to see her. Even the girl-of-all-work, she who was nobody and who saw nothing, is gone now.

Everyone is gone.

For the first time, Leo and Clotilde are truly alone. Or rather, *we* are alone, the three of us. Because of course I am

there, too; though I do not yet exist, I am a determining presence. I turn with my mother, revolve with her. We wax and
wane together, she and I, on the worn-out cushions of the sofa.
We seek a point of compromise. Seek and do not find.

Around us all is disorder, disarray bordering on squalor. With
Mary gone there is nobody but my mother to do the cleaning
up, and Clotilde does not clean. And so, everywhere: piles of
books; old newspapers; my father's sketches, pencils, paints;
boxes, half unpacked, with half-eaten plates of herring balanced
on their lids; discarded stockings; half darned pillowcases with
the needle and thread still in them; a hairbrush knotted with
tangles of blond hair; a comb likewise, knotted with dark;
stained shirt collars, stained shirt cuffs; scissors; opened envelopes; sealed envelopes; cold toast; and bills. Bills from the grocer, the butcher, the fishmonger, the coal merchant, the surgeon,
the chemist, the tailor . . .

Leo and Clotilde survive on credit. On good will. On air.
Mostly.

Downstairs, in the kitchen, roaches dine languidly on weeks-
old bacon grease and drippings.

It's not my problem, of course. We are together, we three, but
their struggles are not my struggles. I am safe and well fed,
turning silently on my tether, leeching off my mother, tethering
her to me, opposing from within: rotating left when she turns
right, then right when she turns left, migrating down when she
stands up, and up when she lies down . . .

In this I mean no harm. It's just my nature, something I can't help. Despite this, how she complains about me:

Oh, Leo, it's so awful . . . this thing . . . this awful thing . . . it's so heavy . . . I can't put it anywhere . . . I turn here and it kicks there . . . turn there and it kicks here . . . I hate it, the little monster, and it hates me . . . look at the size of my ankles! Bring me a pillow, will you? A lemonade? My Papa's book? . . . Oh, it's so dreadfully hot in here, Leo . . .

In the green light cast by the vines of the climbing roses, my father regards his wife, the beautiful smooth globe of the belly, the mystery of what lies within. What am I? He doesn't know. I am an unknown substance. She doesn't know me either, though she has her suspicions.

Such an awful thing . . . I wish I could get rid of it.

She still makes these bitter remarks, but without the old conviction—her physical assaults upon me are a thing of the past. Though she tosses and turns, rages, complains, calls me *this thing . . . this awful thing . . . this terrible thing . . . the little monster . . . the beast within . . .* she has fully acquiesced, in her way, to my presence: all the self-inflicted bruises have healed, her body ripens unimpeded, expands, blushes, softens, even seems to emanate a radiant light—

Thanks to me she has become even more lovely than she was before. Not that she is grateful. There's no gratitude in her. She will go on, calling me names, even after I am born. It's true: on the day after my birth day, she'll hold me to her warm, soft, milk-scented breast, dangle her lovely blond curls in my face, stare speculatively, and say: *What an awful, ugly thing . . . it don't favor me a bit, does it, Leo? It's biting me something awful, the beast.*

· · ·

But this is still in the future, as well as in the past. For the present moment we are still one creature, she and I. I still dance at the end of her umbilicus, though not for long now.

Leo, my back hurts! Leo, will you rub my back? Oh, and my feet, too . . . will you rub my feet?

In the green twilight he adjusts her pillow, rubs her back, rubs her feet, then brings her the book written by her Papa, which she does not read but holds idly, the pages wilting in the heat.

That is what we're all doing: wilting in the heat. Wilting and waiting. We seem to occupy a timeless space, he and she and I. Expectation hangs heavy above the River Esk. It hangs in all the five corners of the three pentagonal rooms of the Birdcage, fifteen corners in all.

Here are neglected Turkish carpets eaten with mold. Butterflies crumbling on their pins. Unlabeled pupae that will never hatch. My mother averts her eyes from those.

Only the river moves. It moves faster than ever—roaring and rushing, boiling over with the rotting offal of the entire city. It stinks to high heaven—stinks so badly even I can smell it, I who only provisionally can be said to have a nose.

The river is what reminds us that time is truly passing.

Leo—are you going out? Where are you going, Leo?

Pregnancy has heightened all my mother's senses. She can hear my father upstairs in the bedroom, tying his shoes. She can practically hear him breathing, from any room in the house. She can sense, if it so happens, the acceleration of his heartbeat.

He does not answer her, but then appears suddenly in the turning of the stairs, unbuttoned, black hair raised up at the crown of his head in a careless, unintentional crest. Poverty has ungroomed him.

Just out to the shed.

Can't you stay and read to me? Please, Leo?

If you like.

He is mild, does not resist, sits with her on the sofa, her feet (the toes like little pink shells) resting in his lap. He will read aloud to her from her Papa's book even though she does not really want to hear it, because he knows (and I know, too) that she is afraid.

My mother doesn't like to be left alone with me. Not since the day, a week ago Monday, when the midwife came and pressed on me, hard, with her bony, long-fingered hand.

Any day now. She's a'most ready. A big, strong barne. Healthy.

She has prognosticated me. She a sinewy, grizzle-headed crone from among the cottages at the bottom of the cliff—not the same one who sold my mother the hellebore and juniper leaf, but one of that kind. Bony, adept hands. It is she who will yank me out when the time comes, when my mother gets tired of pushing. This is who will attend my birth instead of the surgeon. And there will be no chloroform. Leo and Clotilde cannot afford that.

Leo will avoid most of the screaming by retreating into his shed.

But this is not yet. Not yet. For now he holds my mother's

feet on his lap, the ankles swollen but the toes still small and pink as ever, the soles delicately lined, heels calloused and dirty because she has, of course, given up on shoes as well as on clothes and because there is nobody to wash the floors anymore. A thin, grim layer of grease coats everything now.

Maybe it won't come at all. Maybe it will stay in there forever.

This is my mother dreaming. It is her waking dream of time-lessness, here in the crooked house above the river, in the summer heat, with the windows lit green by the vines of climbing roses. And it nearly seems possible—nearly. That I will never be born. That she will hold me inside forever, will stop time, through sheer strength of will, because she is afraid to let me out.

She is afraid, of course, that I, whom she wanted so badly to kill, will rip her to pieces in the process of being born.

My father says, gently, *It will come.*

He still loves her, you see. In spite of all.

There is a silence between them then. His words are devastating, dream shattering, though this is not intended.

Beneath them the river rushes, carrying clots of blubber and bone inevitably out to sea.

Inevitability. That's the thing. My father has recognized mine, and doesn't flinch from it, while my mother strives to forget. To forget, and to remain suspended in timelessness.

In this, though, her body betrays her. She is betrayed by her body, again. She ripens unwillingly. In the humidity her hair grows thicker and more curly, becomes a mane. Unbrushed, unwashed, it has a strong, musky, not unpleasant smell, such as might emanate from a healthy, fecund animal. This is what she is. What she does not want to be.

Savage!

From the strength of her savagery alone she hopes she may prevent me.

This is her waking dream. Her dreams in sleep are of a different order. Then she dreams of birthing monsters. Flippered things. Faceless. Footless. On awakening she can only remember vague, troubling shadows.

Leo, you won't go out today? You'll stay with me today?

This is how afraid she is. Her knuckles white against the cushions as she lifts herself slightly toward him. Her belly like the sun.

Even he cannot acquiesce all the time. The sense of inevitability from which she averts her eyes has gotten under his skin, eats at him from the inside out. He knows he must provide. Because I am coming. I am inevitable.

I have no one to blame but myself, he thinks. *I shouldn't have stolen from William Cloverdale. It's my own fault. I was careless.*

But he thinks it mainly out of politeness. Really, he blames me.

Beast. Little monster.

Now he works for Harry Owen only, for a pittance, out in the shed. This innovation, the arrival of the bench, and the lamp, and the oven, and the tools—the hooks and tweezers and calipers and brushes of my father's trade—as well as the coal to fuel the furnace, is paid for by Harry Owen. In return, my father makes glass: scientific models, for which he is paid by the piece, if they pass muster.

Sometimes they do. Sometimes they don't.

My mother is unhappy about this.

It all belongs to him—the bench is his, the tools are his, the glass is his—what's in it for us?

He pays me. Defensively. Defiantly even. Black topknot of hair upright.

He pays you pitifully!

Enough to keep you in lace.

She is silent at this. There is nothing she can say. Harry Owen's money has bought no lace, and my father knows it. So where did the money come from? This he doesn't know. Thomas Argument being out of the picture, as far as he can tell. But then, the lace has gone, too: a silent disappearance. My mother has different desires now, desires that must be provided for. Clotilde eats so much now! She feeds me with entire fowls, with roasts, with whole loaves of bread, platters of herring, anything she can get her hands on. She never seems to stop eating.

And so he must make. That is his justification.

Really, though, he loves the glass. The red-hot responsiveness of it. Its lightness contrasted with the cool, heavy iron of the tools. His desire for glass is a tactile desire, a longing lodged in the tendons of his fingers, his arms, it is a physical part of him now. And then there are his creatures. That desire is emotional. The work like a living thing.

. . .

Despite his need for money, he will avoid, as much as possible, that block of Church Street where are located the opposed and facing competitors, Argument and Cloverdale. Were he to go, he'd see that *Leopoldo Dell'oro, Master Glassmaker* is still up on Cloverdale's sign, that Argument's Vesuvius is as eruptive as ever, the lines of those hoping to see it as long, or longer.

It mattered, once, that he was there. But it doesn't matter that he's gone. The relentless mill of their competition grinds on without him, he who was once the grist forgotten now.

That world is his no longer.

I have to go out, Clotilde. I have to work.

When she refuses to remove her feet from his lap he lifts them himself, gently though (he is always so gentle), cupping the rough heels in his palms.

Oh, Leo, must you—

Yes. I really must. I'll just be outside, in the shed.

He won't go to Henrietta Street, seeking help, any more than he'll go to Church Street. No matter what their level of desperation, he will never seek his father's help. That's what he thinks, as he stands at the corner, looking left, then right, dark eyed, the upright crest of hair giving him an appearance of false alertness. He is like a crow about to pounce on a crumb, except there is no crumb, either to the left or to the right. And below him: that is the river, rushing, boulders looming smooth and dark beneath the surface.

He will not work today. He has lied to my mother. Even he cannot acquiesce all the time.

Instead he is headed down the hill, toward the Scaur.

It is a place Leo seldom visits now. He doesn't know that my mother and I visited it often, a certain number of months ago, in our frantic efforts to be rid of each other.

It's difficult to say what he's looking for there. A trace of his childhood self, perhaps, the mark of his own ancient bootheels on the uptilted, striated rock. But it's impossible to leave a mark on the Scaur. It takes a million years to make a mark there. My father, traversing it again, will not find himself there, if it is his self that he is seeking.

Whatever he is looking for, he descends determinedly toward it through the warren of streets, disappearing between the whitewashed walls, then reappearing where the bends of the road open out toward the sea. He marches, his back stiffly upright in the too-old, too-shiny, too-warm suit, too-tight collar chafing just beneath his ears; weaves in and among and past the shop fronts and fishmongers' carts, through shouts of bakers' boys and potboys, past sweet shop and Punch and Judy, is among but not of it, removed by his demeanor (absorbed, distant, off-putting) and his clothes (strangely formal, yet in disrepair). He has taken on the general aura, which has now become typical of him, of wanting to be left alone.

I don't know if it's really what he wants. Or merely what he conveys.

But he *is* left alone. He descends, unharassed, to Harbour Road, then turns sharply right, onto the Scaur. Though it is a hot clear day, the heavy, green sea exhales coldly upon him, breath reeking rot of tide. His feet remember, instinctively, the twisted spine of rock. Despite the constrictions of suit cuffs and collar he climbs the rough stone ably, sure-footed as ever, eyes cast automatically, habitually, downward. Instinctively searching.

The Scaur is the same but also not the same. The rock itself is unchanged, though new cliff-falls pock the cliff face, exposing striated layers of sandstone and marl, seams of jet, seams of bone. But there are bathers here now, in their frilly costumes, and among the jetties on the cliffs: fossil hunters with picks and hammers, pith helmets, bulging bags, the instruments of amateurism. This is different.

This is Felix Girard's doing. It has been like this ever since Felix Girard excised the Whitby Beast from the face of the cliff called Black Cap. Whitby has become a destination. Wealth in a new form now mounts upward, from the seafront, into the town.

My father, though, is not particularly interested in this. His gaze is downward, his focus myopic, his stride, even on that rough ground, is purposeful, if slow. He is heading toward the Black Cap. Occasionally he pauses, stoops, reaches. He is gathering ammonites, their shells, just as he remembers from his boyhood, turned to brilliant amethyst, garnet, pyrite, smoky quartz. He thrusts them absently, almost automatically, into the pockets of his not-quite-shabby suit. It is almost like he is a child again, exercising the habits of his childhood: to stoop and to search, to gather, to collect. To hoard.

In this way he progresses slowly along the Scaur, pockets bulging with rocks. He in his rusty old suit, with his abstracted air.

He's trying to distract himself. He doesn't want to think about me. That's difficult, of course. I am omnipresent, although I do not yet exist. I am paradoxical in this.

When he reaches the foot of the Black Cap he stops. And for the first time in many years, dares to look up.

The old wound is still there—the wound he could not bear to look at, when he was a boy—the gap where the cliff face came down. The wooden stage is still there, too, long abandoned now, where Felix Girard gave his first lectures on the Whitby Beast. The beast itself, of course, is gone: surgically excised, taken away to London. Leaving behind a massive scar on the face of the Black Cap. A scar within a wound. Sliced out of the slick, dark rock.

My father gazes upward, at the place where the tree roots still dangle, exposed, black, snaking arteries, the still-living trees green and precarious but still clinging to the cliff's edge.

That is the churchyard up there, St. Mary's; the coffins that were also unearthed, and hung exposed like ragged rotting teeth, are gone now—rescued—replanted somewhere safer.

This is where my parents met. Not so very many years ago. But also a lifetime ago. She up on a scaffolding with her darling Papa, assisting in the excavation of the Whitby Beast; Leo down below, in the rocks, with his pencil and sketch pad, watching. Her golden hair. And her mocking cry. *Papa! Who is that ridiculous bo-oy?*

My father bends down, hefts a rock, despite the unhelpful constrictions of his suit throws it at the cliff face, watches, with silent satisfaction, the cascade of shale produced thereby. Then disgorges, from within his right front pocket, a small ammonite, the coil perfect, of fool's gold. Turns it over in his palm. Admires this, the living tissue turned to stone. Stopped in time.

If only I could make them in glass.

Petrels fumbling moodily in the updraft.

Meanwhile I, who have been approaching for many pages, am about to arrive.

In an act of fateful serendipity, my mother is no longer lying on the sofa. She has gotten up; she has even, in my father's absence, put on a frock; has even, for the first time in a month, hefted herself awkwardly down the stairs, this a major endeavor for her as she cannot, in fact, see past the vast planet of her belly even so far as her feet—so she feels for the stairs, first with her toes, then with the ball of the foot, then the heel, her palms braced against the walls for balance; edging me sideways past all those belongings of her father's, past the rolled-up carpets and the specimen trays, the taxidermied alligators and the ocelot, those lifelike, no-longer-living things that occupy so much of the Birdcage's limited space. She edges and inches until she reaches the fragrant nether realm of the abandoned kitchen, which she prefers not to see or to think about, and then maneuvers herself, with great effort, out, into the yard. Glancing surreptitiously at the shed, into the street. Upon the edge of which she stands, like a beacon, hugely.

Passersby do not pause, but they do stare a bit.

I'd like to say that she emerged because she knew I was coming— that, prompted by a premonitory pang, she sought help for us both, in the fast-approaching hour of our mutual extremity.

But this she did not.

No. It was rather that she happened to spy, out the window, a figure, tall, dark, slightly stooped, passing along the brow of Bridge Street; and this figure she wished to pursue, in spite of, or perhaps *because of,* her bulging belly.

In the time it has taken her to edge us down the stairs, though, the object of my mother's desires has disappeared, up the brow of Bridge Street and into the town. Whether turning to right or to left: unknown.

My mother is not perturbed.

She begins—not to run, that is impossible for us now—but to trot, very swiftly, with a sort of rolling motion, a sideways motion, none too smooth, her vast prominence balanced carefully in her palms, hair loose, frock flapping. Thus we make our way together, she and I, on one of our final excursions of the sort, to the corner of Bridge Street and Grape Lane, where my mother, sensing or, perhaps, even *scenting* her man, with that uncannily acute perception her pregnancy has granted her, correctly chooses the right-hand turning.

We arrive just in time to see a tall, stooped figure hovering at the entrance of the Custom House tavern.

Tom! Tom! my mother calls. There is an urgency in her tone, so much so that Himmelfarb the old-clothes man looks up sharply from beneath his many hats, the acrobats tumbling on their carpet under the Custom House awning pause in their tumbling, Punch misaims his whack at Judy, and Thomas Argument (if indeed it is he), apparently failing to hear, recedes all the more quickly through the tavern door.

Tom! cries my mother. *Tom!*

Angrily this time. There's an edge to her now.

She would willingly follow him in—she has already begun trotting again, gaining momentum, palms beneath belly, the entire street crew of onlookers urging her forward—*That's the way! You tell him, missus!*—except that now comes the sudden, warm, wet gush between her legs. All at once, abruptly, like a folding chair collapsing, my mother sits down in the street. Under her breath she mutters, so softly that only I can hear it: *Beast!*

And then:

Quick, she says, from her apparently helpless position, *somebody fetch Mrs. Marwook!*

It is a credit to my mother that even in this, her most abject moment—big bellied, tear streaked, her frock soaked in amniotic juices, ignored by her lover, down on her nates in the middle of Grape Street—mercilessly kicked, in short, both from within and without   she is still beautiful—more than that—she is compelling. Nor has she lost her presence of mind. *Mrs. Marwook!* she cries, *on the double!* And the butcher's boy, feeling himself commanded by beauty of irresistible aspect, immediately drops his tray of steaks and dashes off to fetch the deft-fingered crone who will, very soon, usher me into the world.

I will not dwell on the details of the birth—the extended battle between me and my mother, lasting the better part of eighteen hours, fought in the big bed in the small pentagonal bedroom on the third floor of the Birdcage—nor mention how it galled her, in the thick of it, to feel beneath her thigh, through the scrawny mattress, the hard jabbing edge of the traveling trunk she never got to finish packing. I think that even then, even as I was making my struggling, strangling, stumbling way down the birth canal, my mother was mentally packing that trunk—*six dresses, two corsets, three petticoats, five pair of stockings, gloves, evening gloves, blue hat with an egret feather, black hat with a maroon lace, cambric hankies, dress boots, waterproof boots . . .* No surprise that there developed, during certain moments in the struggle, a controversy as to whether she was trying to

keep me in, or thrust me out—*Push, missus! Ye're distracted!*—
which Mrs. Marwook, prodding sharply with words and hands,
urged her to resolve as quickly as possible, and in the right
direction.

My father, coming up from the Scaur with his pockets full of
fossil ammonites, hears the screaming, and retreats to his shed.
He will spend the entire night there, nervously sketching sea
urchins in nearly impossible detail—the fragile test, the inching
tube feet, the purple anus, the mouth (*Aristotle's lantern*), the
hollow black spines, pinching pedicellaria—occasionally thrusting his head out the door, then ducking just as quickly back
when he hears her: screaming still.

I must emerge, of course, in the end, despite my mother's reluctance. When I do arrive, finally, noisily, at around half past
eight in the morning, I am grasped by the head, tumbled
brusquely upside down by the capable Mrs. Marwook, dabbed
in every pit and orifice, and swiped between all my digits with a
rough wet cloth, then swiftly wrapped in swaddling clothes.
Thus properly cleansed and restrained I am set to nurse, despite
the warning in my mother's hostile eye.

It's a large barne, Marwook says, not entirely without sympa-
thy, pulling the swaddling clothes tighter, as if by binding she
can shrink me. *A girl. Ginger hair.*

Clearly Marwook does not entirely approve of ginger hair

or large girls, together or singly, but neither does she disapprove—not entirely—or so her tone, one of mild restraint,
implies.

Put it in the cradle, says my mother, wearily. She does not
bother even to glance at whatever is upon her breast. Maybe she
is afraid to look. Then, too, she can still feel the edge of her traveling case through the mattress, pressed hard against the back
of her thigh, and she isn't too tired, yet, to resent it.

So Mrs. Marwook takes me up, and lies me down.

It is only later, when all has been silent a while, that my father
deems it safe to enter the bedroom and examine me.

It resembles Felix Girard, he says contemplatively, laying his
index finger gently upon my tightly swaddled chest. My mother,
sleeping, does not hear him. Which is unfortunate, since it
might have been a consolation to her to learn that I did not
resemble somebody else.

As for me, I am unconcerned. I know that I resemble nobody
but myself, that I am the eating, sleeping, shitting, screaming
center of the universe—*Carlotta omphalos.*

Red! Over here, Red! Walk my way!

Except that I'm not. The universe being larger, and more complicated than I can, at this moment, comprehend.

.   .   .

I express myself—a first, tyro's effort—and from my mother receive no reply.

I think it needs to be fed, my father says, removing his finger from among my swaddling in response to certain noises I have made.

It is a first time, but it will not be the last, that it is my father, not my mother, who responds to my utterance. My mother never seems to hear, or maybe she cannot understand me. It is only after my father has applied his Rosetta stone to my vocal hieroglyphs and produced an interpretation (*It is hungry—it is wet—it is tired—it is bored*) that my mother acknowledges my efforts with a grudging *Very well*, and presents her breast, which is not the less beautiful—pink as it is, warm, and engorged with milk—for being begrudged.

(In one of those odd inversions that she manages so well, my mother seems to move farther away the closer she comes, so that when I am placed at her breast I suck, along with the milk, the hollow sensation, unidentifiable as yet by me, that presages not her living presence, but her impending absence; and not knowing what it is that I have swallowed, I am lulled to sleep with uneasy dreams of things I have never yet experienced: the weirdly elongated shadow of a pheasant perched on a stile at sunset in a silent empty field; the dead carapace of a crab, tossed and tangled with seaweeds; a chair abandoned in a cobbled yard, with a single glove resting on its seat.)

I wake fretting.

Red! Over here, Red!

You see I am desired. Just not by her.

I think it needs to be changed, my father says.

He has to repeat himself several times before my mother hears, and then finally he gives up, and changes me himself. His hands, though rough, are deft and precise; he turns me over carefully, unwraps me and then wraps me up again, neatly, every detail in place, as if I am a piece of glass he is forming at his lamp, while my mother, who is sometimes nearby—in the same house certainly, sometimes even in the same room—wonders how much longer before she can get back into her strictest corset. Not too much longer now. She is a beautiful woman; she has kept her figure. The mirror is back, its cover removed. We are reflected in it together—here we are: she, smoothing her dress down tight over her narrow waist, turning from side to side, blond curl pendant over bare, white shoulder. I am behind her, a blur in the cradle. My mouth is open wide, oral apparatus on display, tongue first, tonsils behind. In reflection no one can hear me screaming. The reflected me is the one my mother much prefers.

She is usually someplace nearby. Almost always in the same house. Sometimes in the same room.

Out in the yard, sometimes.

Although I am the omphalos, the center, I am sharply aware of my mother in all her peregrinations, those orbits that take her in a series of ever-widening gyres away from my cradle—at first, harmlessly, just downstairs, into the sitting room; then, from my perspective more unnervingly, two floors down, into the kitchen; then, more ominously yet, through the door and out into the yard; then, inevitably, into the shed where my father is working; then, at last, terrifyingly, out of the yard, into the street—foreign place of neighing ponies and rattling cart wheels, of roaring river, from where, despite all, above every other squeak and whistle and rattle and thump, above every catcall and cry, above the passing songs of balladeers and barrel organs, I can hear the distinctive ring of my mother's bootheel on the cobblestones as she recedes up the street.

I don't know where she is going.

Away. Away from me.

Still fresh in the memory of an earlier time, a time when she would, by necessity, have taken me with her everywhere, I grieve at being left behind. The physical tether binding us has dissolved, only to be replaced by a tangible, finer, yet equally strong filament of connection; and I am exquisitely sensitive to every tug upon it. Yet it seems that, in spite of all, she is free of me. I am bound, but she is free. With what carelessness she shifts her orbits, moving farther and farther away from me.

I rage, loudly, at the unfairness of life.

My father, putting his mild finger inside my wrapper, says, *I think it is wet,* and proceeds to unfurl me—finds me dry, and furrows his brow. He doesn't know what's ailing me—let alone that it's the same thing that ails him.

When she is nearby we are both aware of her, we two; exquisitely aware. There is her scent: the perfume, yes, but beneath it, more importantly, the earthier odors of her body, the sweet commingling of sweat and milk, armpit, neck nape, and cunt. We are always aware.

My mother. His wife.

   She is moving away from us. Downstairs. Outside. Out into the street.

Birthing me has hardly changed her at all. She is, if anything, more beautiful than before. Unlike me, she sleeps soundly every night, the gentle, white curve of her brow unperturbed by the various songs I have composed for the purpose of gaining her attention. She is unconscious, slumbering. My father gets out of bed and slips my coral into my mouth. For a while I will suck on it, this hard thing, calcified exoskeleton surrounded by four jolly bells that jingle and jangle softly as I suck, *ring-a-ling-ling-a-ling-ling!* My mother does not wake; undisturbed, she sleeps on, sleeps profoundly. *Ring-a-ling-ling-a-ling-ling!*

   I think it is hungry, my father says at last.

   My mother awakens then and is cross. Her nipples are red and sore. *It's biting me something awful, the beast.*

   At last she feeds me, briefly, before laying me back down and returning to bed herself.

As is true of all things distant and desirable, the farther away she moves, the more we want her back. We are in the bedroom, my father and I, amid the chaos of disheveled sheets and squandered pillows, sunlight and rose vines knitting a shadow trellis up the wall—my father is at the window, looking out—a silhouette against the windowpane. *Where is she? Where can she have gone?* Another day: I am in my pram, she has tucked me in herself, her hands gentle but uninterested, her curls tickling my face, her perfume my nose; she parks me on the cobblestones in the yard, just outside the back door, and then she recedes, hands and curls and perfume disappearing into the periphery of my swaddled vision, which has no real periphery, no side to side or back, only an above, straight above. I gaze up into the sky. Her figure receding, receding, gone.

A seagull passes.

Another.

Another.

Many in succession.

Eventually Leo emerges from his shed, sees his baby left alone in the pram in the center of the yard, and wheels her back into the kitchen.

A hot day in August. Roses wilting on the vines.

Clotilde, later, is petulant, grows vague when scolded.

I've been to Mr. Kiersta's. Nothing fits me anymore.

But you left baby in the yard.

Did I? Did I do that?

Blinking rapidly, in confusion, her delicate blond lashes.

I'm sure I wouldn't, Leo. I wouldn't do that.

. . .

She did do it; but we forgive her. Like a planet, distant and revered, she has moved away from us for a while; her orbit has taken her away; this is only to be expected; now she has returned. Supplicants that we are, we dare demand no more. Indeed, we are grateful. My father subsides in his scolding; my mother takes me up into her cool, noncommittal hands, loosens my wrapper just enough to see that I am not sunburned, then puts me back down. Turns away. Turns her back.

And is forgiven.

Where will she go, my mother, in the new dress of yellow lace that Lars Kiersta is going to make her? Where is she going, her bootheels ringing on the cobblestones, as she retreats up Bridge Street, away from us, toward the town?

It's a mystery. Throughout my childhood it will remain so. What I remember is a constant game of hide-and-seek, seek and find; even now, when I think about her, she retreats before me, memory itself is rendered unstable, is itself a thing sought and not found. In memory I pursue my mother through the three small pentagonal rooms that comprise my world, searching her out among the remains of my grandfather's collection, which, increasingly, migrate out of the shed and into the house. My mother is always hiding: receding behind a stack of specimen trays, or the tawny ocelot with its fierce eyes of yellow glass, or else she is sifting with her pale, elegant fingers through a tray of ancient Persian amulets in semiprecious stone, or arranging on our dining table, as if she thinks she can reassemble them, shards of Roman terra-cotta decorated with a fish, an octopus, a lion, a goat. She is caressing the remains of her father's world, willing them into coherence with gentle feather-strokes of her cold, elegant fingers. Like me, she is trying to reassemble the past. But the pieces don't fit, won't cohere. She lives among them in my memory as if in a museum, surrounding herself, as closely as she can, with the artifacts of her father's world, as if these things, beautiful and cold as she is herself, can compensate her for her double loss—the loss of her father, and the loss of her hopes of leaving Whitby in search of him.

She finds them an insufficient compensation.

I am her most tangible artifact: as my father was the first to observe, I look like Felix Girard, the resemblance becoming more striking as I grow. But my mother does not caress me, nor does she seem to find, in me, any compensation at all.

Instead, she looks away.

I make her uncomfortable, the same way the ocean did, once.

She regards me, whenever possible, narrowly, from the corner of her eye.

It is getting so frightfully large, she says. *I can't lift it anymore, Leo, it hurts my back so!*

I will lift her, my father says, grasping me by the armpits, hoisting me up and out of a box of my grandfather's old books, which I have found, and opened, and climbed into, and

rummaged through, and bent, and torn, and otherwise rear-
ranged to suit myself.

*It is hurting my Papa's things! Why must it always hurt my
Papa's things, the beast!*

She doesn't mean to hurt them. She's just a child.

How big it is! Look at its feet! So ungainly!

Meanwhile slipping into her own very delicate shoes.

Or:

It is like a giantess, she says, as she puts on her petite grey
gloves, one slender finger at a time. *I was never like that at her
age. Will it ever stop growing, do you think?*

It's true: I am not like my mother, with her graceful, slender neck,
lithe body, golden hair. Even at this early stage I am an ungainly,
large-footed creature. I alarm myself as I outgrow, one after
another, each of my childhood frocks. One day my blouse fits; the
next day I thrust in my arm and burst a seam. I can't fit my feet
into my shoes, my neck into my lace collars, my rump into my
pantaloons. My toes poke out through shoddily mended stockings. And I have, what's more, a wild, curly mane of ginger hair
that licks behind me like fire when I run. And I do run—as often
as I can—on my long, sturdy, fast-growing legs: up and down and
around those spiral stairs, from the kitchen to the parlor to the
bedroom, from the bedroom to the parlor to the kitchen, and
again, leaving in my wake butterflies off their pins, upended
orchids, despoiled carpets, the terra-cotta heads of gods and goddesses rolling, wide eyed in surprise, all around the parlor floor.

Qu'est-ce qu'un sauvage! my mother cries. She has dropped her pearl earrings, a gift from Thomas Argument. They have fallen beneath the vanity in the bedroom; she cannot find them. She is on her hands and knees in her new yellow lace with her golden curls loose, unpinned. She is crying. And it is my fault—always my fault.

Go! Get away! Go bother your father for a change!

At least, that's how I remember it. I don't know if it's true. Memories are tricky things.

She ought not be blamed. She is so unhappy.

Down there on the floor, looking for her earrings.

Later, though, she'll go out again. That's always the way. She's gone out! She's gone! She's put on her gloves. She has taken her umbrella today, because today it is raining. She has put on her veil because today it is sunny. It is hot. It is cold. She has put on her boots, because there is snow. She is wearing her shawl. She's forgotten her muff. Where is her hat? She's gone. Again.

Where does she go, in the evenings, when she leaves us? The sound of her bootheels echoing on the cobblestones, echoing, relentlessly, til it dies away altogether, the sound along with her receding up the brow of Bridge Street.

Such an unhappy woman.

. . .

For a long time I try to find her in the boxes of her father's books, or, if not there, then somewhere else . . . among the crates of fossils from Mongolia, lately opened, in the center of the room that serves, in the Birdcage, as dining room and parlor both; or else in the closets, the drawers, the cupboards, even in the great, cold, black, cast-iron belly of the neglected claw-foot stove. From which I emerge, covered in ash.

It is fruitless, of course. All fruitless. My mother is not there. She is a planet, moving away from me. I track her orbits; I trail behind. I am the fiery red tail of her comet. I come close sometimes; but very seldom do I touch. Less and less often, as I grow.

And so I try to win her by charm.

(What would come naturally to any other child isn't natural to me; charm rests uneasily upon *my* broad, red brow. But I try.)

Four and twenty tailors went to kill a snail, the best man among them durst not touch her tail . . .

In response to which song my mother turns away with a sigh, retreats, wringing her hands, into some other part of the house.

It's no use, no use, any of it. The singing, the trying to keep my feet in, keep my pleats straight. Beside the point, all of it. It is all avoidance, changing the subject.

. . .

Here I am, Jumping Joan, when nobody's with me I'm always alone . . .

No matter. No matter. Her back is turned. Head inclined. White nape of neck exposed, hair swept up, bound tight. She isn't listening. This isn't the kind of music she likes. She likes music played on a spinet, on a *darling little piano.* Accompanied by one voice only. There's only one she can hear; could hear—ever.

Oh, Leo—can't you make it be quiet? I've got such a dreadful headache!

She seems so fragile sometimes. Brittle, even. The milky-white translucence of her skin. Every molecule gleaming. There is less of her on some days than others. Sometimes, I feel like I can see through her. Straight through.

My mother is going to leave us.

I know this without knowing. It's already inside me, her departure, lodged like a bubble behind my sternum. There is a hollow

place, a gap, a fissure. A missing piece. Tap hard with my finger
against my chest and I can hear the echo. Nothing I can do is
going to change it now. It can be neither swallowed, nor dislodged. I have always known it without knowing. Thus my cries
as she moved away from me.

Inevitably away.

There are signs.

One day, I find her at the dining table, papers spread out before
her. She leans over them, chin cupped in hand, with an appearance of intense concentration. Approaching from behind, I see,
over her shoulder: the blue of an ocean unknown to me, yellow
dots that must be islands, the curving, black lines of latitude and
longitude, a distant hemisphere divided up into wedges like a
piece of fruit; notes that I can't read, written in an unfamiliar
hand. My mother hears me; quickly, she shuffles the papers into
a stack, the map disappearing among them. She rises. The chat-
elaine jingles at her waist. Keys, thimble, scissors, tumbling.
Without looking at me, pretending not to notice, she turns to
mount the stairs.

Another day: I enter the bedroom. I don't see her at first; I think
I'm alone. Well: I have often been alone, in her company. Then,
movement—her blond head, white shoulders. She is kneeling;
the bed is between us. Her body is obscured. But I can tell what

she's doing: she's shoving something under the bed, something heavy. Before I can see what it is, she says, *Out! Out! Go find your father!*

So I do.

He's in the shed, working. That's usual. He's always in the shed. That is where I find him. Here he is, my father, in the shed, in the dark, or rather in the not-quite-dark, it isn't as absolute as that, so: in the semidark I find him, here he is, sitting at his bench. Light does come in, but randomly, through chinks in the walls (there are plenty of those), bright random motes and beams, alive with galaxies of dust; pencil-thin rays fall around my father like shooting stars, spatter his shoulders, his hair, fall uselessly to the floor around his feet; then, too, there is his own light, my father's special light, that is to say, the light of the lamp. So though it is dark, it is not absolutely so. In the semidark, then, my father, hunching over the lamp (this, too, is usual), holding a rod of glass in the flame. I who have slipped in, between the motes, stand silently, watching, as he turns the rod in the flame, turns it, turns it, nipping here or there with his special tools, which gleam wickedly even in this obscure light; then he pulls, and suddenly the rod expands, a bulb appears, elongates, flattens, grows ovoid, gravid, shrinks, twirls, expands, rises—this is my father's magic, this is what he does, the glass responds to his touches, to his teasing pokes and prods, in a sort of dance, a call and response from which shapes emerge, mysterious shapes; undefined things; insinuations; bodies of glass;

fleshly glassine enigmas. What is my father making? On this day, it is impossible to tell. With a single, swift blow of the pliers he severs the rod so that the body, whatever it is, falls into the crucible. He does it with a slight, shielding movement of his arm, protecting whatever it is he has made, hiding it. Only then does he turn to me.

From this it may be seen that he, too, has his secrets.

But his secrets are different from my mother's. They shimmer, glassily, are refractive, harder, and yet, at the same time, are vaguely apologetic, suffer from uncertainty, and perhaps, even: from shame. Unlike my mother, he does not always shut me out; rather, he shuts me out and takes me in, simultaneously, because he knows that shutting me out is wrong. Nodding at the honeycomb of cubbies where the rods of glass reside (packed tight between and among the stacked remains of my grandfather's collection—though these have been moved, more and more, into the house, at my mother's insistence), he says, gravely, *The blue one*—. Gravely says it; stretches out his hand. It is a severe hand, severely offered. Where has it come from, this severity? My father is not usually severe; only when making glass; then he is severe, as his father was severe, too, carving jet. The severity is my cue: I know if I am not quick enough he will snap his fingers once, twice; and then I might panic, hand him a rod of the wrong color, or even fumble, and drop it. This must not happen, for the glass is precious—precious as living things are precious—therefore the rod must not break. I understand this; and usually it is all right. As it is this time: all right. I hand my father the glittering blue cylinder of glass, and stand at attention in my too-small dress, my hair a complexity of knots and mats and frizzes and curls because no one can be bothered to comb it, feet aching in too-tight shoes because nobody can be bothered to buy me new, watching my father work. I take very seriously my role as assistant. But he isn't noticing me; not anymore; because it has begun again, his dance. Undistracted, he bends over the lamp, stretching out from the narrow rod of glass the beginnings of whatever he might be making, coaxing from his low flame the first blue, tonguelike extension of some mysterious object; he works with such slow, minute seriousness, eyes narrowed, shoulders hunched, what little movement there is concentrated in his hands only, hands moving gently in the darkness. There he is, in his apron and goggles, turning and turning the delicate bit of liquid glass, creating, from its hot, malleable heaviness, something that will, when it hardens, become, paradoxically, light as air, and infinitely more breakable. Stained with enamel. Chromate of potash. Sugar of lead. Gold chloride. Copper oxide. Bone ash. Arsenic. Oxide of manganese. Saltpeter. From these hard things beautiful colors are made. Hard things, ground up, melted together, then, inside the oven, in a clay crucible. Which I must not touch. Which I will not.

It is very hot, my father says. *It will burn you.*

He doesn't have to tell me. The flames themselves tell me this.

. . .

He is making me a toy in the flame of the lamp: a tiny fish, blue, flawless.

It is his apology to me; though I don't realize it, at the time.

(This is how I remember him, now that he is gone—)

Later, in my excitement, successfully distracted, I will run to show it to my mother. *Look what Papa made me! It's a fish!*

She's at her spinet. Because of me she has dropped her sheet music. Now it's all on the floor, hopelessly disarranged. She cannot put it right.

A fish? she cries. *A fish! Of course it is! What else would he make! Your Papa is a very great man, for fish!*

She shouldn't be blamed. She is so unhappy. It does not go well with her.

For my father is spending a great deal of time in his shed, more than before, working. Harry Owen has written, request-ing more glass. There has been an influx of money from an anonymous patron—*taken with your work*, the letter says, *A patron is taken with your work*—as if the work is an illness, a contagion, by which someone can be *taken*. Taken away? Taken hold of? Taken in? And suddenly there is greater demand. This, for my father, is pressure. *Hornsby is elated—can't you, for God's sake, Leo, send me more glass?*

Strange, isn't it—how the opening of a wallet in London can change my father's life? And my mother's?

Can't you, Leo, for God's sake, send more?

My father, unused to demands, is very slow about it. The letters from Harry Owen arrive at regular intervals, distinguished from the usual post—mostly tradesmen's bills (*To Mr. L. Dell'oro, A bill in the amount of 4/3 for one pair of ladies boots. To Mr. Leopoldo Dell'oro, 5/- outstanding for the purchase of bread. Mr. Leopoldo Dell'oro, 6/3 for 1.5 dozen oysters purchased Saturday last. Mr. Dell'oro, Please pay 6/0 for three weeks' delivery of coal. Dear Mr. Leopoldo Dell'oro, in regards to the amount of rent owed, currently overdue on the cottage called "The Birdcage," the amount of 12 s. 4 d. Mr. Leopoldo Dell'oro from Mr. William Cloverdale, Glassmaker, in consideration of the glass you stole from me when you were in my employ. This is my third letter*)—by the fine, thick creaminess of the paper, the official Montagu House stationery with the return address decorously embossed in the upper left corner—and are left to pile up unattended on the dining table among the other detritus of our lives, the uncleared unwashed plates, the toys, my mother's combs, my father's papers, whatever part of Felix Girard's collection my mother has lately unearthed, played with, grown bored by, set aside, and forgotten.

He does not immediately read these letters, my father, despite all. Sometimes he slits them open, peers inside, and extracts a check, leaving the letter itself for later—or for never—

Though he doesn't think of it that way. He knows he ought, he knows he must, and he believes he will. The thing is, he has set himself to the solving of a problem—several problems—out there in his shed, and he doesn't want to be distracted. Or rather: cannot allow himself to be distracted. Or rather: he's fallen into something, and he can't stop himself, even though he knows he should.

He's got something he's tinkering with, out there; he's got it wrapped in cloth, tenderly wrapped, gently wrapped, secretively wrapped; he began it in a moment of boredom, as a distraction, between commissioned objects, then set it aside; but he couldn't set it aside, not really, because it nagged at him too much; and so he unwrapped it—carefully drawing apart the grimy layers of cloth, one layer at a time, then laying out, on his bench, one by one, the pieces, each piece a secret in itself; all very surreptitious, for it is of the utmost importance that my mother not see; I, of course, have seen, but it's nothing to me, not now, I am a child, easily distracted by a new toy, a new treasure, a glass fish, or a swan, these being the currency of my father's attention, a hard, warm currency that I can carry in my pocket, pausing every now and then to touch, not realizing until later, much later, the dissatisfaction of such things, the emptiness of the currency, of the object without its maker; I am a child, I take my gift and go, leaving him, always, to his other, his *real* work . . .

He's got the kaleidoscope out there, the one Thomas Argument gave to my mother—that very small first gift—and he's taken it to pieces. He's removed the lenses, has laid out in a row its small, cunning mirrors, he's got the colorful glass innards out of their chamber, in a heap sometimes, at other times spread out on the bench like the pieces of a puzzle, each piece almost but not quite touching the next, and he ruminates over them, these pieces, rearranges, holds them up to the light, thinks about them, puts them back down, puts them away, wraps them up carefully, like objects of value, like gems. Then, too, he's got the pocket mirror Thomas Argument gave her, in which she'd seen the reflection of her dear, vanished Papa; he's taken it apart, has picked all the shards of broken mirror out of the silver frame. Even the yellow glass bird is there, carved and filleted on his bench, the wings removed to expose the delicate mechanism within. He's studying, very carefully, each of these objects, and others, Thomas Argument's gifts to my mother, studying in depth, contemplating, learning, or trying to learn, *how they work.*

This, of course, does not satisfy my father, even when he has these objects, innocent in themselves, bared to the bone, as it were; there's something here he can't penetrate, not even once the cold mechanism has yielded its secrets—and they do yield, eventually, these objects of Thomas Argument's, though they don't do it quickly; no—there are challenges here, even for my father, who, with his Dell'oro *tendenza*, is an indefatigable scratcher at and ferreter out of secrets of the mechanical kind— though he is less perspicacious with other types, secrets of the flesh or of the emotion, for example. No—apart from the purely intellectual rewards my father derives from understanding, fully, the mechanisms of his rival, his explorations leave him unsatis- fied. Carving them down to the wire, to the nuts and bolts, to the mirrors and lenses, still—unsatisfied. But this is the Dell'oro condition, is it not?

He can discern how the mechanisms work, but he cannot discern *how they worked on my mother*—this, no baring of mechanism will reveal; the secret cannot be reached this way; no merely mechanical penetration, however deep, can ever be deep enough to fathom this mystery. In the gloom of his shed, though, my father does not realize his efforts are in vain; indeed, does not know just what it is that he is seeking—it's a shadow, something somewhere on the periphery—though he knows very well he isn't finding it; and so he continues with his dissections. Harry Owen and Montagu House are forgotten (at least until another envelope arrives, and then another; but even these are mere nagging presences, nits buzzing in the ear, pests, to be waved away) in the shadow of this other, more urgent, undertaking.

What a fool my father is, in his shed, with all this tinkering, tinkering, tinkering. He has learned nothing, it is clear, about my mother, or about the high price of neglect. Monsters are fathered that way. He got off lucky the first time. Who knows what's next. But that doesn't occur to him; he's working, that's all, there's nothing else, just the work.

In his own odd way he's not neglecting her, of course. As far as he's concerned. More like, he's forgotten where she is. He's groping blindly, he's lost. But it's her he's thinking of, all the time, every time he turns a screw to recalibrate a mechanism, or reaches for his soldering iron, or examines a minute cog and wheel with the aid of a magnifier that belongs to Harry Owen, and Montagu House. Every time he starts the bellows, bends over his lamp. Because of course he can't be content just taking Thomas Argument's gifts to pieces. He's a Dell'oro, after all.

There's always got to be something more. He's going to do
something with them, these gifts.

It's taking him closer to her. That's what he thinks.

I remember his hands moving, gently, in the lamplight. There's
nothing left but his hands. That's what he's reduced to: it's
memory's work. The spattering of sunlight across his shoulders,
that's part of it, and his hands, moving, moving, gently, desperately (except I don't know that yet, I am still a child), in the
semidark dark. He cannot continue, yet continues. Ever in the
attempt to penetrate that which cannot be penetrated. That
which moves away at his approach. Closer is farther. Cold is
warm. Glass is flesh.

This is what love has made of him. A creature part flesh,
part fire, he's been winnowed down, has winnowed himself to
just lamp and hands, a face partially occluded by goggles (eyes
invisible, shielded), neck a thin, pale stalk beneath the un-
trimmed mane of his curly black hair, he's bent earnestly in
my memory, bent forever, there in the dark semidark, a suppli-
cant before the flame.

Meanwhile the letters from Harry Owen pile up unanswered,
slip down between the dining table and the wall, lie forgotten
on the Turkish carpet, among the crumbs. Are trod upon at

mealtimes. Beneath her sharp heel, my ill-fitting shoe, his boot with the worn-down sole. *Can't you, Leo, for God's sake, send more glass? Hornsby is keener than ever—*

But my father is too busy. He is rearranging small, gemlike shards of glass in a glass chamber, a small, tightly lidded capsule, of Thomas Argument's making; dissatisfied, opens it, adds other shards, other brilliants, of other shapes, other colors; then he turns his attention to the mirrors, gently alters their angles inside the wooden tube of the kaleidoscope. It was my mother's first gift from Thomas Argument—that which began all. The object that piqued my father's interest in glass. Without it, perhaps, he would never have made glass. Had he never lifted it, looked inside, and, being a Dell'oro, seen the possibilities. Now at last it is laid bare, disarticulated, exposed. With a sharp knife he cuts a convex curve, delicate as a sliver of new moon, from the narrow far end of each of the three rectangular mirrors. Three new moons fall onto the bench, onto the floor, reflect narrow scimitars of light, scintillating blue scythes of sky. Carefully he replaces the mirrors in the tube, the chamber at its apex, the clear lens into the viewing end. Applies his eye to the viewer. Rotates. Sees what he has made, multiplied two, four, sixteen, a hundred, a thousand times. And is lost there, in precise, brilliant geometries of glass.

His work, his real work, has begun at last.

. . .

Carefully he removes the chamber again, once again opens it, and with a tweezer, begins removing small, brilliantly colored fragments. Like gems they glitter in the uncertain light at pincer's end.

He is dissatisfied: always dissatisfied.

My mother, for her part, hasn't noticed the loss of these, Thomas Argument's purely *sentimental* gifts. It is the missing pearl earrings she pursues, down on her hands and knees on the bedroom floor. They, after all, are germane to a secret project of her own. As for the others . . .

They don't matter to her. But I believe she feels their loss. She just doesn't know it. Instead, what she feels is a reduction in her self. Something's gone. But she doesn't know what's missing. She's groping for it without knowing what she's groping for. Finding a pearl earring. Yet feeling, still, the gap, the lack, the fissure. The missing piece.

As for me, I'm growing up in the gap between their two secret, separate worlds—at the juncture of their mutually averted eyes. For all the childish length and breadth of me, I've managed to slip between them, unnoticed by either. Nobody bothers to look for me where I've been dropped. And so I remain, shining, quietly, in the dark, increasingly mysterious to myself, as, too, I am sure, to them. I lie in my trundle bed—the little bed that has become, over time, too small, my self (that mystery) projecting, feet and ankles, over the low drawer that supposedly contains me—lying there, hearing, while it is still dark, the first noises of the morning—the single, cawping gull, then the many; rumble of early cart wheels, clatter of hoofbeats; footsteps on the cobbles; shutters opening, a quarrel starting up early in the house next door; my parents turning, beside and above me, so near and yet so distant, my mother's soft, inscrutable, warm murmurings in sleep; and I, the eavesdropper, aware, always, of the growing mystery, my self, under the rough sheet, the blanket, atop the prickling straw mattress; everything a mystery—swelling breast buds a mystery, my skin a mystery with its unexpected pink blushes, the sudden scrawny, startling growth of red bush at my pubes and the twin tendrils, smaller, in my armpits, all this a mystery to me, all new; I feel myself growing, being built, as it were, piece by piece, expansion of blood, bone, sinew, and also of mind, there beneath the roof of the Birdcage, which it seems sometimes will hardly hold me, so quickly am I growing, and so large—

My mother disliking the duty, as I grow it is I who am sent to the market. There I am a spectacle in all weathers with my mother's basket on my arm, judging, along with the housewives of Whitby, the spoiltness of mutton, the freshness of oysters, the relative percentage of spiderwebs to dough in the bread, whether the butcher's scale is weighted fairly, whether the potboy charges fairly for the ales. The ocean sighing beneath,

shifting its broad, grey back under the sodden, louring tent of
sky. Voices hiss behind me:

Poor barne!

Well! She's a red'un, ain't she?

Yais, terrible red.

Big for her age.

Verra big.

She don't favor her mother at all.

No. Nor the father, neither.

Which father, dear?

Hush. Hush now. She'll hear.

They go quiet as I approach, then resume behind my turned
back. There's a joke that I don't understand. The word *argument*
is meaningless to me, in the sense that they intend it. What does
it matter? I am spectacular here. I am a youthful, ginger giantess, a startling and incongruous figure, possessing the broad
back and large feet of my grandfather, Felix Girard; spectacular,
in Market Street with my basket, my child's breath rising on the
frosty air as I jostle earnestly in and among the housewives.
While my mother remains at home. Tending to other matters.
Or none.

It's quite a misfortune, ain't it? About the hair an' all.

Yais. And them feet. On a girl. Pity.

Yais. Such a pity.

But there are other attentions, too, which contradict the first.
Old Leng at the fish stall, who reaches across his display of bul-
bous, gape-eyed, put-upon herrings, his prawns and smelts and

winkles, to grasp with grubby fingers a curling tendril of my hair. Elizabeth Hendley in the dry goods, a kind woman usually but in my presence suddenly uneasy, broad rump shifting nervously behind a counter thick with buttons and spools, needles, handkerchiefs, bits of lace. I have come to buy my mother a spool of thread. *Here's trouble coming. You can see it in them blue eyes, a'right. Give it a year or two. It's coming sure eno'.* Her own eyes small, black, evasive. Then the carriage that one day follows me home in the rain, all the way up Bridge Street, until finally at the gate I turn to look—only then, the driver spurring the horses on, does it rush past, the blurred ghost of movement at a drowning curtained window the sole hint of the interest within. The maids who pluck and pull at me in the market, saying, *Aww, it ain't real, is it? She's like a doll or sumpin'—I'd like to take her home wi' me—*

From which I come to know about other species of desire than the sort that I, as a child, feel—to bite sharply through the fibrous, exotic caul of an orange so as to receive upon my tongue the tangy, shocking gush of pulp; or to hold in my own hands the warm, frantically pulsing body of the pullet newly beheaded by the butcher's remorseless blade.

These are my desires.

Hey, Red. Walk my way, why don'cha?

From which it may be seen that there are continuities, old world to new.

. . .

Among my admirers it is the boy who is the most persistent.
The others leave off, lose interest, after a time. But not him.

To understand this is to understand that in the absence of my
parents' attention, in the gap that they have created, I am swept
out into the streets—into Whitby's damp, convoluted alleys and
passages and tunnels, its secret staircases made of stone, winding down toward the sea. I am in the company of other children
who likewise swarm there, some as lost as I am; no, not that, it's
untrue what I have said, in fact very few are lost; most are the
subject of someone's urgent though temporarily distracted
attention—I imagine anxious mothers of six, with husbands,
lost or not, at sea. Except of course for the boy, he seems as
orphaned as I am—I, orphaned by anticipation; he, by fate; this
interpreted by both of us as freedom, while being, really, something else, something we'd rather not think about, not yet, at
least; no, not yet. We are too young for that, still.

　　I notice him first one morning by the fishmonger's stall. It is
raining again—always raining in that place; and cold—the sky
aslant with coruscation of sleet. I have just settled a damp sleeve
of plump, deeply pink langoustines into my—my mother's—my
housewife's—basket when I see him, though without seeing,
hunched at the corner of the stall. It is the son, I think, if I
think anything, of the man who pulled my hair; but really I
think nothing. I am moving on, moving on, barely noticing.
Then, though, I see him again, in the afternoon, as I emerge

from the bakery with three small lemon cakes wrapped in a towel for tea. Then and most disconcertingly in Sandgate Street as I lean in close to the window of Cariole's toy shop to get a better look, forehead touching glass, angel of breath appearing under nostrils, I am so intent upon what is there—a mechanical duck that, when fully wound, quacks, preens, then shits a pellet of dark green wood—there he is, reflected in the glass beside me, this boy, his reflection alongside, on top of, practically merging with, my own—

It is only then, I think, it strikes me that I have seen him before.

He is ubiquitous enough to be invisible, almost. Like other Whitby boys, he has sandy, indistinct hair, pale blue, nearly color-less eyes, translucent white skin, sharply raised cheekbones across which meander a few noncommittal pinkish-beige freckles; and a malicious ferret's grin, absent one or two teeth. He wears a grimy, formerly white, untucked shirt, trailing in the back, open at the neck to reveal a painfully concave hint of breastbone, and nubbly, hand-me-down knickerbockers a size too large. There is, in other words, nothing to distinguish him from many others, all approximately of my age, none achieving my height or anything near to it, whom I encounter in the course of my daily errands, or in the street wanderings, eclectic as they are, that follow.

I turn around, and he's gone.

Just like that.

He always did have the knack of disappearing like smoke. Hip, that is. Hippolyte.

What kind of name is that? say I, on hearing.

What kind of name is Carlotta, says he. Ferret's sneer so quick it does not occur to me to ask how he knows my name, since certainly I have never told him it.

But we have advanced by then, Hip and me. I am ahead of myself now.

It is, I suppose, not quite credible that I should have an admirer: I, a child, a ginger, a giantess. Unsubtle of foot. Nonetheless, it is true.

Though not immediately. I must chase him first, through all the passages and tunnels, vast and various, that constitute the underneath of Whitby. There is great pleasure in the play of giantess's legs, hot in pursuit of that-which-must-be-pursued; and the boy is always ahead of me, a grey figure in a grey ground of Whitby winter: up, over a wall, into somebody's yard, scattering buckets and nets and tarps and ladders, startling chickens, setting the dogs to barking; up over another wall, up an alley, past a shut-up, still-stinking latrine, a smallboat wintering in a mummy's wrap of canvas, a garbage tip heaped with bones, it's death here, all death. We are mocked all the while by the icy, tinkling chatter of frozen laundry hung out on a line, a man's voice shouting *Stop that din or I'll whang ye, I will!*—the angry gestures (shaken fists, upraised elbows, pointed fingers, others) of housewives surprised in the act of smoking bedbugs out of mattresses—we create our messes, he and I—wheelbarrows thumped, pots tipped, spilled milk mingling with spilled bitter, night soils unceremoniously scattered; and all the time, just ahead of me, the tantalizing tail of the boy's grimy shirt as he rockets over another wall, around another corner, over another cesspit—and then finally, inevitably, one day, at the corner of Grope Street and Lantern Lane, down, into the passages.

I've heard about those. Pirates are said to have inhabited the passages once. Now there is just the cold, strangely stilled air, smelling deeply of brine; the echoing drip, coming from somewhere, of water; and endless, deep sighings of the sea. Then, too, growing farther away with every moment's hesitation, the galling patter of footsteps in the dark, the single laugh, high, clear, contemptuous, carried up from below. It's because of this that I finally make the leap.

Then it is footfalls pinging in the dark, mine and his, his and mine, spiraling down through the dark, dank, sea-spattered brickwork, grey harbor glimpsed in chinks and gaps, until at last I emerge, alone, huffing, into the tarpaulin-shrouded boatyard with its towering piles of timber, raw mast and spar and decking, giant spools of canvas, rigging, the boats themselves up on blocks, waiting for spring. Skeletal creak and twang, clank of winch, soughing of wave, that is all; not even a laugh: he has evaded me, again.

Such a long walk it is, back up the hill, to the remains of my shopping, which I've dumped in my pursuit: the salmon stiff with cold, egg yolks stuck to the cobblestones, onions muddied but salvageable. Lurking then around the door of my father's shed I hear at last the hot, reassuring breath of the bellows; he is working again, on his rightful work, that is what I think, creating his glass. His glass ocean. I do not try to enter. I am distracted anyway, with puzzles of my own.

.   .   .

What a peculiar thing it is, this admiring and being admired. For me especially. After all, I'm an anomaly. Not like other girls my age. Though I don't know it.

If I knew others my age, I'd know. But I don't. They aren't where I am. Very few girls like me, out there on the streets.

I am *otherwise* and *elsewhere*.

As I am still young and ignorant, this is not yet painful.

It is he who comes to me, in the end. I return from marketing one day to find him crouched like a small, brown animal, very still, in the deep bruise of shadow at the corner of my father's shed. With his northern knack for colorless ubiquity he has very nearly succeeded at blending in there, though the windy *flap-flap* of the buttonless knees of his plain-woven knickerbocker pants gives him away, so that I hear before I see him as I round the corner out of Bridge Street; but then I do see him, with his eye pressed up to a gap in the wall of my father's shed.

He with his mischievous sneer, his eyes the color of water, of sky, of no color at all. He will press me up against the brick walls and half-timbers in the alleys, between the market stalls where the sellers hawk their marrows and crockery and bolts of cloth. We will linger together in the recessed doorways and cobbled yards until the housewives chase us out, brandishing their buckets and their brooms; or in between the higgledy-piggledy pews in ancient crumbling St. Mary's Church, where the ossified finger bone of the saint herself reposes on a cushion inside a glass and silver reliquary. Many times we'll gaze upon it with a kind of silent, half-mocking awe, then run away, giggling, jostling, tickling each other nervously in the armpits, on the ribs, around the belly. We'll fear the saint is judging us, perhaps; touching us, unbearably, with luck, or with madness.

His eyes the color of ocean, of air, of no color at all. His indistinctness a distinction. It is so easy to lose him. With his help I will continue the exploration of who and what I am and who I might become, until he decides that he is done with me again, and disappears until next time.

Until next time. Whenever that is, it all will have changed by then—next time, the when and where of it, all will be up in the air, and myself, too, back arched against the ancient bricks, unseeing of the future.

He saunters as if being caught spying at my father's shed is nothing.

What's doing in there? This nonchalantly said.

I am openhearted, unaccustomed to spies.

He's making, say I. *Making glass.*

As if this, too, is nothing to marvel at. This as well as the strange yet tender experiment we are about to launch upon, by which we will create, with fumbling hands and lips, the outlines of each other, and ourselves.

But not yet. Not yet. It hasn't started, yet.

He reaches out then, and removes a tangle from my hair. So things begin, by small gestures, incrementally.

Is your Ma in there with him?

Nah. She's in house.

The cold rain is coming down on us, sharp with icy insinuations.

Golden, is she? Your Ma.

Yes: she is golden. Very golden. With her white skin, slender body, tiny, delicate feet. The whorl of her ear like a seashell. Her teeth are pearls, her lips are corals. Hip grins his rat-toothed grin and I feel myself stung with something—some nettled, tangled thing inserting its hooks, they won't come out easily. They will rub and rub me now, chafe. I haven't been jealous of her before, not like this. Other ways, but not this way.

She's in t' house, playing piano.

Oh. Disappointed breath upon the air. *I thort I saw her, is all. You didn'.*

My basket is on his arm by now, we are making our way down Bridge Street, over the rioting turmoil of the river, toward the market. He will accompany me, or so it seems. Except when we reach the turning for Grape Lane, suddenly he says he must tend his master's horses. It is hard for me to imagine this. I try to picture him with currycombs, buckets of mash, raking out the warm, soft straw, none of this is possible. Hefting his master's suitcase. No. No. Not he. He does not work at anything, though later he will attribute certain of his absences to *My master's travels.* Hip has no master, I feel this strongly, a form of intuition. Work leaves its mark, and he doesn't have it. He's been marked by something else. I don't know what.

Nonetheless, very quickly, with an action like the dissipation of smoke in air, a conjuror's trick, he is gone, and I alone as usual must make my way wherever it is I am going.

I grow preoccupied then, once I am alone, without him to distract me. I haven't thought of her this way before, the way he has just made me think of her. Certainly, I have thought of her attention, all directed elsewhere, not on me; anywhere but on me; and have been pained thereby. Never, though, have I considered the attention of others, drawn away from me, inevitably, onto her.

Of course it's inevitable.

This stings, now that I know it, it's like a burr up my sleeve, something I can't get rid of. I know I'll think of her this way again, perhaps always, it's unfortunate. She was one thing, and now she's become something else, both more and less than herself.

I see him often, after that. A galvanic process has taken place, a fusing, however imperfect, by which we find each other again and again in the dark winter afternoons and the nights aglow with the cold reflective sheen of snow, white nights, during which a girl may lose herself in the secret alleys and passageways of this city, in the many places where a boy may be met, or not, depending on his mood, and hers, outside the watchful gaze of parents' eyes—particularly if those parents are not watching—if they are turned away, eyes averted; father at his bench, mother at her spinet, not bothering; everyone knows mothers watch best and closest, though in my case, not at all.

I seen your Ma, he says, *in the window, her hair were like a shiny rope, hanging down.*

It clutches at me, around the heart.
   She weren't in the window, say I.
   She were.
   I know it is a lie.

In this manner a new year begins.

It is my first outside, in the street.

   Tonight it is the New Year's night,
   tomorrow is the day,
   And we are come here for our right,
   O sing Hagmena-heigh!
   O sing Hagmena-heigh!

Snatches of song are borne back to us on the wind, along with sharp, stinging flakes of snow that have begun to fall in the

dismal twilight, borne inland off the metallic convexity of the
sea. They touch coldly, cling to hair and brows.

If you go to the black-ark
bring me an X mark
Ten mark, ten pound
Throw it down upon the ground,
So me and my friends may have some,
Hagmena-heigh!

From up the river comes the dull *thwuck-thwuck* of hammers in
the shipyard; and up above and behind us the lamps are being
lit, street by street, the ghostly blue flames of gas illuminating
doorways and windows, alleys and passages, the curving stairs
and sea-stinking grottoes of Whitby—as well as the haphazard,
glittering, guttering, peripatations of the snow.

It is four o'clock in the afternoon, dark already, on the eve of
the brand-new year.

Despite the weather and the darkness, the streets are busy, the
housewives hustling home with their bundles, the cook-maids
straight from the bake house with fragrant, warm loaves of bread
wrapped and cosseted beneath their arms. Just outside the tantalizing, gaslit window of the milliner's shop a puppet show is
enacted, accompanied by hectic strains of hurdy-gurdy: a skeleton, stark white, dances, bones departing one by one across the
tiny stage until only the skull remains, gyrating wildly, upon a
background of worn black felt. Snatches of song rise up—

Tonight it is the New Year's night, tomorrow is the day—

And just as quickly fade.

Groups of children, roiling together like schools of fish, tight packed, jostling, in threadbare coats and trailing scarves, emerge from the ill-lit alleys, disappear shrieking down damp and ancient passages descending toward the sea.

We are abroad, Hip and I. The foam that trails the wave. From shop to shop they go, begging money; we do not beg. It is something else that we are after.

If you go to the bacon-flick, cut me a good bit
Cut, cut and low, beware of your maw
Cut, cut and round, beware of your thumb,
So me and my friends may have some!
Sing Hagmena-heigh!

The detritus is what we are. Unstable stuff. Left in the wake.

We don't want what they want.

Come on, says Hip, *you mus' see this!*

His eyes of any color or no color at all glint eagerly in the gaslight, transparent yet simultaneously opaque as coins, as flat. Shifting. Coins on black felt. His fingers graze my elbow. I feel a sensation, as of bubbles rising rapidly through dark water, silver spheres rushing upward around me, and myself sinking, sinking through the cold and black; this is a premonition, though I do not know of what.

Come on!

He is always finding something for me to see. Last time, a house at the top of the cliff, half burned, outer wall peeled away like the skin from a skull. Remains of a life laid bare: the unmade bed and upturned chairs. Scorched dresser. A painting still hanging from a wire on a blackened wall. This was fascinating, he could not look at it enough, it was like theater, he said. There was a woman's nightgown tangled around the legs of a chair, and a hairbrush on the dresser. Were there strands of hair in it still, stuck among the bristles?

A story.

I wonder what will it be this time.

We make our way up Church Street in the spitting, sparkling snow. This is where he takes me. Argument's Glasswares is ablaze with light. But Hip has gone to the other, darker window.

Look. You mun see!

It is glass eyes in a wooden case, sizes and colors various, watching us watching them.

Tonight it is the New Year's night, tomorrow is the day—
Look! You mun see this!

Now he is at the other, Argument's blazing window.

Come on!

We shouldn'—

Nonetheless, above our heads a bell tinkles with irresistible cheer.

It is warm, inside.

Look!

We are surrounded by mirrors. He stands me in front of one; peering in I see myself: there I am, the ginger giantess, in my too-small winter coat, wrists protruding from sleeves (how long they are, my wrists, such embarrassment), and then there is the hair, the mess of mats and tangles, and the pale skin, flushed red from winter's cold; and as if this unflattering object in its collective singleness is not bad enough, I see it reflected ten, twenty, a hundred vertiginous times in a hundred scintillating mirrored surfaces. I am made and remade. Hip has positioned me perfectly for this, clearly he has been here before.

It's you!

But which is me? This is unclear. There are so many.

He does not laugh really, rather bares his teeth in a soundless, mirthful grin.

It's you! Now me—

But he will never take his turn. Suddenly there is a movement. From behind a curtain at the back, a tall, thin man emerges, long of limb, dark of eye, smoldering.

Run!

There is a crash, reality splinters, my reflection multiplies, contracts, disintegrates before me in a waterfall of glass; the water rises around me, a deluge of black and cold, bubbles race past white and silver buzzing in my ears like bees, in the distance somewhere there is an incongruous sound, a cheerful, ridiculous tinkling. I am being plucked at: Hip has my sleeve, he is pulling me back to the surface. Reeling me in. *Come. Come on. Run!* A dash upon the pavements and we are lost then in the roiling crowds. A right, a left, and suddenly we are in the tunnels with all the rest, two among many like ourselves, breathless, singing children. Except I am a giantess, and prone to be noticed.

We are come here for our right, sing Hagmena-heigh!—

.   .   .

I chide him later for the rock. I think he ought not have thrown it. The rest is lost on me, all his work. He says, laughing, *Let's not have an argument about it—*

For days I await the repercussions. But there are none. After all, Thomas Argument won't come to our house, no matter how many mirrors I break. I have been dropped again, effortlessly, into the invisible space formed by three intersecting and averted glances. I have slipped through again unscathed.

It feels like magic. I am so many, so big, so red, so hard to find. Invisible.

Hip is hard to find, too, after. I won't see him for a while. A shift of earth and time has taken place, all but imperceptible. A subtle mechanism, working.

Thus the turning of the year.

Winter in Whitby is perpetual twilight, perpetual rain edged sharply with ice. Roses long since nipped from the vine, the vine itself gone, shriveled against the whitewash, fallen. Grey twilight packed against the windows where green vines used to be. Inside the Birdcage we are held tight by clouded twilight, like the delicate objects of glass wrapped in cotton wool—those my father sends to London, those he doesn't. Sunrise at half eight;

sunset at half three; Hip gone; nowhere; absent. The three of us,
then. Together.

Curtains drawn tight. Block it out.

I am upstairs in the bedroom, on the Turkish carpet, surrounded
by what have been, in my life, companions: Señor El Galliñazo,
formerly brilliant wattles greyed with time, peering down skepti-
cally from the top of my mother's dresser. He is not my only
audience: there is a cayman, too, gap-toothed grin beneath wicked
yellow eyes, coolly carnivorous. These do not unnerve me.

From downstairs voices filter up, muffled by the carpet,
fragmented by the roar of the river. I can't make out the words,
just rhythm, cadence, tone. Three voices, two male, one female.
Two low notes, one high. Untamped by either rug or roar: fragrant, unfamiliar aroma of tobacco, winding its way up the spiral staircase.

And I can hear my mother laughing. This noise, too, floats
upward, the unaccustomed sound of her happiness making its
way among and around the clamorous disharmonies of the river,
buoyed, somehow, instead of drowned, by the sound of the
water. It washes over me, this tide of my mother's laughter.
Hearing it makes me aware how seldom she laughs.

Downstairs, they are talking to Harry Owen. A stranger, he
has entered unexpectedly through the kitchen door, bringing
with him blast of cold and wet, spackling of sleet, black umbrella
half furled, dripping; boots clinging with leaves; small earnest
spectacles blurred with the weather; soaked mackintosh slick as

a second skin, which reveals, when removed, tweed, a dark serious wedge of beard, deep resonant voice, smell of cinnamon and tobacco. Cigar tamped out at hearth, new one lit. Leather satchel, overbursting with books and papers, belted once, crosswise, belted again, lengthwise, as if he fears that left unrestrained it might fly apart, releasing its contents to the wind. But in the Birdcage it is safe; he leans it against the hob, along with the umbrella, once he has it thoroughly buttoned and contained. He is my parents' friend; but he is nothing to me, a stranger who takes my chin in his fingers, turns my face from side to side, then runs his fingertips lightly over my skull, beginning at the forehead, then back and up, behind the ears.

She is the image of Felix Girard! he says. *Same broad regio frontalis . . . same cranial vault . . . same strong orbital structure . . . prominent chin . . . and then too the shoulders, the chest, the membri inferioris . . . everything! Remarkable resemblance! Young lady, you will have a large brain and a strong body, just like your grandfather!*

He has not mentioned the adventuring spirit; I have that, too. But do I really have a grandfather? Felix Girard is a mythical creature. We do not speak of him.

Harry Owen lets go. I take a step back, stare; we stare at each other. Already I am as tall as he is. I feel conscious, under his scrutiny, of my long, gangly legs, my big, uncoordinated feet, my large hands, but then, too, of the small, tender new breasts, feel all of it taken into his gaze, examined. Critically? This is unclear. Clinically? Yes. He is a stranger. I don't see the friend in him yet.

But I feel the excitement he has brought with him. My parents have sparked with it, their eyes bright, smiles relaxed, mindful, suddenly, of a distant place I can't even imagine. It's just a name to me, a place packages come from. Chromate of potash. Sugar of lead. Gold chloride. Copper oxide. Bone ash. Arsenic. Oxide of manganese. Saltpeter. Colors are made from these. They are the spark, the snap, the heat of my father's glass.

Harry Owen is the source of all these, the source of the glass, of bench, of the tools. Of whom my mother has said: *It all belongs to him! What's in it for us?*

Despite this, though, she is smiling now, cheeks brightened with excitement as she stands by the door, the flowers Harry Owen brought her cradled in her arms. She averts her eyes as I am examined. Her eyes are on the window above the cast-iron sink. Through that occluded glass nothing is visible except the clattering torrent, rain laced with ice.

I think of her differently now, my golden mother. Does she think of me the same way?

When the examination is over and Harry Owen has released me she says, *Carlotta, go upstairs now.*

Sharply. A bright, cutting tone.

This is my cue. I curtsy, just as she has taught me. I do not, in this instance, trip over my too-large feet.

Remarkable! Harry Owen says. *Remarkable!*

He does not say: *What a lovely young woman.*

Rather: *Remarkable regio frontalis!*

By which he means to admire my broad, bulging forehead, recipient of a Felix Girard–sized brain.

Again I have that sensation, shaft of bubbles breaking upward, opalescent, through black water, a gasp for air, as I mount the spiral staircase, circling round and round and up, their voices growing indistinct below me.

The light notes of my mother's laughter, the deeper tones of the men, of my father and of this stranger, Harry Owen. Feel myself: shut out. Afloat. Cast adrift and carried upward on the foamy roar of the river. Turkish carpet a raft for me and my thoughts. Hip, ah, Hip: where are you? Rising on the flood.

Two words surface from below, bob clear in sound if not in meaning, a magical incantation in a stranger's voice:

Argonauta argo.

The Birdcage shudders, groans with the combined vehemence of wind and water; there is a shift, a change in pressure, a blast of cold air carried up, with a scattering of leaves, brown and brittle, deprived of vital juices, around the winding stairwell; then a slam that shakes the house.

From the window I see the three of them, my mother and father, Harry Owen, wrapped in winter coats, hats, gloves; moving slowly against the driving rain, their bent bodies a series of ciphers. Inscrutable alphabet that I cannot yet read.

The shed door sucks open, then closes, they disappearing within it. I, in the Birdcage alone, rifle through my mother's drawers, withdrawing these secret garments, the corsets and camisoles and stockings, the small cask for jewelry, with which I stretch out then on the carpet, my vessel, legs stretched forward, arms back, making desultory examination of my mother's belongings, then casually brushing, beneath the white fringe of the bedspread, an object. A hard object, large, smooth, resolutely right-angled.

I allow my fingers to play over it for a time, idly exploring. Until an image comes to mind, of my mother kneeling. The bed between us. Her body obscured. She was shoving something under the bed, something heavy. I had forgotten. Now my fingertips remember, passing over the smooth surface of the wood.

It is my mother's trunk. I slide it out from under the bed, undo the clasps. Fingers beneath the lid. It is awkward, even for my large hands.

Inside: Skirts. Bodices. Petticoats. Bustles. Corsets. Nightgowns. Stockings. Gloves. Hats. Shoes. Boots. Shawls. A muff. A large winter coat, much finer than the one she usually wears. All these items appear new, perfectly folded, never worn. They must belong to my mother, though I have never seen them before; it is her trunk, therefore her belongings; yet not a single article is familiar, and when, very quickly, I succumb to the urge to bury my face among them, I immediately miss the familiar scent of my mother's body; there is nothing familiar here; I draw back, having found myself suddenly, uncomfortably intimate with the belongings of a stranger.

Also in the trunk there is a smaller wooden box which, when opened, reveals a glittering universe of jewelry sharply in contrast with the few humble items in the cask she keeps in her

drawer. Here I find a diamond necklace and brooch with match-
ing earrings, which I've never seen before. A tiny, gold ring set
with a green brilliant. A pin in the shape of a dragonfly with a
sapphire thorax and a slender, tapering abdomen set with tiny
rubies. Objects belonging to a mother I do not know.

Also in the jewelry box I find a fine purse of blue shot silk,
large with coin, and containing a single piece of paper, yellow,
carefully folded, bearing at its top the logo of the steamer *Emerald Isle*. Open passage.

These are my mother's secrets, nesting, one within the other,
inside this trunk. With my large hands I open them one by one.
I unpeel her.

If I look out the window, I can see the *Emerald Isle*. It is moored
in the harbor, waiting out the storm. Broad, black bow, red fun-
nel. Gangway withdrawn, stowed. Nosing in among the fishing
boats as if wishing to hide. But really seeking shelter. This, too,
is my mother's secret.

Bound, turning at anchor in uneasy water.

The deck of the *Emerald Isle* is abandoned. Her crew is in the
Bird in Hand, drinking bitter. Her customers have not yet
boarded. Looking out, I do not really expect to see my mother
there, on the deck, a small distant figure in a blue shawl, hands
jammed into a pert fur muff. My mother is here, nearby, in the
shed with my father and Harry Owen. I know this and in spite
of knowing, feel my mother is there, on the *Emerald Isle*, all the

same. If I look hard enough I will see her, my other mother, the stranger who packed this trunk.

A door slams below. Quickly I replace, layer upon layer, what took her years to accumulate; sharp lowering of lid. Trunk slid back, into the dark beneath the bed. Into a place of forgetting.

Except I won't forget it now. The hollow place in my chest resounds with it. With its strangeness. Its stranger-ness.

My mother is going to leave us. I know, although I don't know it.

Here she is, though, sitting by the fire.

My father and Harry Owen are nearby, at the table, talking. Papers are spread out between them, jars, calipers, tweezers, a magnifying glass. My father is leaning back in his chair, sketch pad on knees.

Their voices murmur a gentle counterpoint to the rattle of hail against the windows.

Harry Owen is saying: *A charming little Eolis. It was transmitted to me, alive, by a Mr. David Landsborough, of Saltcoats. Found beneath rocks at low tide.*

They have it on the table between them, in a jar. My father sketches it, makes rapid lines.

Harry Owen says, *It is the only specimen found as yet in the British Isles.*

He says, *It is pelagic. Throws the branchiae forward when angry.*

A soft laugh. It is futile to object.

My father says, *Manganese and cobalt.*

This is the formula for amethyst glass. This is how he will

make it. Another soft, surreptitious life, exposed. Turned hard. Stopped in time.

My mother says, *Leo, I'm bored.*

She is still here, now, by the fire.

Leo, I'm bored. Leo, it's staring at me. Can't you make it stop?

He says, *Carlotta.*

I go to my father, stand behind him, watch him draw. I stand so close I can see the fine, curling hairs at the back of his neck, the red whorl of his ear, his cheek brightened with the heat of the fire.

My mother has packed her trunk. I have seen it, seen the folded clothes, the money in the purse, the open passage to London on the steam packet *Emerald Isle.*

I could tell my father this, but I don't.

What a secretive creature I have become! I stand by my father and watch the drawing appear, *Eolis landsburgii,* the delicate tentacles, the feathery fronds along the double line of the back, the fine details that my father will later fill in with color: delicate amethyst shading to red, transparent violet shading to white, light yellow, orange . . . intimations of a life barely seen, lived in the margins, in the tide pools, in cracks and crevices and sandy bottoms, under rocks green with algae fine as mermaid's hair, hidden places. I have a kinship with this and with all creatures who hide.

I will not tell him.

Later, I'll wonder why I didn't do it when I could have. Didn't intervene. Didn't try to stop her from leaving, when I could feel, already, the exquisite pain of her anticipated departure like a sharp stone wedged behind my sternum. When already I knew that once she left, the tether binding me to her would stretch and stretch, would fray unbearably, but would never break, leaving me bound, always, to a loss, to her loss, to *the loss of her.*

I see my mother as already on board the *Emerald Isle,* in her blue shawl and her muff, with her golden hair bound up for travel, her breath white on the cold ocean air. Her trunk is already stowed in the hold. The gangway has been withdrawn, she is there, on the deck, among a crowd of others, all waving their good-byes as the *Emerald Isle* slips its tether and backs slowly away from the wharf. Only my mother is not waving as the *Emerald Isle* backs away, as it maneuvers, slowly, through a harbor crowded with fishing boats and steamers, whalers and merchant ships heavy with paper and coal. She has already turned away from us, she has turned her back on her point of departure and faces only the future, a future that lies somewhere on a map barely glimpsed from over her shoulder, a map, divided up, like fruit, into wedges of longitude and latitude for her to devour selfishly, alone. It is her intention to devour those distances, those strange places that remain beyond the reach even of my imagination. My mother is already gone.

Maybe it is the strange doubledness of her, the sense that she is simultaneously here, by the fire, and there, on board the *Emerald Isle,* that prevents me from speaking.

She has become an uncanny thing. A thing of two faces, and none.

And me? How many faces have I got?

. . .

My mother. Saying, *Leo, I'm bored. Leo, can't you make it stop staring at me?*

While outside the window there is wind, hail. Hip, somewhere. Inside, the fire. The smell of Harry Owen's cigar. The scratch of my father's pencil.

But these things are temporary, illusory, a scrim through which may be discerned the shadow of her other life, the place where she really lives, the place she'd really rather be.

She doesn't live here with us anymore. Even I know that.

She is a ghost.

She inhabits insubstantiality, makes ghosts of us all. My father is not real, the warmth of his body where I press against his back is an illusion, the curling hairs at the back of his neck are an illusion, the pencil he sketches with, the paper he sketches on, none of this is real; nor is Harry Owen, tapping his cigar and saying, enigmatically, *Onychia platyptera*, strange words that my father recognizes, nodding—not real.

Nor am I.

This is the effect of my mother's presence, which is really an absence.

Harry, she says from her seat by the fire, *stop talking about those stinky fish of yours, and tell me about London. Have you seen my Papa's friend, Mr. Petrook? It is a very long time since I have seen*

Mr. Petrook. He never writes—he never sends. Has he forgotten about me, do you think?

The stranger's whiskers stiffen into a fleeting expression of distaste, quickly and scrupulously hidden.

I haven't seen Arthur in some time. He's been traveling, I believe. You know how it is with Petrook. Always off after something or other.

Yes, says my mother. *It's true. He was always off after something or other, wasn't he? Just like my Papa.*

She falls silent, stares unhappily into the hearth. It's like she's been reminded, suddenly, of something she wanted to forget.

She reminded herself.

Harry Owen says, *Ommastrephes sagittatus.*

My mother grows translucent by the fire. Her fine, small hands, slender arms, white neck, diminutive bare feet, all these, already pale, grow paler, as if, in the moment of remembering what she could not forget, some further percentage of her has disappeared.

Is disappearing, while I watch.

They don't notice. Neither one notices. My father draws. Harry Owen produces papers from inside his leather satchel. Bound and then unbound, lengthwise and crosswise.

She is lit from within. Staccato of firelight falling not on but through her. Glass in the crucible at 2,500 degrees. Her substance is elsewhere. On the deck of the *Emerald Isle* she turns away from Whitby. Finally she faces the sea.

Does he hear from my Papa, do you think? Does my Papa write to Mr. Petrook, and not to me?

This makes them look. They don't want to, but now she's left them no choice.

My father says, gently, *No, Tildy, he doesn't write.*

He is a kind man. He doesn't say, *Felix Girard will never write to anybody, ever again.* Even though that is what he thinks.

Deep unease of Harry Owen. Nervous tamping of tobacco. Shuffling of papers.

I think I will write to Mr. Petrook myself, says my mother, *and find out.*

My father says, in a mild tone, *As you wish.*

All the time his pencil is moving.

How can he not know that my mother is disappearing?

Bit by bit. Another piece missing. She is at sea already.

It is my fault, perhaps. I don't tell him, even though I should. I press slightly against my father's back.

She says, *Mr. Petrook will tell me where my Papa is.*

It is possible she may be smiling. In the glare of the firelight it is hard to tell.

She says, *Mr. Petrook will not hold back the truth.*

My father, still mild, continuing to draw. *Nobody is holding back the truth,* And then to Harry Owen: *We can go out to the Scaur when it clears. There are some interesting shale formations I'd like to show you . . .*

Harry Owen, stiffly formal, with great rigidity of whiskers: *I'd be very interested to see those. I've read Young on the Whitby shales, of course, but I've never had the chance to examine them myself.*

He is frightened of my mother: of her beauty, of her mockery, of her unhappiness. He won't look at her. My father won't either. They're both afraid. They're hiding, one behind his paper and pencil, the other behind his whiskers.

Me, too, I am also afraid. But I do look.

She sees me looking. Doesn't like it.

Carlotta, she says, *why aren't you in bed?*

Away from the fire I feel how cold the house has become. Clatter of hail on the red-tiled roof.

My mother's voice follows me up. *The Scaur? That awful, ugly place? Oh, Leo, must you really? Poor Doctor Owen . . .*

While Harry Owen says: *But you don't understand, my dear. I want to go! After we've reviewed the specifications for the new models, of course . . .*

Oh, of course!

Jingle of harness, later, informs me that he has departed.

My mother, on the stairs: *He's checking up on you. Spying.*

To this, my father says nothing. What can he say?

. . .

I wonder does she know what he's doing out in that shed instead of making the glass ocean that he's promised Harry Owen. Does she know about the things he's taken, Thomas Argument's gifts to her which have gone, or those other objects, my father's carefully wrapped, tenderly cosseted secrets? Does she feel, without being able to identify it, the sense of herself diminishing? Of something being taken away, somewhere beneath her notice? Is that why she's decided to leave us? So as to make the choice herself, which parts of her will stay, and which will go?

I am surprised I haven't noticed this before, my mother's doubledness, the way the light falls through her. Through the shadow that both is and is not her. She is like an image in a kaleidoscope, bright and scintillating fragments coming together, falling apart, beauties and monstrosities forming and reforming, combining, breaking, fleeting away.

I don't think she knows. I think she's a secret to herself. As are we all.

In the morning, early, Harry Owen returns, bringing with him harness jingle and whip of wind bearing stinging bites of cold rain, dry rattling dead leaves that pry like fingers along the jointures in the stone floor, heavy scent of sea stink and brine. Various pieces of gear enter with him as well: heavy oilskin boots, thick coats, gloves, collector's bags, pick and hammer for each, coils of rope, all paid for by the benefactor, she who by her own account has been, by my father's work, *taken*. As one might be taken by an illness. Swept up in a gale. Except this thing is a good thing. There is talk of boats, expeditions, all paid; this frightens me, the ocean is no comfort, a scaled and horned and scornful thing in my imagination now, slithering at the foot of the cliffs, murmuring low and constantly of distances long, black, impossible to imagine.

Harry Owen says, *We shall go out together in the spring. There is a great deal of money.*

Spring: this, too, is difficult to imagine, with the Whitby winter pressed so hard upon us.

My mother stands helpless before the influx, golden braid slack on her shoulder, mug of tea pressed between cold hands.

I'm not coming with you. I won't come, Leo.

This being evident regardless. She is undressed but for a moth's wing of nightgown, shivering by the fire. And anyway, they have not asked her.

But nor does she ask him, to remain.

Instead she and I remain together, in the cold and empty house, while they head off to the Scaur, to *examine the shales.*

I have a new unease with her, it is like being left behind with a stranger who both is and is not my mother. Doppelgänger. Simulacrum. She: present and absent both at once; I: wishing only to be absent, free of the Birdcage and its accumulation of secrets, dead bodies, its low, uneven ceilings and canted walls and doors jammed shut, the sooty sparking closeness of the fire.

This is easy. She will not object.

But once free and out in the street I find myself overwhelmed by the conviction or fear that she has gone already, ceased to exist, perhaps, absent the gaze of my formative eye, as if it is I who create and uncreate her; I want to run back and check, then, just to make sure she hasn't left us, to make sure she still exists, but I remember Hip, *She's golden, ain't she, your Ma? She's golden,* that furtive, half-shy grin, and there is a click, something changes, it's like the closing of a door I won't let myself go back and open, no matter what.

Hey, Red! Over here! Walk my way, why don'cha?

I am used to it by now, early, the cold out in the street. Even the market is not yet thriving, the *Emerald Isle,* down below in the harbor, drowsing on her tether, is unaware as yet of having a role in our small drama; all is cold, silent, still. I look for Hip but I cannot find him, not in any of the usual places or even the unusual, not around the market stalls or the Punch and Judy in Grope Street or the burned-out house at the top of the hill or the stables in Highgate; Whitby is empty of him; he has gone off, perhaps, to please his master, fetch and carry, or some other impossibility. And so I idle about, observing for a while the steaming breath of ponies, then peering in shopwindows at goods I will never have sufficient funds to buy.

Ain't you cold, girlie? Want to warm yerself, don'cha?

This the hawker of chestnuts, gloved hands splayed over hot brazier.

There is none of this in the new world; it is an altogether warmer place, though I don't know yet that this is in my future, cannot possibly imagine the skitter of lizards around my skirts, or the ancient black sickle of the man-o'-war bird, drifting aloft on high, blue currents of air, or even my raven companion, she who enters at the screen door and tells me it is time to go; all this is yet to come; what I have now is my forehead pressed painfully against cold plate glass, fog of my own breath blinding me like angel's wings, and the bubble of foreboding lodged beneath my sternum. I can neither belch it up nor swallow: feel myself choking. Drowning in it.

Ain'chew cold, girlie? Wants to warm y'self?

In the end it becomes too bitter, I have to return home. All the way across the bridge I imagine the empty house, the vacancy where my mother used to be, this is pain and pleasure both and so compelling that I do not linger as I would, usually, to look at the dark, indistinct things looming beneath the surface of the Esk, too turbulent ever to freeze, but hurry instead in dread and anticipation, undignified as ever on my long legs, imagining the abandoned spinet, the empty chair, the vacant mirror, she gone, self and shadow both. Yet when I arrive she is as always in the parlor before the fire, and though I look for it her transparency is no longer evident, she has disguised it, pulled close her veils, except there is a slight blurring around the edges of her, a softness, which may be smoke or the frost on my eyelashes or something else—I don't know what. I was so convinced she would be gone I can't believe she is there, it takes me a moment to realize it, and then I am either disappointed or relieved, it is unclear which. In this way I am a mystery to myself.

My father and the stranger, Harry Owen, are there as well, beaten back off the cliffs early by the cold. Nobody but the stranger looks up when I enter: I am not invisible to him as yet. Immediately he asks if he can measure me.

This peculiar request brings no reaction from my parents, my father intent on his newly collected rocks, my mother staring broodingly into the fire, as if she has lost something and thinks she might find it there, so, shrugging off my coat, I accede.

He measures me gently, with a piece of string. The circumference of my skull first; then the lengths of my arms, in separate measures: wrist to elbow; elbow to shoulder. Then my legs: ankle to knee, knee to hip. Measures each of my feet. My hands, each of my fingers. He is so clinical it is impossible to find anything improper in his touch, which is light and dry, like paper, though, too, I can feel his warmth, his tweediness, can smell his cinnamon and tobacco, can hear, even, the intimate, measured ticking of his pocket watch almost as if it is his heart tucked away safely beneath his waistcoat. Carefully he makes note of all my measures. He can rebuild me now, if he wants. Replication is possible.

He says, *Remarkable!*

This is because I am a giantess, not out of any other type of longing, or desire, or admiration.

Those belong to my mother, all of them, always. She is not sharing with me.

Indeed, it seems she will not allow me even this, for as if his remark has alerted her to my presence she emerges suddenly from her reverie, blinks, sees me, and says, *Carlotta, run to the bake house and buy me a loaf.*

And so I am out again, into the cold.

Outside I feel lighter, relieved of a burden. It was not just the heat from the fire, or the tightly packed, tensile warmth of my grandfather's creatures pressed close around us, threatening to spring.

It was, is, something else altogether.

Weight of secrets, drawing us downward. Stones in our pockets. That is what I think, passing again, at my mother's bidding, above the murmurous river.

. . .

In the night it snows. The stranger returns to his room at the
Bird in Hand; but in the morning it clears, and so he returns,
early, before it is light.

They will attempt their expedition again.

My mother says:

Take Carlotta with you.

I am both too surprised and too delighted to respond to this
unexpected largesse; but then my father says, *No, she can't go out.
It's too icy.*

My mother scowls and turns away. But really there is
nowhere else for her to turn; there is only this one place, these
people; so she turns back.

My Papa used to take me with him on all his adventures, she says.
But nonetheless: *It's dangerous. She could fall.*

So I am left behind again. My mother and I watch, together,
from the parlor window, as my father and Harry Owen emerge,
heavy with gear, onto Bridge Street. It is a white morning,
bright with ice, Harry Owen and my father black figures upon
it, dark, moving hieroglyphs upon a stark field of white cross-
hatched with shadows.

The ice is bright from within, like hot glass emerging from
my father's furnace. Yet this light is confusing, because it has no
clear source. I watch as my father and Harry Owen cross the
bridge, grow distant. My mother says, yawning, *It's too early. I'm
going back to bed.* The moth's wing of her gown brushes against
me. She is a stranger again in the strange cold light, the ice light.

Her face is altered. She isn't really here. She has already boarded the *Emerald Isle,* awaits, impatiently, the moment of *casting off.*

She says, *Find yourself something to do.*

Then she goes up, round the spiral. I do not follow. I am left alone in the parlor, with the ticking of the clock, the soft hiss and spark of embers in the grate.

Recalling the bitterness of the day before, I decide I will not go out. I will *find myself something to do.*

This is easy, in the Birdcage. The general deterioration, the softening of order, the laxity—the boxes half unpacked, overspilling with Felix Girard's creatures, the papers scattered everywhere, the books, the journals, the crumb-laden plates, the discarded clothes, on the dining table, on the chairs, on the floor—there is opportunity in this. There is a box I've had my eye on. Inside it I find a collection of sea fans, their brittle labyrinthine branches separated and preserved between thin sheets of crumbling paper on which someone (my grandfather?) has written:

Gorgonians. Holoxonia.

They release, as they emerge, a shower of sand, broken fragments of fragile coralline limbs, scent of brine, of rot, of sea. I spread them carefully on the floor. They form a delicate two-dimensional forest, a fading peacock's tail of pink and red, violet, yellow, orange. Some are very tall; all are very flat, rigid, skeletal; the hard, dry bones of something once vibrant and alive. Gently I trace a path with my finger along their tangling, interwoven copse, then walk it in my mind: a path along a seafloor dense with shrouded things, hidden detours, forbidden turnings, movements sensed rather than seen; scuttle of claws, flash of fierce, cold eyes . . .

. . .

I am awakened, abruptly, by the slamming of a door: tumult, footsteps on the stairs, a man's unfamiliar voice roaring, *Are you ready, Tildy?* Then: *Oh, hello. Who are you?*

He stands and stares at me, long-legged gangling thing that I am, sprawled out half-asleep on the floor: a yellow-haired man, young, leonine, with a large, proud mustache, ruddy, ripe, almost womanly lips, camel overcoat bearing the raw, snowy scent of outdoors, long, pale, womanly hands. On his left pinkie he wears a gold ring set with a tawny flashing stone.

My mother says, *Oh, that's just Carlotta.*

She has come downstairs in her traveling suit, the short, sharp jacket of grey velvet lined with red, the trim, gunmetal-grey skirt, the petite black boots, the soft, narrow, calfskin gloves, which she adjusts over her slender hands; her hair is bound up tight beneath a blue hat trimmed with a trailing black feather.

Really? Is she yours?

He stares at me more intently now, with a fierce, hard, pale stare, interested, yet devoid of feeling, as if I am one more specimen among my grandfather's variously arrayed exotica.

She's a big girl. Awfully damned red, ain't she? Ain't she?

My mother ignores this. She says, *Carlotta, this is Mr. Treanor. He is an explorer. He is coming with me to the Gulf of Mexico to look for my Papa.*

Mr. Treanor says, *God, Tildy, ain't you got any luggage? It's a frightful long journey, you know. You might want to change out of those things.*

He smiles a wicked smile, revealing strong bright teeth among the golden hedge of his mustache.

My trunk is upstairs. It's terribly heavy.

Not to worry. I'll send Samuel up for it. From among the folds of his overcoat he produces a watch, which he examines critically. *By God! We'll be late if we don't look out! Samuel! Get up here and shift Mrs. Dell'oro's trunk! Come on, Tildy. Don't want to miss the damn boat after all this.*

My mother doesn't look at me. She has never looked; she isn't going to start now. She stands at the center of the room, carefully pressing her fingers into the fingers of her calfskin gloves. Then she says, *I've left your father a note, Carlotta,* and I see that it's true; there's an envelope on the mantel, leaning against the terra-cotta head of a goddess.

Be a good girl, now.

She bends to kiss the air above my forehead.

Then, suddenly, with a clatter of boots, she is gone.

Mr. Treanor, though, lingers. He stands, taut with attention, at the top of the stairs, toes over the edge, like a man getting ready to jump; except he looks back at me, speculatively, and he doesn't jump. *I say, Tildy, is it awright to leave like this? The kid? Tildy?*

Tildy? Then: *Well, by God!*

Thrusting his hands deep in his pockets, he jangles off down the stairs.

Then the servant comes, and takes away my mother's trunk.

The house shudders; I hear the springs of the cab in our yard quaking beneath the weight of my mother's luggage, the snap of the cabman's whip, the sharp urgent ring of hooves against icy cobblestones. The spark struck: then off.

In the harbor the *Emerald Isle* has come alongside the wharf. She is tied fast, shored against the buffeting sea. The gangway is lowered. Soon enough the cab will disgorge them, my mother, Mr. Treanor, the servant, the luggage. And they will board. Boarding with them, on this foul day: A farmer bound for Hull, with his lunch wrapped up in a cloth napkin. Two spinsters recently departed from the Ravenscar Hotel, now bound for Colchester, each carrying a soft-sided, paisley suitcase. Their black terrier bitch, long nosed and indifferent in a plaid traveling coat.

In other towns others unknown to me will join them, and together with my disappearing mother will endure bump of wave, shift of tide. While I remain behind, on Bridge Street, waiting for my father to come home.

It will seem like a very long time. A long time, to contemplate the distances of ocean she is putting between us. And I, paralytic on the sofa by the cold, black hearth. Sea fans spread out on the floor at my feet. My grandfather's notes my only company. *Gorgonians. Holoxonia.* Ticking of clock.

I will have a long time to contemplate the distances of her ocean. A lifetime. During which she will never stop drawing away from me, distance growing greater, growing unbridgeable, growing unfathomable, becoming unbearable. Never ceasing to grow.

It is a long time. But I don't know that yet.

I think: I could have prevented it, but I didn't. I should have said something. Yet I both hoped and feared that she would go, and so I said nothing. Now it will be my job to break the news. I don't look forward to that. Maybe I will never hear the footsteps in the hall. This is what I hope, then fear, as the morning draws on. I wander lightly through the empty house. It is hard at first, then easy; I have done this before; this is how I imagined it. So many times my mother has gone, drawing on her gloves, her boots, her shawl, her muff. Leaving me alone. Crouched among my grandfather's seashells and stones, his pressed leaves and pinned butterflies. This is usual.

Then I remember. Sudden waking. Opening of the distance. The Birdcage empty and strange, and I, too, in it, strange and empty.

At one o'clock the snow resumes, at first sparse, tentative, then heavier, insistent. Now my father will come home—must come home. Enveloped in the sparkling, suffocating caul. Even so it takes a while. It's after two when I finally hear clank of gear in the yard, stomp of frozen boots in the kitchen, voices drifting upward.

Damn cold in here, ain't it?

Damn cold!

The stove's out. She let the stove go out again.

Clotilde!

The unanswered call. Soft laughter. Scrap of conversation tossed up above the roar of the river.

. . . off on another one of her adventures.

Is that so?

Murmurs. Rattle of coal in the scuttle.

I imagine them downstairs, snow-burdened coats stripped off, grimy, wet boots puddling on flagstones, wet scarves steaming. Red palms slapped together for warmth. Nape of neck goosepimpled, laid bare to unexpected cold. Raw smell of ice. Specimen bags encrusted, glittering, shedding their wintry second skins.

Clotilde! Carlotta!

You'd think she'd have lit the fire, at least, before she went.

I listen as if from very far away. I am far away. I am on the third floor, in the bedroom, sitting on the stale, unmade bed, surrounded by my mother's turned-out dresser drawers, the clothes scattered, rejected, left behind among the sheets, on the pillows, on the chair, on the rug.

I, too, left behind. Scattered.

Squandered.

Clotilde?

He is working his way up, through the house; he hasn't seen her note; walked past it; stands on the threshold, gazing down at me. At me and then past me, at the mess she's made.

From the glazed, anguished look in his eye I know he knows it. I don't have to tell him. The chaos tells him, the crumpled stockings, the dumped camisoles, the emptied dresser. Without a word he turns away.

Leaden footsteps on stairs.

She's g-gone.

Gone? Good God! Are you sure?

There is a silence; some shuffling.

She's t-taken her father's book!

Muffled voices, descending toward the kitchen.

I am forgotten. I have slipped through once again. I sit on the bed, shadows stretch out across the room, a finger of winter-killed vine scratches at the window, snow sluices down, filling the casements, stilling the vinescratch, the outside world begins to disappear, bridge, street, harbor, sky, all consumed in a torrent of white, edged with lozenges of crystal. The only sound in the house is the sound of the river: hollow, mindless *boom-broom!* of water, storm maddened, tumescent.

My mother is on the sea.

My mother is not on the sea.

She has put on her boots, her gloves, her shawl, her hat, her muff. She has gone downstairs, into the parlor; into the kitchen; out, into the yard, the shed, the street. She has gone into town, walked down to the churchyard, the marketplace, the dressmaker's shop. She is lengthening her orbit, moving away from me.

She is not coming back. She has taken her Papa's book.

She *is* coming back. I am confident of it.

She has never left.

My mother is and is not on the sea.

Meanwhile I am waiting. Snow is whispering. I am alone and at sea myself, adrift in the storm.

The silence in the house is also a tension that must not be broken. I sit very still so as not to break it. The slightest movement might shatter everything: then we will fly apart, all of us, like improperly cooled glass.

Eventually I dare to go downstairs, silently, so as not to break the tension, which is all that holds us together. As I pass through the parlor I see the envelope my mother left on the mantel. It leans against the head of a goddess. My father hasn't seen it, not yet.

I should tell him, but I don't. He is in the kitchen, sitting in front of the stove. He is deeply sunk in his chair, chin on chest, legs extended; deeply sunk into himself. He doesn't look up when I come in. Because his posture repels contact I do not go to him as I would like to do. Instead I go to the settle, sit. We are paralytic, both of us. Harry Owen is the one who moves: energetically, around the kitchen, producing bread, butter, cocoa powder, milk.

You must do something—must look for her—find out, at least, where she has gone—

My paralytic father doesn't reply. His chin sinks lower.

—why she has gone, what she thinks she is doing—

It's funny, isn't it? That they don't ask me? That I don't say? We are in collusion, we three.

Abruptly my father says, *I'm going out.*

And then he does, putting on his boots but neither hat nor

coat nor gloves, slamming out into the storm, a fringe of snow entering in his wake, scattering wavelike across the kitchen floor. A subsequent creaking of hinge informs us that he has entered his shed. The lamp he lights there, which my mother once sought in a moment of trouble, is a dulled spark, waxing and waning behind swirling clots of white.

In silence Harry Owen and I consume buttered toast with cocoa.

He will emerge from his shed only sporadically in the days to come, entering snow shouldered, silent, disinclined to interact with either one of us.

Harry Owen says, *We must do something!*

To which my father replies, savagely, *I* am *doing something!*

What is he doing? He is in his shed. He has taken apart, left splayed out on his bench, Thomas Argument's gifts to my mother. All the delicate innards exposed, mirrors and springs and coils, guts, butchered remains, glistening offal. And he is making glass. Manganese and cobalt fused with sand and lead oxide at 2,500 degrees; violet shading to white, amethyst shading to red; initials formed in gold enamel around the delicate turning of the un-imaginable mouth: CGD'O, CGD'O, CGD'O.

Lamp and furnace, furnace and pot and lamp and lehr.

He hasn't seen the note on the mantel. It stands as she left it.

The sea fans, too: still spread out on the floor, just as they were in the moments before I fell asleep. A line of demarcation. This is how the world used to be. Now the parlor is a room to pass through, hurriedly, on the way to somewhere else. Scene of an accident nobody wants to revisit. The wrong touch could shatter everything.

Though we'll have to clean it up eventually.

Harry Owen's beard is sharp with urgency. *You must do something about Clotilde. You must find out where she's gone, with whom, to whom—she could be hurt, in danger, ill, needing our help and our intervention, our, our aid—you should at least tell somebody, report it—check the station, the harbor, the constabulary—*

I think about the rough sea, and my mother on it. The distance between us opening up, opening wider. The black waves, the depths beneath. And what inhabits them.

This is exciting.

My father, though, is obdurate—rising from his chair, deigning at last to put on his large coat, which he wears rucked up carelessly in the back. He is returning again, compulsively, to the more certain warmth of his furnace and lamp, to the glass that is more responsive to his loving ministrations than his Clotilde could ever be.

He is ready now. His work, his real work, is about to begin.

. . .

He can do amazing things with glass, turn the rod in the heat of
the flame until it grows soft, caress it with his tools to form the
bulb, the bud, the first perfect, translucent body upon which he
will practice his art, from which he will conjure, with a series of
small but eloquent gestures, other bodies, other forms, embed-
ding as he does, within each of them, her initials.

It doesn't matter. It's useless, all of it.

Harry Owen wonders, gesticulates, grows emphatic, spastic.
Froths at the mouth practically. My father says nothing, nor
do I.
    We are in collusion, we two.
    Finally, painfully, Harry Owen stops asking, sharpens his
beard instead over books by the stove.

Her absence has become a wound nobody wants to look at.
    Meanwhile the snow is replaced by a sullen, dark dripping;
the sea reclines on the horizon, an indolent, silver-scaled beast,
cold thickened, slithering slowly: forward, back; forward, back;
into the harbor, out; into the harbor, out. I am lethargic, too, my
numbed fingers awkwardly fumbling the buttons of my dress
in the frigid bedroom where nobody bothers to light a fire
anymore.

Nor is there a fire in the parlor.

Nor are the lamps lit.

The fifteen corners of the three pentagonal rooms of the Birdcage are stale, contain, suddenly, strange, unexpected pockets of abandonment that hover like ghosts, cling damply to the skin when passed through. Smelling of dust, of fur, of feathers, of formaldehyde; of unbrushed hair, unswept fingernail clippings, unread books, undrunk tea, uneaten food, unriddled cinders.

In this way, it seems, we are haunted.

It is a reverse haunting, though: instead of a presence, an absence. Trembling of air. Attempts at conjuration fail: descending the spiral stair I see her from above, sitting at the table. I hear her: footstep in the pantry. Voice—a single word—short, sharp, impatient, imperious: *Carlotta!*

But I am mistaken. It's just a shadow. Vinetap on windowpane. Snippet of dream. I wake up; she isn't there; things fly apart: the molecules will not cohere.

My mother is gone. She isn't coming back.

Finally though, one day, after many days of tense silence, through a blue filigree of frost I do see a figure after all, dimly familiar, lurking at the gate, indistinct in the sleeting; from its slouching, clowning manner I realize it cannot be my mother, yet just the same I feel a sense of relief, of breath inheld released: I have been waiting for this, too, without realizing. It's Hip. How long has it been? Long enough: he won't know she's gone.

There's relief in that. Wrapped in a thick, greasy parka, tongue protruding teasingly from the gap between his teeth, colorless as ever, his breath white upon the grey-white freezing air, he is a shadow, unlike others, that grows in solidity as I approach. It is easy enough for me to slip out to meet him, to disappear, myself, into this monochromatic world; to slip between; nobody, after all, is looking. In the shed the bellows respires, smoke rises greyly through roof vent into grey sky, this is my father at work; Harry Owen, reclined by the fire, has buried his spade of a beard deep in the pages of a book and will not be aroused. So I slip past, slip through. What is one more disappearance, after all?

Quickly I cover my hair with a shawl, and become invisible. A ghost myself, gladly conjured.

I won't tell him she has gone. In our shared world, she's still here. This is magic.

I am barely through the gate when he says, *You got to see this!*

Again?

Yeah. You got to see.

This is how it is with us, it is as if no time has passed since the last time. Time with Hip is a single blink, or several parallel worlds he is interweaving. Only he can see the thread.

What is it?

Of course he will not tell me. He never tells. Surprise being of the essence. I know this, in itself it is no longer surprising. The thing he shows me, that is what will surprise.

Come on!

He touches my hand lightly, ghost tap on ghost flesh, distantly apprehended.

Naw. Hold up. It's too cold. I don' wanna go.

C'mon. Why not?

I don' wanna, that's why.

Nonetheless, of course I'll go. This is what I do, what we do, he and I, together. Beneath us is the Esk, boiling and freezing simultaneously, dousing us with its cold contempt.

At the corner of Bridge Street we turn, head down the hill single file, unspeaking. He grows indistinct in the sleet, as if vanishing behind a scrim. Then pausing to wait for me he grows solid again at my approach, a veil is lifted, it's like a game, molecules flying apart, coming together.

I can depend on this.

I won't tell him she has gone. In this way she can accompany us, a ghost among ghosts. I feel her absence at my back, it is loyal, like a thing on a leash, tugging lightly, playfully, though Hip can't see it.

He senses it, perhaps, my silence giving shape to that which is missing. I know this but can't help myself, having nothing to say.

Fortunately he is magnanimous, has no wish to unmask me.

So we will descend, three ghosts together, into the warren.

The sleet is so thick that today even this is abandoned, mean figures and mean, low buildings emerging darkly from ice and wind, then sinking away again, the streets narrowly turning back upon themselves and each other in a circuitous dream of stucco and stone that has for its accompaniment the rhythmic, angry music of the sea.

It is right below us here. The ground trembles with it. We are a heartbeat away from the wave that could dash everything to pieces, all of it, all of us, ghosts then, in the sea.

Instead we turn another corner, and another, this is Hip's territory, the sea's an impersonal menace, it does not care about us, and I myself am lost, getting in deeper with every turning.

Imagining her there, on the sea. Distance growing greater.

Though at the same time she is with me.

My mother is and is not on the sea.

Come on. This way. Over here.

How does he find these things? When has he the time? His master, if there is such, is certainly a lenient one. Somehow Hip has memorized these streets, follows them by touch or smell or some other sense uniquely his own, by the cobbles beneath his feet, perhaps, the cant of them, the curve, the rough and smooth spots, or, like a jungle creature, by a trace he left the last time he was here, undetectable to all but himself. Me he leads with gentle touches, hand on wrist, hip, shoulder, this is palpable enough.

I haven't been here since she carried me inside her. She has dislodged me at last, I suppose. Having held her grudge longer and better than I ever could have imagined, she has left me her ghost only, to carry with me from now on. This is another of her inversions, I left to bear the weight of nothing, an empty space that, as it cannot be emptied, will only grow heavier with time.

Over here, says Hip, *look at this!*

He has brought me to the window of a little music shop where along with the flutes and mandolins there is a woman seated behind the streaked glass, playing at a small keyboard; the music issues out to the sidewalk in brittle gusts through a gap in the door, which is narrowly ajar. We are not alone in watching; a small gathering, children, one or two women, stand before the window as well, staring intently.

We are silent, all of us, watching, waiting.

Two days she's been here, Hip says. *Ain't that something? Ain't it?*

Behind the glass the musician lifts her arm to turn the page of her score, shifts disjointedly, with a roll of eyes resumes her play, which is awkward, the flanges stiff in the fingers though those fingers are slender, pale as flesh, paler, the nails small and delicate and rosy.

Look! cries Hip. *Ain't that something? She looks just like your Ma! Don' she? Don' she? When she turns her head like that?*

She don', say I. *Not at all.*

I can be discriminating now, even if at first something did jump up in me. Blue of eye, whorl of ear, tilt of neck, slope of shoulder, all these resemble, but being lifelike without life, point up, instead of resemblance, its opposite: the lack, the gap, the fissure. The distance between.

Growing larger.

This is not my mother. Despite the golden hair.

Though the eyes are blue.

My mother is gone.

My mother is, and is not, on the sea.

Unable to bear her absence I must bear it some more.

Hip is disappointed now.

If we go inside, he says, *they'll show us the motor. D'ya want to see it?*

Naw.

That's all right. I seen it already.

With the crowd we stand a while and watch, as the sleet comes down on us, until I cannot stand it anymore. It grows horrible, watching, in the end.

Let's go.

At the top of the hill Hip says, *I thought you'd like it.*

Tone injured, slightly defensive.

And then when we are at the gate, *Do she always watch you like that?*

Who?

Your Ma.

She ain't watching.

Is too.

Isn't.

He gestures by jut of chin over my shoulder toward the

house; turning toward the Birdcage I see the light on in the parlor window, and my mother there, having pressed back the curtain, watching. From where I am standing I can see the glint of firelight on her hair, the outline of her cheek, this is clear as day almost, despite the sleet and the impending darkness; I can even see, behind her, the row of terra-cotta heads on the mantelpiece above the hearth. Abruptly then, as if she has noticed us noticing, and doesn't like it, the curtain falls.

She's beautiful, your Ma, Hip says, with a rapturous expression. *So golden.*

He touches me then, my hand with his hand, my lips with his lips. We are warm together in the cold.

This is a thing of mixed feelings. My mind is elsewhere.

I think, *My mother has returned.*

When I get inside, though, the fire is roaring brightly, and my mother isn't there. No one is there but me, with the empty space behind me. I lift the curtain and gaze out into the liquid blue unraveling of the evening, but Hip has already gone— disappeared—not a trace. There is a strange, dull glow to the east, from the sea; it undulates softly, rotates, like a net that has captured nothing.

Then there is a change, a slight but vertiginous disalignment, tilt of sky, horizon, shift of earth on axis; houses descending darkly down the hill, backs turned, the indifferent, whitewashed shrugs of our neighbors. Trembling of masts on the harbor. Shrug of sea as well, with the *Emerald Isle* upon it. Somewhere.

A tremor that may or may not have traveled upward, from the river.

This is slight. Am I the only one who feels it? It is in me, perhaps. Movement, a lurching. Whether inside or outside, I can't tell.

The lamps are lit, in the city. The shades are drawn.

The empty net undulates softly, greybluegreyblue, this is the phosphorescence of storm. Sleet becoming snow becoming wave. It is a white night, tonight.

And I am haunted.

Haunted, yes, certainly I am that.

Of what use is this fire to me. Given the room is empty.

I don't understand how Hip does it. Disappearing like that.

The curtain falls. I let it. There's nothing to see.

It is peculiar, this emptiness of the house. Harry Owen has lifted his beard out of his book and gone off somewhere, leaving this bright fire, the lamps lit, half-smoked cigar on the fender, prawns half eaten on a plate, this all speaks of hurry, the ship abandoned in haste. Or else have I slipped again in time, fallen out of whatever net Hip has been weaving, tumbled at a blink into a world of which I am the sole and lonely occupant? Upstairs does nothing to dispel this feeling or fear, it, too, is empty, the bed an unmade tangle, my mother's things still strewn around because nobody has the heart to put them away, the cayman grinning through the armhole of her old corset, wicked, toothy snout where the pale, slender, seemingly translucent arm used to be. This cannot be real, certainly I have slipped through again, fallen unnoticed into a strange, soft space I cannot get a purchase on, which nobody will ever bother to lift me out of. The river throbbing through the floors, up into the soles of my feet, my chest, my throat.

Through the back window, though, I can see light in the shed, the orange glow outlining the door, and the smoke still rising thinly from the metal vent, though riverthrob occludes what might or might not be the warmer thrum and throb of the bellows.

My father is out there, that is what I think. My father is out there working.

But nor is this true. When I enter I find the stove lit, the lamp warm, my father gone. It is as in the house, the tools set down as if abruptly, small unfinished objects, half formed, ambiguous, bobbing in the crucible. So convinced am I that my father's absence is only temporary that I wait there at the bench in the dark, cave-like space, my father's space, listening to the hiss of the sleet against the walls and the strange, surreptitious rustlings within, as of small furred creatures making their way through my grandfather's boxes, small, furtive gnawings and hungry peripatations, restless susurrus of warm bodies turning in tangled, acrid knots of dream, these going still, suddenly, at my approach.

My giantess' footfall and large shadow portending an unknown danger.

Then moving on. Peaceful resumption of nibblings, gnawings, dreamings.

My grandfather's boxes, never fully unpacked, do constitute a
kind of forest, one that sways slightly, like a real forest, settles,
seems to respire. Of course this is just the wind, entering through
chinks and gaps and fissures. How many years have the boxes
been here now? Many. There are traces of my mother's gnawings, boxes she has opened and from which she has extracted bits
and pieces of her patrimony, taking what interested her, leaving
the rest for the mice.

The rest. Thousands of stilled breaths there, in these boxes.
Thousands of lifeless, formerly living things. And that soft sibi-
lance: the sound of specimens breathing.

I wonder if my grandfather, Felix Girard, the collector, the
explorer, the naturalist, he whose remarkable *regio frontalis*, *regio
orbitalis*, *regio zygomatica*, large feet, long fingers, thrusting
elbows, broad back, and ginger hair I have inherited—did he
ever hear the sound of his lifeless specimens, breathing?

Maybe that was why he collected them—why he grabbed
and gathered and piled up as much and as fast as he could,
why he disappeared over the edge of the earth, still desperately grasping and clutching and snatching—going over—
past the edge—taking my mother with him, in the end.
To obtain the company of these many strange, lifeless respira-
tions.

To replace a single, beloved, *living* breath that had gone
away?

. . .

No. He preferred these. This is hardest of all to understand. Though there is much company here, among my grandfather's boxes. This I acknowledge.

Imagine the ghosts!

I walk between them, think, what are these to me? Though the wind rattles fiercely, causing all my father's flames to flicker. This is not a reassuring thing, when surrounded by ghosts.

But then, of course, I have my own ghost, I take her with me everywhere. Sometimes she even speaks to me, or so it seems.

Carlotta.

Soft susurration of wind.

Carlotta!

Irritated now. Impatient. Peremptory.

Oh angry ghost.

Burst of wind, gust, sudden upspark of flame, tinkling, sighing, coruscation of glass. The boxes sway.

Carlotta!

Finally I see her, just a glimpse, between the stacks. Tangled gold gleam, pale smooth cheek, whorl of ear. Pink and white. *She's beautiful, your Ma.*

Carlotta!

There is another fierce burst of wind and the door flies open, Harry Owen is saying, *It's a damn fine vessel!*

My father is less certain. Though Harry Owen thinks they should take advantage immediately.

But, he says, *you must make more glass. She won't go on like this forever, you know.*

Yes.

My father admits that this is true.

Nobody will give money for nothing, says Harry Owen.

I emerge then, into their company, and Harry Owen tells me that the patroness, she who *has been taken,* has donated a small, seaworthy vessel for their use, his and my father's. It's wonderful news! *And a diving suit,* he says, *the latest thing. Rouquayrol and Denayrouse.* Great excitement, expressed as bristling of beard.

Less so for my father. *I'm n-not an ex-p-plorer, Harry.*

Eyes large and dark, thin, pale gesture toward a neck. I look at him closely: he's a stranger, too. He notices me looking. Expression turns evasive.

I'm d-doing the best I c-can, Harry.

This is for my benefit also.

Anxiously rubbing one wrist against the other.

A sensation as of sinking through black water, bubbles rushing upward, colliding, humming as of a thousand bees in my ears, or is that just the wind—

The wind.

The shed door banging in it. Clatter now, of hail on the roof. I have seen what I should not see.

The fine, translucent hands, delicate fingers, nails like seashells, tiny, perfect. Mother of pearl.

This has been his real work.

My mother is and is not on the sea.

Harry Owen says, *Come! Let's go inside. We can discuss it further in the morning.*

Some things, though, cannot be discussed. My father locks the shed door behind us, carefully slips the key into his waistcoat pocket. In the new world, the gangway has been lowered, my aunt's hand is on my shoulder, she's pushing me, a gentle hand but insistent, the moment of embarkation has come, *Carlotta*, she's saying, *Carlotta, it's time to go.*

IV.

———✦———

ON A WINTER NIGHT
A TRAVELER

On Christmas eve, late, I mounted the East Cliff in the rain: a ginger giantess, orphaned now, hugging my thin coat around me, carrying my sole remaining possession, a broken suitcase tied with twine. Below me, as I climbed, Whitby spread itself, the same sea-spittled, brine-slicked place it had ever been, stinking of rot and ocean, the harbor with its ships groaning restlessly at anchor, the cottages huddled stoically together like barnacles on a rock, backs turned, windows bundled, releasing only, like errant fingers beckoning, thin shafts of light that hinted at the hidden lives lived behind the tightly closed shutters and carefully drawn shades. I could not see the Birdcage, from where I stood; perhaps that was just as well, for it was my home no longer. I couldn't see the *Emerald Isle* either where I knew it must be, turning at anchor, restless in the tide. Whitby was a place I knew, and yet I did not: it had been made strange for me; there was no longer, here, a door I could knock on, and expect to be let in, except, perhaps, for one. Penniless I mounted toward the Ravenscar Hotel and my future, whatever it might hold. I had been summoned there, and so I went.

As for that place, which had loomed large and mysterious over my childhood, it burned like a torch above the darkened city, threw off mad sparks of light and laughter and music, and gravel, too, from beneath the churning wheels of carriages ricocheting up and down the long drive—blurred faces turned toward me behind frost-covered windows, gawked, then were carried swiftly past, rocketing forward as I persisted in my own slow, orphan's trudge: I a spectacle again as always, on the verge of the road with my flimsy case, my hair disheveled, my frock a baggy enigma in wool, my shoes unsuited to the snow, and yet.

And yet this was the one place in Whitby where they must let me in—which they did—though there was, it's true, an exchange of glances at the threshold, the eyebrow raised. *Does Madam wish a room? No. Does Madam wish to check her, ah, bag? No—.* But the mockery of porters and bellmen, refined to the point of abstraction, were easy for me to step over and past, and I found myself, rather quickly, and for the first time ever, in that glittering, mythic lobby, where a tannenbaum stood, starred tip nearly touching the distant eminence of the dark-paneled ceiling, candles burning low and dangerously among the needles, branches festooned with gold garlands and glittering ornaments shaped like planets, seashells, saints, stars. Revelers, moon faced themselves, clustered like moons at the foot of the tree, festive hats tipped back at dangerous angles on seal-sleek heads, clutching their stemware as they toasted together giddily over the fizzing fruit of the second fermentation.

Anybody who cared to look could have seen that I didn't belong there—gawky goony bird that I was, with my shabby clothes and my twined-together bag; but nobody looked, or else they looked quickly and then looked carefully away, in the usual mannerly violence of exclusion that is practiced in such places. Stranger in a strange land, that was I.

Until finally, from among one of the groups surrounding the tree, a single figure detached from the many, came toward, extended.

It was a woman, with long, straight, dark hair, wearing a snug, black velvet sheath with a low-cut bustier, droplet of pearls at the white throat, tapering black gloves, wristlets of marcasite gently tinkling, giving off those characteristic cold, black sparks.

I did not take her hand.

Sound of amusement at the back of the throat. The hand withdrawn.

You're like your father in that, she said. *He was stubborn, too.*

Of course it was she: I had recognized her immediately. It was Anna, my aunt.

She knew me, too, of course, there was a conflict of eyes between us then, as we sought and found in each other that which was familiar conflated with that which was strange; then she took me by the arm, and moved me away from the crowd. They were glancing at me curiously now that she'd made me visible by acknowledging me; they were gawping at my ginger frizz, all right, judging me, surreptitiously, over their shoulders, through their lorgnettes, from beneath the glittering brims of their holiday hats, oh yes, they were taking me in, every inch, with a smirk, and finding me lacking. So I performed the curtsey my mother taught me, holding out, with the tips of my fingers, the edges of my ill-mended colorless skirt, so as to expose my laddered stockings, and taking a bow, low and deep, and holding it, that bow, right foot forward, left knee bent, just as Clotilde showed me, until, in consternation and embarrassment, they were forced one by one to look away, and hotly to reconsider the bubbles in the depths of their champagne.

She, of course, did not look away, but instead looked more closely, with an ironical lift of a single, darkly penciled eyebrow eloquent as a hieroglyph incised on pale marble.

I hoped you'd come, she said, quite calm, as if she'd assumed it all along.

Which was presumptuous: for I had debated, when I received her letter. More than six months my father had been gone, by the time she finally wrote me.

You should have come to me, said I, tartly I fear, *after all, I'm the one who's orphaned and alone, my world emptied out of protectors and friends, and I only sixteen—*

She said nothing in answer to this, but her grip on my arm tightened, and I felt, in the place where we touched, a soft shudder, by which I knew my remark had struck home. She looked down, hair sliding forward to hide her eyes, large and dark, which so resembled my father's. *Come*, she said, and began to propel me, not quite against my will, through the glittering public rooms of the Ravenscar Hotel. Each room was a new chapter of festivity, here diners tucking into venison and chestnuts, there dancers moving together at a leisurely pace, like dreaming, ladies' gloved hands on gents' arms, all of us somnambulating, they and we, through a sweeping diminuendo that took Anna and me all the way to the broad, red-carpeted staircase, then up, through and around a complication of hallways like lovers' knot. Mirrors blazed along the walls, reflecting, as if at a great distance, pale intimations of movement that I recognized as ourselves, mounting yet another flight of stairs. Finally Anna paused, fumbled at the wall, and disappeared into a rectangle of light.

With only a moment's hesitation, I followed.

Behind the door of Room 301 I found her, once my eyes had adjusted to the glare of the gaslight, sprawled out on a bed richly wrapped in softly ambiguous undulations of vermillion and gold; she had taken off her shoes, and comfortably stretched her toes in the direction of the hearth, where a fire fiercely blazed.

Relax, she said. *It's all mine; I've rented the entire floor. Make yourself at home.*

A gesture urged me to come join her in that luxuriant wilderness of pillows, but I chose, instead, a nearby upright chair of red velveteen that clashed brilliantly with my hair.

She laughed. *You're just like him*, she said, *he wouldn't have sat next to me neither, at least not yet. Though you don't look like him much, nor much like her, for that matter.*

There was something, I thought, derogatory in the way she'd pronounced that *her*, which, for all that it was justified, caused me to jut out my chin, pridefully as I could. *I'm like my grandfather*, I said, *the explorer, Felix Girard.*

She laughed again, and finished me with a smile that disarmed somehow any perturbations I felt, so that I slipped lower in my chair, and took a moment to contemplate the room in which we sat, taking in the plush, enveloping cossetingness of it, the thickness of the carpet into which my feet had sunk, and, seemingly, disappeared; the veritable mummification of the windows beneath layer upon layer of curtains that served to disguise utterly the distinction between windows and wall, all of it vermillion and gold like the soft ambiguities that swathed the bed, and all of it hectic with reflected gaslight. The tops of the bureaus, of which there were many, were crowded with knickknacks, hairbrushes, powders, pins, jewelry spilling from casks, pictures in silver frames, all of it suggesting that the occupant of these rooms had made herself thoroughly at home. The mantel above the hearth was likewise crowded with objects, some of which looked strangely familiar: small, ambiguous, glassy shapes, strange bristlings, my father's work.

My father's things! I cried.

They're mine, she calmly said, stretching out her toes toward the fire, *I paid for them. I was his patroness, you know. It was I who paid your bills. It was wonderful of me, was it not?*

She patted her pillows again, which invitation I once again ignored.

You can look at those pictures if you want. Go ahead! Put your nose in among 'em if you must—they won't bite. You're a Dell'oro through and through all, though you don't look like un. I'll put the pictures in your hands then if I must—

And jumping up from the bed in a single, catlike movement she joined me by the fire, and began gently, oh very gently (these objects, clearly, were precious to her), taking up the daguerreotypes in their silver frames and, making good on her threat, forced them, one by one, into my reluctant hands. Why did I resist? I don't know—why do we do anything? As I had no choice now, I looked at these pictures, which were of strangers, but familiar to me. Here was one of two children, a boy and a girl, standing stiffly in their Sunday best; here a stern-faced man gazing out from behind glasses like twin silver moons; here a little boy standing next to a pony on the Scaur, his eyes directed off somewhere, away from the camera—

Oh! It was me he was looking at in that one. Mama never forgave me for ruining it. His birthday it was, his tenth. We had a lovely day that day.

She caressed the picture fondly.

He must have talked about me, she said. *I was so angry when he left. He left me, you know. High and dry on Henrietta Street, without so much as a word, and went off to sea with that awful man, your grandfather, and that awful woman, your mother—yes, high and dry he left me, high and dry.*

But I'm over that now. I'm not angry anymore. Not for a long time.

My father looked for you, said I. *It's we who were all alone, after she left us—and he looked for you—in Henrietta Street—and all the other streets—up and down, at the top of the cliff, at the bottom, on the Scaur, everywhere—all over Whitby. You were gone.*

Yes, she said slowly, taking the picture from me, and putting it back, and perching herself on the foot of the bed, among the wraps and cossetings. *That's right, I was gone by then. I was married by the time Leo came back. As you can see, I've been left a wealthy woman: widow now—an orphan—alone—like you. He paid for all this—*

She made a gesture encompassing the room in which we were sitting and, perhaps, too, by implication, all that lay beyond it, the empty hallway outside, the Ravenscar Hotel, Whitby, the cold, white-capped North Sea with the *Emerald Isle* turning upon it, unseen, in the dark; and maybe more than that; maybe, even, the vast reach of all the space that had opened, and opened, that was opening still, vertiginously, between my mother and me, between my father and his father, my father and Anna, small ships all of us, fanning out, upon cold dark oceans of our own. Outside, as if in reply, the Christmas wind rattled at the windowpanes so that, inside, the thick, warm curtains billowed inward, toward us, then receded, softly, into the casements; inhale, exhale, a soft, tinkling tremor, then a settling; a sparking up and then a diminution of the gaslight, a sudden relaxation of vision, the pupil dilated in the dark.

—and for your father's glass. My late husband. All his various goods and chattels.

Against my will almost I found myself drawn then toward the other things, my father's things, those small, self-contained ambiguities that proved, on closer inspection, to be very specific indeed: a delicate yellow nudibranch, a prawn striped red and white like a candy cane, and something else, resting on a tiny pillow, like a reliquary itself or the finger of a saint, delicate and perfectly lifelike, down to the blush of pink beneath the nail. I had seen something like this before, picked it up now, held it in my hands, turned it over, my father's work certainly. Though she whose finger it resembled was no saint. I am sure, could I have examined it closely enough, I would have seen, in a thread of gold, her initials, CGD'O.

But I could not; and as I held it the clock struck twelve, the curtains exhaled again, cold blasts without, spackling of rain against the windows, and fragments of sound filtering up to us from below—laughter, "Carol of the Bells," doors slamming, a woman's voice crying out *Oh, no, you wouldn't*, a man's replying, *Oh, yes, I would!*, heatless sparks thrown off some distant source of incandescence—it was a party down there, corks being popped, songs sung, dances danced (awkwardly, skillfully, gracefully, reluctantly), troths plighted and plights complexified amid the tinsel and party hats and streamers. Another world it was. It was for others, not for us, this celebration. And then she asked me, as we were each other's only family now, what gift she could give to me for Christmas.

I want to sail, I said. *I want to find my mother. And my father.*

For I still believed, as I do now, that he was not dead, but had slipped away somehow, in search of her; disappeared, on some pathway multifarious and branching, in pursuit of his obsession. He is a Dell'oro, after all; as am I.

And so I find myself at the point of embarkation. Mother I have none, father neither; both gone; missing; having stepped off, as I am about to do, over the edge of the world.

Acknowledgments

A number of literary, historical, and scientific sources were invaluable to me in the creation of *The Glass Ocean*. These include Philip Henry Gosse, *A Naturalist's Sojourn in Jamaica*; George Henry Young, *A Geological Survey of the Yorkshire Coast: Describing the Strata and Fossils Occurring Between the Humber and the Tees, from the German Ocean to the Plain of York*; Lyn Barber, *The Heyday of Natural History, 1820–1870*; Judith Flanders, *Inside the Victorian Home*; Isobel Armstrong, *Victorian Glassworlds: Glass Culture and the Imagination, 1830–1880*; R. H. Dana, *Two Years Before the Mast: and Twenty-four Years After*; Sidney Waugh, *The Making of Fine Glass*; Geoffrey Wills, *Victorian Glass*; and Barbara Stafford and Frances Terpak, *Devices of Wonder: From the World in a Box to Images on a Screen*.

I would also like to take this opportunity to thank the Corning Museum of Glass and Cornell University Libraries for allowing me access to the papers, drawings, and works in glass of Leopold and

Rudolph Blaschka, whose lives and art provided the initial inspiration for this book.

With especial thanks to Harry Mathews, Melanie Jackson, Ann Godoff, and to my husband, Peter Gale Nelson, without whose loving support and editorial guidance *The Glass Ocean* could not have been written.